I0708987

BLOODY WAR

by

Terry Grimwood

Bloody War
by Terry Grimwood

Publication Date: April 2011

All text copyright Terry Grimwood 2011

Cover art by David Rix

ISBN: 978-1-908125-03-3

www.eibonvalepress.co.uk

Acknowledgement:

Thanks to Imelda May who gave me the idea when she appeared on BBC Radio 4's 'A Good Read' last summer. Her chosen book was 'All Quiet on the Western Front'...

And, of course, sincere thanks to David Rix at Eibonvale for believing in this novel.

Suffolk-born Terry Grimwood started his working life as an electrician and is now a college lecturer, having travelled full-circle from doing the job to teaching it (which he prefers). Along the way he has been a quality assurance manager, project manager and technical author. He is the author of numerous short stories and reviews which have appeared in *Midnight Street, Bare Bone, Murky Depths, All Hallows, FutureFire* and Eibonvale Press's own *Blind Swimmer* anthology among others. He has written and directed three plays and runs the Exaggerated Press which started when he published his first collection, *The Exaggerated Man*. His novella, *The Places Between* is available from Pendragon Press and his novel *Axe* will be published by bad Moon Press in late in 2011. Terry's web site can be found at http://exaggeratedpress.weebly.com. *Bloody War* is his first full length novel.

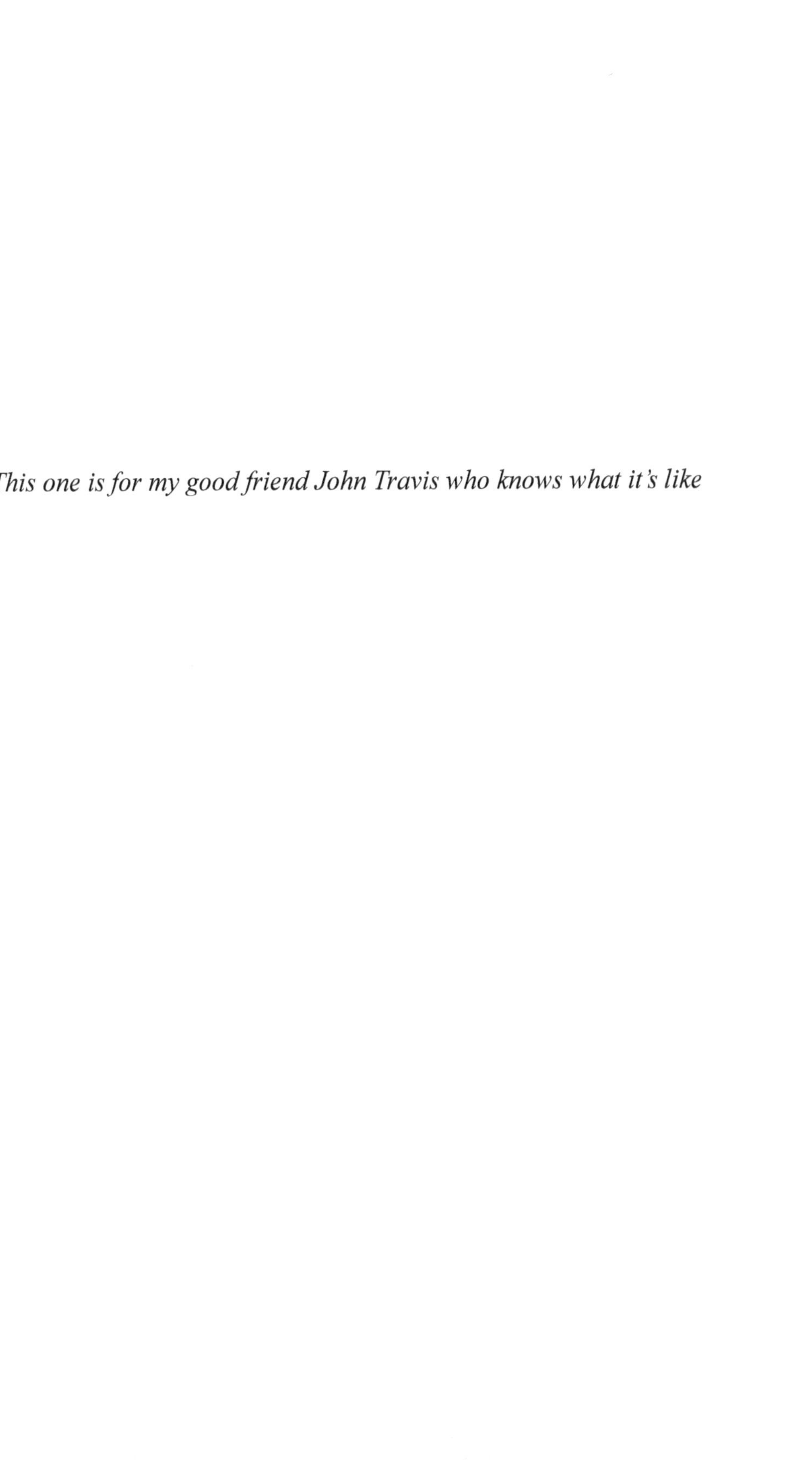

This one is for my good friend John Travis who knows what it's like

Contents

"Don't you know there's a bloody war on?"

- World War 2 film cliché

There _Is_ a War On

I know what's wrong now, it's the curtains. They're no longer the smooth falls of velvet over lace beloved of my wife, but solid, black and ugly, jarring with the rest of the room, something Ruth would never countenance.

So why should I care about bedroom drapery? I'm just a middle-aged, ex-biker who grows his hair too long and has faded "Black Sabbath" and "Thin Lizzy" tattoos on his arms. Curtains are curtains aren't they? You pull them together to keep the light out and pull them apart to let it in.

But these bastards worry me. In fact, they worry me so much I clamber out of bed, naked and bleary-eyed, and cross the room just to touch them. The rest of the family are already up. I can hear them downstairs, having breakfast. Normality. It should be reassuring. It isn't.

The curtains are heavy, stiff. Like I said, wrong.

I pull them apart.

And find another wrong. Several wrongs in fact.

There's white tape on the glass, a big diagonal cross on each pane that partially obscures the view of our back garden.

And there's smoke, beyond the row of pre-war semis that abut our own, two huge, thick columns that join the earth to the November-grey clouds. We live in Northwood, so the fires must be in Ruislip, or possibly Northolt.

Plane crash, it must be. There's a constant stream of Heathrow-bound airliners in that piece of sky. One of them must have come down, or a pair, a collision perhaps. Christ, all those people.

But it doesn't explain the curtains or the tape.

How the hell did I sleep through that? There must have been one hell of a bang. I mean, I was woken up by the great Hemel Hempsted fuel dump explosion back in 2006, and Hemel is lot further away than Ruislip, so why not this one?

Even the bedside phone managed to wake me.

"I'm very sorry," a woman's voice had said. Then added; "Wrong number."

Thanks, I may be going back to work today, but they've told me to come in when I'm ready, so I could still be asleep now, warm and snug while my wife and kids struggle out to face the bleak, cold world.

I sit back down on the bed and absently run my fingertips over the scar. It's one of many. Motorcycles are unforgiving brutes, plus I was a big bastard when I was young and big blokes make big targets. This one, though, is new. Appendix. And there were complications, an infection that kept me in hospital for two weeks longer than normal and off work for a month, well, out of the office that is. I started working at home as soon as I was able. Sickies are not what they're cracked up to be, they are, in fact, bloody boring.

I've left the curtains closed. I don't want to see that smoke because it's means dead people. And lots of them.

It's only when I get out of the shower and finish drying my face and hair that I see that the flower-patterned bathroom blind has also been replaced and that there is tape on this window as well.

I'm still buttoning my shirt and tucking it into my grey suit trousers as I clatter downstairs and into the kitchen-diner. A tie is draped round my collar, to be knotted after I've eaten because I tend to use ties as bibs. AlphaTech requires its staff to look smart, so I do. A job's a job and I'm not throwing it away over some stupid long-ago promise I once made to myself that I would never, ever, wear a suit for work. Anyway, we all have to compromise, didn't Robert Plant accept a gong off Prince Charles and Mick Jagger a knighthood? If my heroes can make sacrifices like that, surely I can wear a suit for work.

The family is sitting at the dining room table. It's one of Ruth's Rules. The family always eats together at each end of the day. Ruth has a lot of rules and they're all good. The two girls are at peace, which is rare. Amanda, the older one, is fourteen, blonde and already frighteningly beautiful. However, looks aren't everything. My sweet little Amanda has turned into a sulky, explosive and utterly selfish princess. But there are moments when the other Amanda, the kind one, the funny one, wins through. Rachel sits opposite her, she has my dark hair but her mother's brains, thank Christ. Rachel is bright and sharp and a little too serious. Still, she's only twelve, she'll lighten up when she's good and ready.

I sit next to our son, Dominic (not my choice, I'd have called him Steve). He'll be eighteen on Sunday. He's dark too, and like his younger sister, has his mother's wit and intelligence. He's got a job as an apprentice electrician and is doing well at college and with his company. No girl friends yet though, well, none that he's ever talked about or brought home.

"Has a plane crashed?" I ask as I reach for the toast.

Everyone looks up.

"There's smoke, over Ruislip."

"There was a raid last night," Rachel says.

"A raid? What terrorists?"

"An air raid," Dominic says. He glances at his sisters. "We've had them every night this week."

"You mean, Ruislip's being bombed?" The idea is so incredible I can't even believe I'm asking the question.

"Yes," Dominic says. He glances at his mother this time. She's in the kitchen, making coffee. "Dad, the whole of London is being bombed. The whole Country's under attack."

Amanda rolls her eyes in that exaggerated American way girls have adopted nowadays, the look that really irritates me. "The war Dad? You know, like, The War."

"No, I don't know like the war. What war? What bloody war?"

My irritation startles them.

"*The* War," Ruth says and makes it sound as if that explains everything. "Pete, are you okay? Maybe you're not ready to go back to work."

Christ she's beautiful. We've been married for twenty years and she still stops me breathing sometimes. She's wearing her plain and practical teacher's roll neck sweater and trousers, but she makes it look like the sexiest and smartest outfit on earth.

"I'm fine," I say. "Look, humour me, who are we fighting? Who is bombing us?" I swig the coffee Ruth has handed me. It tastes foul.

"The EoD." Even Rachel sounds impatient now.

"E, o...?"

"The Enemies of Democracy," she explains, as if to a five year old.

"But...I mean...We weren't at war last night when we went to bed were we? The curtains were..."

"Pete, we've been at war for eighteen months."

Suddenly they all look as frightened as I feel, not of the EoD, but of me. My daughters in their school uniform grey, my son in his thick work-worn sweatshirt and carefully messed-up hair, my wife. They all stare at me, no longer eating.

"Yeah," I say. "Yeah...of course, the war. I forgot. You're right Ruth, I'm not feeling too good...I get confused, perhaps it's the anaesthetic." I offer a smile that feels like a grimace. "Darling, this coffee doesn't taste right."

"Powdered milk. We used up our milk ration yesterday, don't you remember?"

No. "Right, yeah, I remember."

Ruth serves up scrambled egg and that doesn't taste right either. I don't ask because I have a feeling that the answer will involve powder.

Ruth sits down beside me. "Perhaps you should phone in sick."

"No, I've made up my mind. I'm fed up with moping around the place and feeling sorry for myself. Anyway, my Country needs me."

Silence.

"That isn't funny," Amanda says. Her eyes are shining, welling up. She stands, suddenly and flees. I hear a sob as she crashes through the door.

I look round, horrified. "I'm sorry. I...I wasn't thinking." About what?

"Well I suggest you start thinking Pete." Ruth is up now, following Amanda, calling to her.

"I'm going to work," Dominic stands. He is subdued, pale. "See you Dad."

And he's gone. Now there's only Rachel and me, though not for long because in a moment she mutters her excuses and flees. She doesn't want to be alone with me and that hurts.

I can't finish my food, so I go out into the hall, grab my coat off its peg and open the front door.

"Make an appointment to see a Doctor, Pete."

Startled I turn to see Ruth. She too is pale and strained. I want to ask her what the matter is, what I said that upset everybody so much, but I can't. No more questions. I want to get out, to be alone so I can pull myself together again and try to work out what's happening. I simply nod and mumble that I'll phone the surgery when I get to work.

Outside I can smell the smoke. It hangs in the frost-cold air, a tang, a taint. It scours my throat and makes me cough. In the end, I light up and swallow some smoke of my own. My hand is shaking because being out here is suddenly frightening, the front garden, the pavement and the other houses, all seem like part of an alien planet. As I walk I catch glimpses of the flames at the bases of the smoke columns. Even from this distance the fires look immense. The raid must have been terrible.

Every window I can see is taped, every house and shop, wearing sets of white crosses. They look self-conscious somehow, as if there's a competition, like those Christmas light feuds that break out every December, only this time it's to see who shows the *least* amount of light. I decide that the bigger and more elaborate the taped X's, the thicker and more solid the blackout curtain behind them.

I reach the neat, village-like main street.

There is a gun, located outside the tube station, surrounded by sandbags and pointing skywards. The barrel is dark green, solid, real. Soldiers in camouflage and berets lounge around. One of them smokes. The commuters ignore them. I try to, but it's hard because this is an anti-aircraft gun – at least that's what I think it is, it *is* pointing at the sky - set up outside Northwood Underground station.

A fucking anti-aircraft gun.

I swipe my Oyster card and walk down to the platform. I don't have to wait long for the train, which is packed. Okay, this is rush hour but I can't remember the last time I had to stand in a Metropolitan Line carriage. Then it occurs to me, if eggs and milk are being rationed, then so is petrol. The tank in our Focus was almost empty yesterday. If that hasn't mysteriously changed overnight, how do I fill it up again?

Powdered petrol?

There are soldiers, and airmen and sailors, spattered among the more anonymous dark suits and winter coats. We really are at war. All we need are Vera Lynn and Glenn Miller.

The train jerks into motion and I hang on tight. Even though I commute every day, I do not like the tube. Today is worse because I haven't used the Underground since I went off sick and I've almost lost my nerve. Thank Christ the Met Line carriages are taller and bigger than a lot of the others, but they are still steel and glass coffins to me. Now it's a crammed and crushed coffin. I can't move and I can barely breathe.

I pull a tatty paperback from my pocket. Robert Silverberg, a collection of his short sf. I always read on the train. Reading stops the walls closing in, here and before, when that violent bastard Allman was finally banged-up on remand and he was shut in a cell at night and almost went insane…

Harrow-on-the-Hill, Preston Road, Wembley Park, Finchley Road. The train leaks passengers at each stop then re-fills, replacements always outnumbering losses. Perfume sweat, bodies, bags, uniforms and huge backpacks press into me. No one speaks. I close the book, too worked-up to read The tube rattles and sways.

Then stops, in the tunnel just outside Baker Street. I stay calm, which I do by breathing deeply and slowly and telling myself that the train will move again in a moment.

Just a few more seconds.

I can endure this. I'm big and tough and I used to be a biker, I've got tattoos and scars under this suit. A little claustrophobia isn't going to hurt me. A few minutes stuck in a metal and glass coffin, filled to the brim with sweating, breathing, frustrated and potentially panic-stricken and hysterical humanity is nothing for me to worry about. So, be tough, be cool, come on you stupid bugger, grow up.

A nasal, barely coherent voice erupts out of some hidden speaker.

"Sorry for the delay but there's an air raid alert."

Air raid? A fucking air raid and we're all stuck in here unable to move even if bombs start to fall on Baker Street.

The other passengers groan, frustrated rather than frightened. This is just another inconvenience to them, not possible fiery death or premature burial under tons of bomb-blasted rubble.

I look round as best I can, most of the faces I can see are pressed up close against mine. I see pale skin, I see wide eyes, and I do see fear. I'm almost grateful, at least I'm not the only normal person in here. Someone sobs and someone else starts to pray.

I fill my head with images of Ruth, blonde and lovely and so delicate in my arms. She tastes sweet. I'd never known such a thing until I met her, that a woman's skin can actually taste sweet.

Seconds, minutes, days, fucked if I know how long we're there. I stand, propped up and held in position, I breathe and lick dry lips and nod reassuringly to the young Indian women against whom I am crushed. She attempts a brave smile.

Then the train lurches and so does my heart and we're moving again.

Finally I walk through London Wall's glass canyon towards the bland monolith that houses AlphaTech Software Solutions. That's what I do these days, cut code as they say in the trade, write software. I used to repair cars and motorbikes in a series of downbeat, and often dubious side-street garages. The jobs I liked best were auto-electrics. A lot of mechanics didn't want to touch them, so I got to do most of the rewire and fault-finding jobs.

When I was put inside, after a drunken brawl during which I clouted a police constable, and I was sure that my life as a free man was over, I was not only introduced to the printed word, but also put to use repairing things, including the new gadgets called home computers that were owned by some of the warders.

By some miracle, my industry, good behaviour and new literary bent persuaded the judge to pass down a suspended sentence.

Those months spent in that hell hole not only pushed me nearer to the edge than I'd ever been before, it also opened my eyes to the fact that I have a brain in my head, that it works a hell of a lot better than me or anyone else realised and using it was only thing that was going to save me.

Meeting Ruth was the last, and most important piece, of the jigsaw that was the redemption of Peter Allman because once she had my heart, given willingly and beating in her hand, there was no way I would ever crash off the rails again.

Now reading fills the empty spaces and keeps the dark at bay and messing about with computers pays my mortgage.

Every pane of glass I can see, right up to the top floors of the monsters that border the Wall, every shop front and restaurant window, is decorated with crosses of white tape. There are soldiers everywhere. Armed, alert, on guard I suppose. People hurry round them, as if they're rocks in a river. Everyone keeps their head down. No one catches anyone else's eye. There are few vehicles and what there are seem to be mostly commercial and military. Petrol rationing must be keeping private cars off the road. The soldiers are a mixed bunch, young, middle-aged, some the same age as me by the look of them (that's forty-four).

So why aren't I in the army?

Helicopters clatter over the strip of sky visible between the buildings, their staccato drone replacing traffic as London's audio backing track. When I get to the building that houses AlphaTech, the security is much tighter than usual. My pass is actually checked by the receptionist on the foyer desk, my face scrutinised against the photograph. A curt nod is my permission to proceed to the lifts.

Well, there *is* a war on.

Finally I walk into the office, one of those huge open plan areas in which individual teams are hidden within a maze of shoulder-height, padded partitions. Pig pens we call them. I don't think we invented the name, but it's appropriate all the same.

At least the office hasn't changed, apart from the tape on the windows of course. There are a lot of windows, in fact the entire east side of the floor is glass. That's a lot of tape. The view is fantastic, despite all those giant white crosses and distant columns of smoke.

My own desk is as I left it, thank God, and Andy Taylor is there as he should be. Overweight, balding and not caring about his premature disintegration one little bit.

"You're late." He sounds pleased "Hendy'll have your guts mate."

"Thanks for the welcome back," I answer.

Andy grins and shakes my hand. "I'm surprised you *are* back, you looked bloody awful when you were taken ill."

"Can't think why, it was only a burst appendix."

"Being sick all over my desk was a bit thoughtless but, hey, what's a few diced carrots between friends?"

"At least I didn't throw up over my own desk," I say.

"Very good point. Fuck me, you must be bored to come back here."

"I missed you too much to stay away a moment longer. And I especially missed Hendy."

Tony "Hendy" Henderson is our Team Manager. He takes his job seriously, which makes it very difficult for those of us who don't.

I fire up my computer. There is no browser icon. I look at the programs menu, not there either.

"Where's my internet gone?" I ask.

Andy looks round at me and frowns. "What do you mean where's your internet? You know where your internet is. It's been closed down"

"What?"

"There *is* a bloody war on, in case you hadn't noticed."

"Oh, yeah."

"Come on Pete, wake up."

Frustrated by lack of access to news or information or anything at all that could help me understand this waking nightmare, I open up my current project; a new database that holds customer details for a big accountancy firm. Simple but huge.

We're at the testing stage. I pull the 80-page schedule from my in-tray. It's laborious, mind-numbing but absorbing enough to stop me thinking too much.

The database seems bigger than I remember it, the test list longer even though I've done a lot of it at home.

"Hello Pete, nice to see you."

I look up to see Frances Simmonds, Hendy's second in command, peering at us over the top of our partition. Frances is perfect, red-haired, green-eyed and porcelain-pale. She's another one who takes work far too seriously.

"Thanks," I answer. The correct response is probably, "It's good to be back" but I can't bring myself to say it.

"So, what day is it gentlemen?" Frances says.

"Oh shit," Andy says and gets to his feet. "I know, I know. I was just so engrossed in this highly important work I clean forgot"

"What has Wednesday got to do with anything?" I ask.

Frances rolls her eyes. "Very funny. Come on Tony's waiting."

Always Tony, never Hendy.

"For what?"

Andy pauses, looks down at me. "Team meeting, highlight of our week."

"But that's Thursday –"

"Not anymore," Frances says. "Pete you really have to snap out of it. The Team Meetings been moved to mid-week. Don't you remember? Tony has to brief the MoD on Thursdays."

Hendy briefing the MoD? God help us.

"Oh yeah," I say. "I'm feeling a bit rough this morning, not thinking straight."

"Well don't overdo it Pete." Frances is all concern now and this unaccustomed softness in her voice suddenly makes her disturbingly attractive.

Andy and me follow Frances down to Hendy's office. Andy is staring at Frances's legs. He likes her legs, particularly in the winter when they are encased in silky, dark nylon which he insists are stockings but I'm sure are plain old tights.

Hendy shows his disapproval by looking up sharply and frowning as we come in and sit down. There is a lot for him to disapprove of. We aren't his favourites, we're late for his meeting and worse, we don't take things seriously. Hendy is barely thirty, has a smooth, soft face and wears glasses, which he glares over, schoolmaster style.

There are seven of us in the room, me of course and Hendy, Frances, Andy, an old stager called Tommy Lawson, Katie and Jamie. Katie's a quiet, large, young woman who takes the minutes and seldom seems to gather enough confidence to even speak let alone contribute. She's good at her job though, precise and patient, and she's fun when she's drunk, which is a mission Andy and me undertake assiduously at every Christmas party. We call it the Katie Challenge. Jamie is about the same age as Frances, sharp, cool, always butting in with an opinion or idea and is unpleasant without me being able to work out why. He's what is called a project manager.

"First, I'm sure we'd all like to welcome back Pete," Hendy says. "How are you feeling?"

"Not so bad." Noncommittal, best way.

"Good, good. Uh, right, okay, now a bit of bad news I'm afraid," Hendy says. "Aryan Abyar has been killed in action."

Solemn nods and whispers.

"I'm sure our sympathy goes out to his family –"

"Wait a minute," I say. "Aryan, from IT support?"

"There's only one Aryan in the company Pete," Frances says.

"But what happened? I mean, how was he killed? Christ's sake it's Aryan." I can't stop babbling. I'm too shocked to think straight. Aryan is…*was* young, bright, and likeable.

Aryan was here yesterday, I talked to him on the phone. *I fucking well talked to him.*

"We don't know how and when he…he died. That's restricted information, you should know that."

There's just so much I should know isn't there.

Hendy turns his attention back to the group. "As you know Aryan didn't have to join up, computing and IT professionals like us are a reserved occupation, but he was determined to serve his Country."

I look up sharply. I said something like that, this morning, at breakfast and it had upset everyone.

"Shall I organise a bouquet for his family?" Frances asks.

"Yes, yes please."

Hendy's solemnity seems genuine enough. There's an awkward pause. Then Jamie speaks up.

"The good thing about it is that Aryan's death puts us in the top one hundred of the MCLT."

"What?" I ask.

"The MCLT. The Medium Company Loss Table. The league table for war sacrifices made by companies, yeah?"

I must still look as blank as I feel.

"It's calculated on a company-member-volunteer to death-in-action ratio."

"Oh," I answer. "Yeah." and I want to squash the smug bastard's nose all over his clean-shaven face.

"Well he was a stupid little bugger if you ask me," Tommy growls from his corner. Tommy always growls.

"I'm sorry?" Hendy says, primly.

"What the hell did he want to join up for? He didn't have to. He must have been mad."

I like Tommy. And, something tells me he's right, even though I haven't a clue why.

"Language please," Hendy says. "You know how I feel about swearing."

"Sorry," Tommy says. "But I'm pissed off. What did he die for, eh?"

"For his Country," Francis says and there is threat in her soft-but-clipped tone.

"His Country." Tommy shakes his head.

"I suggest you're careful with your opinions," Hendy sounds a little frightened.

"Aren't we fighting to keep our Country free?" Tommy asks.

"Of course."

"Well that includes free speech."

I stretch out on my too-small, fully-adjustable office chair, and settle down for the entertainment.

"Not in time of war," Hendy says." We all have to be careful what we say."

"Careless talk costs lives," I say. I know I shouldn't but it just comes out.

"Exactly." Hendy seems oblivious to my sarcasm. More unsettling still, no one else sniggers or looks at me sharply. They all agree with me. They think I'm serious because there's a war on and that seems to render such clichés acceptable.

Only Tommy sees through me and offers me one of his maliciously charming grins.

Katie writes it down.

"Now, to business."

This mysterious and obviously brutal war hasn't improved the sheer tedium of team meetings. The Minutes of the last Meeting are both interminable and made incomprehensible to me by both the war and my extended absence from work. The briefing from the senior management team is also interminable and the individual reports from each team member are even more interminable, especially those of Francis and Jamie. I keep mine to "Still testing, I'll be finished tomorrow morning. I've been working from home."

"I'm glad to hear it," says Hendy, "Thanks for your efforts Pete, but even so, we're a week over our milestone."

"There *is* a war on," I try, tentatively. It appears to work. No one argues.

"I understand that," Hendy says. "But the mod –"

"The who?" Tommy's pun gets no reaction, except a smirk off me. I must be the only one in the room old enough to get it.

"Something you can't touch, see, hear or feel Tommy," I say. Still no reaction other than irritation

Tommy laughs. "Very sharp Mr Allman, very sharp. So what've mods got to do with it?"

"The em-oh-dee," Hendy explains, unnecessarily I think. "Ministry of Defence if you're still confused Tommy."

"No that clears it up nicely thanks Hen – Tony."

"The mod are getting impatient. They've been giving me a hard time. They need the database as soon as possible. We have to remember that we're part of the war effort here, we have to react accordingly."

MoD? So that's why the database is different to how I remember it. Along with everything else in my universe, the database is no longer a commercial project carried out on behalf of an accountancy firm but a government contract. I say nothing because I've displayed enough confusion and ignorance for one day.

*

Later, when I'm back in my pen, testing, and Andy is doing his part for the war effort by playing a game on his computer, I suffer a panic attack.

It's not a bad one, but bad enough.

Suddenly I'm scared, shaking. The world has literally gone to hell, and not just my world, the whole world. I don't understand, I'm a stranger, I don't know what to do, what to say, how to act. When I glance out of the big east windows of the office I see columns of smoke. I see tape. Everything has changed, surreal, a nightmare, all bathed in threat.

I swallow hard, breathe deep and slow. My fists are clenched so tight I can only open them by sheer force of will. I'm sweating, my mouth is dry.

Think. Come on you stupid bastard, think slowly and carefully.

This is a hallucination. The operation went wrong, or perhaps it's still going on and I'm either suffering an anaesthetic dream or in a coma. It's like that television series about the police officer who gets knocked over by a car and wakes up in 1972.

Or maybe it's a flashback. I took LSD when I was a teenager. They say you can suffer hallucinations for the rest of your life. Whatever it is, I'll wake up and the world will be back the way it should be, far from perfect but perfect enough for me.

Won't it?

Christ, *won't it?*

"This thing is bloody slow," Andy moans.

"Call IT Support, they'll sort it out for you." Diversion, a focus, something bland and neutral that's what I need, that's how it works for Peter Allman.

"Very funny."

"As supports go they're not bad."

"They're all dead Pete."

I look round at him. He's studying me intently, a worried look on his face that I don't often see.

"What do you mean?" I ask, even though the meaning is perfectly clear.

"IT support is only a reserved occupation if there's no more than one engineer available to a company, in our case, overworked and underpaid Aryan. He was only allowed to join up because some management consultant came in a said we don't need any IT support. The army had already taken the rest of the team for *their* computers, don't you remember?"

"But that Albanian one, Anton, he was only seventeen."

"Well, yeah, until he turned eighteen. They wanted him so bad they sent him his call-up papers a week before his birthday. He had to go the day after. Nice present from Uncle Mod." He shakes his head, becomes uncharacteristically solemn. "Poor little sod won't be having a nineteenth birthday."

Eighteen.

The number is like a thorn in my brain, it hurts, it stops me breathing. It greys out the world.

Andy's face turns pale. "Christ Pete, I'm sorry. I didn't think. I mean…you're…"

My son, Dominic, is eighteen on Sunday.

"Are electricians a reserved occupation?" I can hardly get the words out.

"No, none of the trades are. It's only managers, people in financial services, the software industry, the media, the arts, that sort of thing. Pete, Dominic's probably already got his letter."

"Letter?" The word comes from somewhere distant, spoken by someone else.

"You know, his call-up letter…"

"But he's my son…"

"Are you okay?"

I can't answer him. My son, Dominic, my graceful, friendly, capable son, who is enjoying his job and already thinking about how he can start his own electrical business once he qualifies.

He can't go to war.

Andy and me sit in *The Hammer and Nails*. It's a big pub, lunchtime-busy, dark, anonymous, and illumed with deliberate inadequacy by electricity as well as by green and red splintered light allowed in by the stain glass windows. We manage to grab a table as a couple, both married, though Andy is adamant that it isn't to each other, get up to go. "Too dopy," Andy declares. "If I sat gazing at my missus like that she's want to know what I'd taken and if it was legal."

I manage to laugh because it's better than crying. Or thinking.

"This is getting to you," Andy says at last. We've taken those first silent sips at our London Prides and now it's okay to talk. "And I'm not surprised. Look mate. I haven't got kids so it's not going to happen to me, but it must be shit to face something like this."

"Shit? Yeah, that's some of it." I pause, debate whether to ask the next question then do it anyway. "What war is this Andy? I mean, I went to bed last night and everything was fine, I wake up this morning and we're at war and I have no idea who we're fighting or why or for how long. It's like, I don't know, like being on another planet."

Andy suddenly looks worried, seriously worried. "I think you should go to your doctor. That operation you had, perhaps something happened to you, you know, while you were under the anaesthetic –"

"'Life on Mars'," I say. "'Ashes to Ashes'. I've already thought of that."

"What are you talking about? David Bowie or Gene Hunt?"

I look at him. He's a good work-mate. He's trying to help. I appreciate it.

"It doesn't matter," I say. "Just hurry up and finish that pint so I can buy you another. Then we can go back to the office smelling of booze and you know how much that really pisses off Hendy."

I wrestle my way to the bar and wait my turn. Like the tube and the town and everywhere else, the pub is full of military personnel.

And a tall, skinny man with short-cropped fair hair and a laughing devil tattooed on his neck.

Dave.

I stare, startled, shocked. Dave Miller. He's here, in the Hammer and Nails, with a group who're sitting in a corner by a tape-crossed window. They talk, quietly as if hatching up some conspiracy and all wear the same style of dark suit and open-necked dark mauve shirt. They are avoided, they are close, and they do not seem approachable. I notice that one of them has an arm missing, the sleeve of his jacket neatly tucked into the pocket, another of them has a huge red stain over half his face which I realise is a burn scar.

The drinks arrive and I take them back over to Tony.

"I've just seen an old mate," I say. "Back in a second."

"Who is it?"

"A biker mate from way back when." I nod towards the group

"Are you fucking crazy Pete?"

"What? It's only a mate –"

"They're Veterans."

"What do you mean Veterans?"

"War Veterans, wounded, discharged. No one talks to Veterans."

"Why the hell not? Is it illegal?"

"Not illegal exactly, but it's not a good idea okay?"

"If I want to say hello to a friend then I'll bloody well say hello to a friend." I get up. Andy grabs my arm.

"They won't want to talk to you."

"How do you know?"

"*Why* don't *you* know?"

"Because my war only started today, remember?"

"Christ Almighty Pete. Why can't you leave them alone and sit down and just drink your pint?"

I shake his hand off my arm. "After I've gone over there and said hello to my mate and talked to him about the weather."

As I approach the group one of them notices me and stands. He's the amputee, stocky, shaven-headed and looking as if he wants to rip my head off, even though he's only half my size.

"What do you want?" he growls and blocks my way. Other customers turn to watch.

"I want to talk to my mate." I nod towards Dave. He looks round.

"He doesn't want to talk to you. None of us do so piss off."

"You his bodyguard?"

"Leave us alone, okay?"

"Pete?"

It's Dave, he's looking in my direction, but there's something wrong with the way he's looking, his eyes are not focussed on me, in fact, they're not focussed on anything at all.

He's blind.

I can't answer him. I can't take it in, understand it.

"I'll get rid of him," the bodyguard says.

"No Gary, leave him alone, he's all right."

"Dave," the stocky one, Gary, warns. "Best to send him away."

"I know, I know." Those sightless, screwed-up eyes haunt me already. "Pete, you have to go."

"What happened to you?" I can't help asking. This is a lifelong friend, I can't just accept that suddenly he's gone blind and doesn't want to talk to me anymore.

"I'm a fucking Veteran, what do you think happened to me?"

"A vet…But I talked to you last Saturday, on the phone…" Except I didn't, did I, because here he is, an ex-soldier, blinded in some battle or other, sitting here with his Band of Broken Brothers, cut off from me by an experience I cannot even imagine let alone share. They *are* broken, every one of them. There's a shaker, the burn victim, another amputee, same arm as Gary in fact, and a poor, young bastard whose face is so misshapen and scar-mapped he's barely recognisable as a human being anymore.

"Pete, go away." Said gently, but the words are formed around steel.

"You deaf?" Gary the self-appointed bodyguard says.

I don't answer. Sometimes it's best not to.

"I'll phone you," I say.

"Don't" Dave answers.

I return to Andy, conscious of the curious, and, in some cases, mocking stares that follow me.

"I warned you," Andy says.

"Yeah, yeah, shut up and drink so you can buy me another one."

Shaking his head, Andy does just that. Alone, I can't help but join the pieces of the puzzle that link Dave's blindness to Dominic's imminent conscription and come up with a picture too terrible to contemplate.

Half way back to the office, just as we round the corner by the London Museum, a mournful wail rings out and I freeze. The sound is shockingly evocative. I've heard it before in countless war films and documentaries.

"What the hell's that?" The question is stupid because I know what it is.

"Air raid siren," Andy says and carries on walking.

"Aren't we supposed to get into a shelter or something?"

Andy stops walking and turns on me. "You run to the shelter if you want to, me, I'm fucked if I'm going into one of those stinking hell holes." He makes to carry on walking.

"It's better than being bombed –"

He stops again, turns once more and with infinite patience says: "They never bomb this part of London."

"There's always a first time."

He shrugs. "Maybe, but not today."

"How do you know that?"

"I can feel it in my water. Are you coming or not? Hendy is going to be wetting himself if we don't get back soon."

I shrug and catch up with Andy. He is the expert after all, he's lived this war, he knows its etiquette and unspoken rules. So I follow him, conscious all the time of the amount of glass around me, thousands of square feet of it. One explosion and the whole street will become a hurricane of jagged shards. I don't believe the tape will be of much use in the event of a direct hit.

An aircraft roars overhead. I catch a glimpse of something dark and triangular.

"One of ours," Andy says, laughing. "Jesus you're jumpy. It really is one of ours, Pete, a fighter, chasing the bad guys."

I hear a distant, heavy thud and realise that it is an explosion. A bomb has been dropped, and buildings are shattering, people dying. Another thud follows, another and another. Then everything is drowned out by jet noise.

And still no one is running or scared or making any attempt to gain whatever shelters are available. There is, in fact, a sort of defiant cool, an affectation of unconcern, as if to show any fear will bring scorn down on your head, and surely that's much worse than a brutal fiery death.

For Christ's sake what is wrong with people?

Up on the AlphaTech floor, I can see the raid through the big eastern window. I stand in front of it, not caring about the curious stares locked onto me, and the sniggers and puzzled, murmured conversations. I have to see this. I have to watch.

The enemy bombers are specks that dot the heavy grey cloud. They circle then break into shallow dives that take them across the distant skyline. Flame puffs upwards in their wake, white then orange then melting into dense, black smoke, ten or twelve thick columns of it, climbing skywards to merge with the cloud.

I glimpse a new explosion, this one in the sky. A fireball arcs earthward, leaving a trail of smoke as it falls. The impact is marked by yet another orange and white blossom.

"Taking in the view?"

I look round to see Frances.

"What do you think?"

"Long lunch then a bit of plane spotting, it's all right for some."

Yeah, especially for those who aren't about to lose their sons to a war nobody seems to understand but everyone accepts.

"How many people do you think that air raid has killed?" I ask.

"Best not to think about it."

"Why?"

She stares at me. "Because…well, there's a war on and people get killed in wars."

"That's okay then, as long as it's not you, as long as it's *on* over there and not here or in Islington or wherever it is that *you* live."

Now she looks hurt. "I don't choose where the EoD drop their bombs."

"But doesn't it affect you? Look at it? There's fire and smoke and there must be dead people under it all."

"How's the testing getting along Andy?"

"Change the subject why don't you."

"There is nothing I or you or anyone in this office can do about it, except get on with our jobs and hope what we do makes some sort of difference." She sounds close to tears, covering it with righteous, corporate anger. I feel guilty now. As irritating as she is, Frances doesn't deserve to be upset by some hulking bully like me.

"I'm sorry," I mutter." It's getting to me."

"It's getting to all of us," Frances snaps back.

She's upset now. Perhaps she has a boyfriend, a brother, out there, wherever *there* is, doing his bit.

I shrug. "I'll be finished testing by tomorrow lunch time."

"You'd better be," Frances says and turns to leave.

"Or what?"

She flinches back, unused to being challenged I suppose. "You're not irreplaceable." She closes in, glances around the office then lowers her voice. "Be careful what you say, Pete, cynicism is a luxury these days."

*

As I walk through the front door of my house I wonder what I have actually achieved today Yes, I've carried out nearly all the testing I need to do, but what the hell for? Suddenly what I do seems trivial and useless while people are dying in full panoramic view beyond the office window. If my best mate Dave is of fighting age, then so am I, yet I'm testing software in a comfortable office while people who actually make, repair and build things are out there dying or coming home in pieces, like Dave and his gang of Veterans.

I still don't know who we're fighting and I still don't know where the war is actually happening,

My family is scattered, as usual, over the house, Rachel, in her bedroom doing homework, Amanda slumped in front of the sitting room television, which is showing the news. I sit down beside her to watch and am surprised to see the same smoke and flame I had witnessed this afternoon. "Another air raid hits London, the fourth this week, the enemy apparently concentrating on the densely populated areas in the east of the capital. Two enemy aircraft were shot down by RAF fighters. Their crews did not bail out." Footage of a dog fight is shown, specks, in the sky, the flash of missiles, a puff of fiery smoke. "Birmingham and Manchester have also suffered heavy bombing this afternoon. Casualty numbers have not yet been released but the figure is expected to exceed a hundred. Our political correspondent Alamgir Hussein spoke to the Defence Secretary earlier this evening."

Cut to a night-time Parliament Square and The Secretary, muffled in an expensive looking coat. He puffs condensation as he speaks.

"Our forces are doing an admirable job of taking the fight to the enemy and have our complete support –"

"But more and more EoD aircraft are breaking through –"

"Let's put this in context. Only eighteen percent of EoD bombers actually penetrate our defences which means that the damage inflicted on our cities and towns is insignificant compared to the devastation we are wreaking – no, let me finish please – the devastation we are wreaking on EoD training camps and strongholds."

"Are we any closer to victory?"

"We are always closer to victory. Every day, indeed, every hour in which our armed forces are actively engaged with the enemy brings us a step closer to our goal."

"Have you any idea when that goal will actually be achieved?"

Condescending smile. "It isn't for me to put a time and date on the conclusion of our mission. We have to trust our commanders on the ground to decide that. Conflict such as this is always full of variables and uncertainties. But, look at what we have achieved so far. We have taken the fight to the EoD, we have caught them on the back foot and left them reeling and in disarray. We have instituted a massive £2 billion rebuilding campaign in the areas of the Country worst hit by bombing. We have increased our military budget by £100 million and ensured out forces are able to deploy the most advanced equipment in the field."

"There has been renewed criticism of the war itself –"

"Of course, and shouldn't we celebrate the fact. This is a democracy, a place where we are free to express our views. Isn't that exactly what we are fighting for?"

More questions, but he smiles, raises a hand, says a jolly thank you and hurries away, flanked by aides and security men.

Then it's back to the newsreader and a story about the marriage of a celebrity who I've never heard of. A glittering occasion packed full of other celebrities apparently. So why aren't they out dying for their fucking Country?

I go though into the kitchen where I find Ruth, still in her work clothes and standing over a large stir-fry.

I kiss her on the cheek. She smiles a tired hello.

"Good day?" I ask.

"Yes, yours?"

"Fantastic."

"That bad."

"There was an air raid."

"On your building? Was anyone hurt –"

"No, no, don't panic. Somewhere out in the East End. It was on the news."

"Ah." She shrugs.

"People were killed."

"Bloody war."

I shiver, because her answer is dead-eyed, compassion by rote.

"Who are they?" I ask.

"The people who were killed?"

"No, the EoD."

She stops stirring the food in the pan and turns to scrutinise me.

"Just humour me," I say.

Scrutiny turns to frown. "The Enemies of Democracy."

"Right, but *who* are they? Al Qaeda? The Taliban? The Icelandic Freedom Brigade? Who *are* they?"

"The Enemies of Democracy. They're...shadowy, a network..."

"With an air force as well as an army?"

"Yes, of course, why else would we be at war with them?"

"Are you sure they aren't led by a bald bloke with a scar and a Persian cat?"

"Pete, I have no idea what you are talking about so why don't you do something useful like lay the table."

"People were killed Ruth."

"Bloody war." This isn't right. Ruth never swears.

"Civilians." I can't help myself. It terrifies me.

"Bastards."

I can't eat. It's because of Dominic. He's not doing anything bad, or saying anything to put me off my food. It's simply his presence at the table. He's matured. The job is doing him good, making a man of him He's telling us about a practical joke that took place on the building site he's been working on.

Two men were digging a hole, one of them a grizzled old labourer, the other a newly employed teenager – a typical combination on all building sites according to Dominic, anyone in-between has been called up. While the youngster wasn't looking, the labourer dropped a 50p piece into the soil then picked it up. "Look what I found!" he said. "What are the chances of that?" The young lad was amazed, then even more amazed when his mate found another 50p then a pound coin, a two pound coin and, finally, a five pound note. By now he was beside himself, unable to understand why he couldn't find any. Apparently he still hasn't worked it out.

"Poor boy," Ruth says.

"That was cool," says Rachel.

"What an idiot," says Amanda.

I try to swallow and not stare at my son. He's shovelling chicken, peppers, mushrooms and courgettes into his mouth, the food barely seeming to register as it disappears down his throat. I want to hug him. I want to tell him to stop eating and talking and think about what's about to happen to him. But I can't. Everyone is happy tonight, a little argumentative in the case of my daughters but no more than usual and most of it ends in laughter anyway.

Ruth looks beautiful, her hair a little out of place and messed up, her face flushed, her clothes immaculate. I want her, for comfort, to make me forget. I can't have her yet though. If I make some excuse and take her upstairs the children will know why and their embarrassment, distaste and displeasure will know no end.

I want to talk about Dominic's call-up. I want to know all about it. How it works, where he has to go. Is it the army or one of the other services? He's bright, good with his hands and quick at maths, surely they can train him up as an engineer, something important that means he doesn't have to do any actual fighting. God, I don't care if they give him a job as commanding officer in charge of laundry and sock distribution as long as it keeps him away from the front – whatever and wherever that is.

I don't talk about it though. It's been pushed to the back of everyone's mind. Tonight is just a comfortable, friendly, family evening in.

Once the table is cleared we retire to the lounge. Ruth showers and comes downstairs, comfortable in slacks and an overlarge sweater.

I'm tense, edgy. If they're bombing civilians, then they could bomb us, tonight, here, smash us and burn us and bury us in our three-bed semi. Would we know about it, would we feel our flesh crisp and vaporise? Would we be aware as we're entombed in rubble and broken furniture, paralysed by the sheer weight of it, slowly, slowly suffocating?

I want to get up and pace.

An aircraft streaks over our roof. I flinch, look up. No one else does. One of ours? Or one of theirs, the bastards, on its way to smash another family.

Ruth and the girls are crowded cosily onto the sofa. Dominic is on the floor leaning against the sofa beside his mum's legs. I'm in the armchair. The television is on. No more news reports, just sitcom followed by a cookery programme on which a celebrity chef shows us how to make-do-and-mend with rationed food.

Which is something else I can't work out. Why are there plenty of non-native fruit and exotic ingredients, but precious little milk, meat and butter? Why is home grown food so hard to get when foreign grown is freely available? How do they get it over here? Aren't there any EoD submarines and aircraft out there, just waiting to sink our ships or knock down our cargo planes?

I doesn't matter I'm too tired to care.

Although, there is something else. A flicker on the television screen, an image that seems to appear every now and then, but is so brief I'm not sure it's even there at all.

There's a stir of excitement. A favourite programme then.

Bloody war.

Military music to a dance beat. Shots of earnest, twenty-somethings clambering up rock faces and abseiling down again and running and jumping and tramping through foggy moorland and dank forests.

Bloody war

I saw it, there, on the screen, bright white letters on a black background.

"Did you see that?" I say, half-rising from my seat.

"See what?" Dominic asks.

"'Bloody war', on the television, come on you must have seen it."

Everyone looks at me, either bemused or worried. Perhaps it's an advert for a forthcoming television programme. I seem to remember a similar flash ad for Big Brother, a glimpse of that stupid bloody eye.

Talking of which, we're seconds into a reality programme, exactly the type of television shite I hate with a vengeance. Who cares about the oh-so-desperate ambitions of a bunch of nobodies? Not that there's anything wrong with ambitions and dreams, just don't shout, cry and die over them in front of me. But everyone else seems transfixed so who am I to suggest we change channels.

EoD bastards!

I flinch, sure I've seen the phrase snap on then off the screen. This time I can't remember the colours, just the words. They flare bright in my mind.

The title of the reality show flashes up, in blocky, military-style text.

"Officer Quest"

There's a voiceover now, serious and gravel-raw, a British version of that ludicrously deep voice used on the trailers to Hollywood action films, the ones that always start with "One man…"

This time it's "Ten ordinary people, each with a passion to serve their Country and be a leader of men in our fight for freedom. Only one will be chosen to win a place at Sandhurst Officer Academy, only the best is good enough. Only one will complete the officer quest!"

The music crashes to an end.

We have no choice.

Then the celebrity presenter appears, bundled in the latest designer faux-military anorak, a microphone in his gloved hand. I recognise him, an actor who usually plays tough guys. He's certainly talking tough tonight, and being tough, shivering out there in the wind and rain.

"Last night we lost Karen." Toughness gives way to solemnity. Was she killed? Christ, just what sort of reality programme is this?

Cut to a head and shoulders, a dark-haired, carefully gaunt young woman. Karen Fletcher, PR consultant said the subtitle. She is brave but obviously quietly upset. "I'm gutted," she says. "I was so up for it. But I've failed." Her voice breaks. She dabs prettily at her eyes. "This is all I've ever wanted, I know I can do this and now…I'm sorry, I've let you all down. I've let myself down…"

At least she's still alive.

Bloody war.

"*You* voted her off." The presenter sounds as if he wants to step out of the screen and punch each one of us very hard.

We're back on that bleak moorland hillside now. "Karen's departure leaves just three contestants. Tonight you will have to vote again. Who will fall this time?"

Now comes a sequence of faces, stills of square-jawed young executives; Mike, Darren and Nadia.

So on to tonight's tests.

A tramp through a forest at night with a squad of real soldiers to lead and command. The solders look sullen, resentful, authentically tough and about ready to shoot their prospective leader in the back. They carry huge packs and have their craggy, careworn old-before-their-time faces daubed with black, green and brown war-paint.

Then there's a cliff to scale and parachute jump into a river and so on and so forth.

There are brave words from the trio of contestants, each miniature speech filled with clichés such as "I'm really up-for-it, I know I can do this, I know I'm going to win this" and so on. Ah, there will be tears and tumbles and laughs a-plenty.

EoD bastards!

I watch, sickened and I can't stop glancing at my son who will soon look as frightened and time-worn and vulnerable as the real soldiers in this farcical crap.

The programme ends with another order from our jovial presenter. We all, and that's every one of us who cares about their Country and their freedom, need to get off our arses – yes, he says arses – pick up our mobile phones and waste credit on a vote for the contestant we want to remain on the show.

To my dismay, my family dutifully produce their phones and for a moment the room falls silent as they text in their votes. Then there's a heated discussion about who they all voted for.

"What about you Dad?" says Rachel.

"You know I never vote in these stupid programmes."

"Stupid?" Rachel is horrified. And, so, apparently, is everyone else, even the world-weary and brutally cynical Amanda.

"But it's 'Officer Quest' Dad," she says. I've never heard such seriousness from her about anything other than the foibles of her friends, boyfriends and enemies.

It's that that makes me fetch my phone. I can't believe I'm doing this, condemning some poor stupid, star-struck sod to death by bullet, shell or fire.

I choose the woman because I don't like her arrogant demeanour.

As soon as my vote is sent I feel guilty. She's probably a decent person, has a boyfriend, a mum and dad, an ambition and a life. I can't change my vote though. A strict not-to-be-disobeyed voice has told me that my vote is *final*.

I wander into the kitchen and switch on the kettle. I actually need beer with a whisky chaser, as many of them as I can fit into my tight-clenched stomach, but coffee will be best for everyone.

Dominic comes in to make himself a sandwich and it's all I can do not to grab him, hold him and cry into his shoulder.

I haven't cried since my mum died and that was nearly twenty years ago.

I go up to bed early, claiming tiredness. I lay on the duvet, still dressed, the light off. The blackout curtains keep the room dark, not one chink of light seeps in.

I hear a tread on the stairs, on the landing.

The door opens and there's a glimpse of diffused light from hall, and a silhouette. The door closes and a moment later Ruth is in my arms, a soft bundle of wool and hair and then soft lips and scalding breath. I hold her tight, quickly aroused. I kiss her hard, rolling her over until she's beneath me. Her breath is urgent, she whispers my name. I work off her slacks and her panties, she lifts her bottom to let them pass by. I tear at my own trousers and in a moment I feel her damp warmth against me and I enter her smoothly and easily.

I lay there, joined to her, and kiss her again, slowly and deeply. She moans and clutches at my hair and I begin to move.

It doesn't take long and when it ends it is a delight and then a dark sadness that makes me claw her to myself and hold her so tight that she eventually protests that she can't breathe.

I hear her whisper that she loves me, and I want her again, slowly this time, gently, easily and languidly. This time I lick her until I hear her stifled groans and then the scream she muffles by biting the pillow.

Then I enter her again and this time I relish her and take my time and touch her and kiss her until I'm spent.

Without Ruth I would be an animal, because that's what I was before I met her.

The two men in charcoal suits and sunglasses arrive at AlphaTech late the next morning. They move quietly through the office, their passing a slight disturbance of air, a whiff of aftershave. I look up to see them sweep by then stand to watch. My head is one of dozens, poking, meerkat-style, over the top of our partitions. The suits, the glasses, all make them living clichés, yet there is nothing funny about them.

The men stop at Tommy's pen then step inside. There is murmured conversation, an eruption of foul-mouthed protest, another quiet word and they reappear, Tommy walking between them. He glances my way and I see that his face is ashen, his eyes wide.

I've never seen Tommy scared before.

I draw back as they pass, in another micro-storm of aftershave, and sweat this time, Tommy's sweat. Our eyes lock, he opens his mouth to speak but no words emerge and in a moment he's gone.

I make to follow but feel a hand on my arm and turn to see Andy.

"Are you mad?" he hisses.

"Who the fuck are they, the police?"

"Isn't it obvious?"

"Yeah, so obvious I'm asking you."

"SSU."

"Right, that explains it."

"Fuck me you're hard to please. Special Security Unit. You do not want to get mixed up with them."

"Secret police then, the British Gestapo."

"Of course not, but SSU trouble is *real* fucking trouble."

Andy goes back to his work, a little more intent on what he is doing – and it is AlphaTech business for a change – than usual. I can't. I stand in my pen and stare at the door through which Tommy was hustled away. I want to go after them, demand to know why they were arresting an innocent man whose only crime was to criticise the war.

Bloody war.

The words, white-on-black flare into my mind so vividly I almost speak them out loud.

That frightens me almost as much as the sudden appearance of the SSU. One brief look at the television and that advert or trailer or whatever it was, is already glued to the inside of my skull and flashing on and off (along with *EoD bastards* and *We have no choice but to fight*) like the neon sign over the entrance to a strip club.

My mouth dries, my heart starts to hammer. I'm angry. I'm going to find out exactly what is going on. I don't care what Andy thinks –

The door opens again, to admit another stranger. This one wears a dark blue suit which looks to be infinitely more expensive and well-cut then those worn by the sunglass-twins. He smiles a light, friendly smile that does not reach his eyes. His hair is neatly combed and dark, greying a little at the sides. He is slight-built. He catches my eye as he passes and nods in greeting. I don't return the courtesy because I don't like him.

The man walks straight to Hendy's office and goes in without knocking.

I sit down and return to my testing schedule. I'm almost finished, the database all-but ready to be downloaded onto its server, Andy's job and one he is very good at.

My phone rings.

"Pete?" It's Hendy. "Can you come into my office for a moment?"

Now I'm scared. I try not to show it. I stand slowly, loosen my tie and roll up my shirt sleeves. I attempt a nonchalant saunter down the aisle. My legs are weak, my heart is thudding.

I have nothing to hide, I have nothing to fear. I've done nothing wrong, Christ I even voted in "Officer Quest" last night. My vote counted, because Nadia is still on the programme. Mike was the loser, a square-jawed Design Consultant or some-such. He broke down and stormed off, shoving the presenter aside roughly. His life, he declared loudly, was over.

"Come in," Hendy responds to my knock.

The man is sitting at Hendy's desk. He rises as I enter and offers me his smooth and perfect hand. I shake it firmly, crush it as tight as I dare without actually injuring him. His grey eyes lock with mine during that moment and I see that we understand each other.

Hendy is standing nervously by the door. Is that to stop me running away I wonder, or to give him a head start if *he* needs to?

"Pete," the man says pleasantly enough. "Thank you for sparing me your time. I'm Daniel Mason, Chief Investigator with the SSU."

I nod.

"We have a few concerns Pete. A few matters to clear up."

I resist the temptation to request a Mister and a surname. Better to smother my pride and loathing and get this over with. Mason represents one of those things I hate, along with reality shows, authority, those who feel that they have the right to declare themselves our masters.

"Well, what do you want to clear up? Like you said, I'm sparing my time and I don't have much of it at the moment."

"Pete!" Hendy snaps from his corner in his best be-polite-to-the-gentleman tone.

"That's all right Tony," says Mason. "I admire a man who stands up for himself. The world is full of the craven, the yes-man. It's the no-man that keeps us on our toes. The why-man. I think you're one of those Pete. A why-man."

I don't answer. I'm not going to take his side against Hendy, who I do actually admire in an odd sort of way.

"The thing is, Pete, you've been asking some strange questions."

"What questions?" Awkwardness, the last resort of the frightened and soon-to-be-defeated.

"About the war," Hendy says, made irritable by his own fear.

"Thank you," Mason says to him and there was no mistaking that his courteously delivered sentence is a request for Hendy to keep his mouth shut. "Yes, the war."

"In what way is that strange? Journalists ask those questions all the time. I saw one of them quizzing the Defence Secretary only last night." I look Mason straight in the eyes and it takes all my will to hold his steady, steady gaze. "Is *he* in prison now?"

"Good point and no, Alamgir Hussein is not in prison but continuing to do an important job very well. But he does not ask fundamental things like who we are fighting and request details about troop movements and enemy air raids."

"You make me sound like a spy," I say.

Mason doesn't answer, just looks at me.

When sufficient time has passed to make me sweatily uncomfortable, he says. "We've been at war for almost eighteen months Pete. It's on the news every night, our triumphs and tragedies, victories and blunders. We're as transparent as it's possible to be in the circumstances." He shrugs. "Surely you understand that we can't possibly tell you exactly where our forces are and where we are fighting."

"Of course not but –"

"You are currently working on a highly sensitive project for HM Government. You are in a position of trust. You have signed the Official Secret's Act."

Another thing on the Don't Remember list.

"Your work is vital to the war effort, it may save thousands of lives and yet you display a cynical and cavalier attitude and waste time asking questions you have no right to have answered." All is delivered in a smooth, almost hurt tone. It works too because, unbelievably I'm starting to feel guilty. "What's wrong Pete? Is it stress?"

"Haven't I got a right to know exactly who we are fighting?"

"Absolutely."

"So who are we fighting?"

"The EoD."

"And they are –"

"There you go Pete, probing, questioning, making trouble."

"But *who* are they?"

"A shadow, a cancer."

"Bastards," droned Hendy.

"Are they Chinese? Australian? Who the fuck are they?"

"Pete." Sharp this time.

"Okay, okay, let me put it this way. My son is expected to go out and risk his life soon. Surely I have a right to know, and *he* has a right to know, who he is fighting and why."

"Isn't it obvious?"

"No it isn't."

"Let's go back to first principles Pete. What happened yesterday, what did you see through those windows? Hmm? That's what we're fighting."

I stop. It's no use. I'm floundering. I'll get no answers from this bastard.

"There is one more thing," Mason says. "Yesterday lunch time you went to the Hammer and Nails, yes?"

"If it's any business of yours, yes I did. So what?"

"None at all, except that you approached a group of Veterans."

"One of them was my best friend."

"*Was*, Pete, that's the key word; *was*. He's a Veteran, he's different now. No one who comes back from a war is the same person as the one who bravely marched away to do his duty. My advice is don't approach them again, not that group, or any Veterans at all. They don't like it and it will be upsetting for you." He stands, pats me on the arm. "We need you Pete, whole and hearty. Your Country needs you. Your family needs you, and in the end that's what we're fighting for isn't it, our own, our loved ones? We're all under strain, this war –"

"Bloody war," intones Hendy, right on-cue.

"– is difficult for all of us. We all question, we all doubt, but we fight on, we renew ourselves, we go forward."

I nod, make myself look brave and resolved. Mason can see through it though. But we understand each other, and what I understand is threat. They took Tommy away to frighten us, perhaps me specifically. Watch your step Allman, that's what he's saying, or the clichés in sunglasses will blow in on an Armani scented breeze and whisk you away as well.

"One last item. The database, how close are we to completion?"

"Pete?" says Hendy brusquely, all manager now.

"It'll be loaded onto the server by lunch time."

"Mmm." Mason nods to himself, he appears to consider this very carefully, then he comes to a decision, a decision I know he made a long time ago but needs this little pantomime to make me feel trusted in some way. "Pete, the database needs to be populated as quickly as possible." He reaches into his pocket and retrieves a small object which he holds out for me to take. It's a memory stick, black and silver and very ordinary looking. "This is it, the information. No more dummy entries, just get it downloaded."

"That's a bit risky," I say. "You could lose the lot, other people are still able to view the database, the security hasn't been tested yet —"

"Leave all those worries to me. I trust you Pete. There are back-ups of course, ruined data isn't the problem. We do not, however, want this little piece of plastic and silicone to fall into the wrong hands."

"It seems a bit vulnerable to me," I say.

"Risk is a part of life. Look after it Pete, continue with your good work, and, as I said, leave the worrying to the likes of me."

"Do you want me to lock it in the safe until Pete is ready —"

"A solid proposal Henderson but I trust Pete."

"Of course." Hendy sounds offended, a little petulant.

My hand closes around the memory stick and I put it in my trouser pocket.

"No copies, no back-ups please," Mason says. "If it becomes corrupted in any way we'll supply you with another. If you lose it we'll arrest you."

"What's happening to Tommy?" I ask, foolishly but I can't resist it.

"He's probably in hospital by now. The man is having a breakdown, but we can't let him stay in an NHS establishment can we, too much risk. He'll be looked after, don't worry." Mason offers me his hand. I shake it again. "Thank you Pete. You're work has not gone unnoticed."

An hour later I witness a series of explosions, again over to the east. The shockwaves pound the window dully, ten seconds after the orange-white flashes. They startle no one else but me, in fact few people even so much as look up. I see the aircraft, black dots that circle, dip then climb away. Other black dots sweep in but the raiders are gone.

Again I stare at the smoke. Again I see rubble and fire crew and a desperate scramble for survivors. My mind-images are monochrome, the clothes and uniforms I conjure, sixty years out of date, fire-engines announce their arrival with clanging bells, hoses pour water onto raging fires, there are women in headscarves, men in old-style military helmets bearing the legend ARP…

It won't be like that though will it. Everything will be in full colour, yellow hi-viz jackets, modern, white helmets, radio-crackle and stroboscopic blue-lights. The civilians' clothes will be Primark, Top Shop and Marks and Spencer, the stench and heat and dust will be real, not archive film remote.

The whole team goes to the Hammer and Nails at lunch time. Hendy wants us to celebrate the completion of the database project. He buys the first round, Frances buys the second. She sits beside him and hangs onto his every word. She looks at him a lot, he glances at her and I realise that despite the wedding ring on Hendy's finger, they are more than just colleagues.

We are loud, we drink too much. We talk about "Officer Quest" (me as well) and make all the same old in-jokes and everyone is happy and warmed by the feeling of being in The Team. Even Katie undoes another button of her lilac cardigan to reveal just a hint of cleavage and is flushed and bright-eyed and sipping at yet another Southern Comfort and lemonade. She can't stop looking at Jamie who ignores her completely.

I let myself fall into the illusion. I let the heat of the pub and the beer swirling around inside me, dull my brain. I go outside for a cigarette. Andy joins me and asks about my interview with Mason. I tell him it was about the database and that he's a creepy bastard.

Suddenly I want to go home because it's Wednesday, only three-and-half more days until Dominic's eighteenth birthday. I can't stand being here, away from him. But I don't know where he is and, anyway, he would hate me to walk onto whatever building site he's working on.

We go back to the office at two-thirty. I carry out one final test then unlock my drawer and pull out the memory stick. I hold it, a small oblong of plastic, coffin shaped, deadly.

I push it into one of the USB ports on my desktop. Then I open it.

My head is spinning from too much lunchtime booze and too many cigarettes. I concentrate. My skull aches. There is a list, three columns. Name, Address, Number. Simple, scant. The names are ordinary enough. B. Seaton, F. Shaw, V Sahramdhani and so on, thousands of names. The addresses look like Post Codes with an additional number as a prefix, 56 – HA4 5JU, 7-LP2 12WL, house number then. The Number column is obviously what this is really all about, a code, but what for? Enemies of the State? People under suspicion? Panicked I scroll back up to A for Allman –

Miller.

D Miller 33A – NW6 7KT , then that number 4765325.

Dave Miller, my biker mate, now blind and war-scarred. Kilburn, that's where he lives, or did live before I woke up to this nightmare, and the number of his flat is 33A. So why is he on there? I scroll quickly up to A. There is an Alsop, an Alstein and an Al Hussein, but no Allmans.

So what do I do?

Mason seems responsible for the safety of this data, seems to be the friendly face of whoever needs it, which means that it has not been collated for any good reason. Does Dave know he's on this list? Does anyone?

I hesitate. I'm shaking, my mouth is dry because I know what I should do but I can't summon the courage to carry it out.

Oh come on, there is a bloody war on you know…

I open my drawer and surreptitiously pick one of my own personal memory sticks from the mess it contains. I look around, about as casual and normal-acting as if I was stark naked. I push the stick into one of the other ports. Its light flickers then comes on.

Will they know? Is there some vicious little piece of software in Mason's stick that will set off alarms or, at the very least, register that a copy has been made?

And my own PC, is it being monitored? Our internet and e-mail traffic used to be, but this is not on any network, the sticks are both standalone. Aren't they?

My hands are paralysed.

Fuck it.

I click on "Select All" then copy the highlighted list on Mason's stick. Then I close it and open my own. There isn't much on this one, plenty of memory. I paste.

The download takes hours, days. I sit, staring at my screen, forgetting to minimise it in my panic, leaving it up, frozen in front of it, as the counter tells me that I am 5% complete and the estimated finishing time is twenty minutes.

"Pete?"

I start and hastily and clumsily minimise the window.

"What were you looking at then?" It's Jamie. He grins. "Brought some porn in have you?"

"Piss off." I concentrate on whatever innocuous document I've brought up onto the screen.

Jamie wants me to sign something. I take it from him and fumble for a pen among my desk litter. He leans over me, reaches for the mouse.

"Let's have a look then –"

I grab the mouse a moment before his hand closes about it. "Don't you understand the term piss off?" This time I manage my infamous you-wanna-a-fight-growl.

"Fuck me," he says, rattled. "Can't you take a joke anymore Pete?" He shakes his head and walks away.

I maximise the window and find that the data has all been transferred. I close my stick, remove it then drop it into my trouser pocket.

"Okay Andy," I say. "The data's in the holding area. It's all yours."

And mine.

Dominic isn't here tonight.

He's staying at a mate's, which makes this a practice run, a meal eaten without him sitting at the table, a house where he *isn't*.

His friends are having a combined farewell and eighteenth party for him, apparently. I was supposed to remember, but I don't.

"This is his night with his mates," Ruth explains patiently. "Jason's parents have that huge house, remember?"

Yes I do, I'm not senile.

"They've agreed to let them have half of it and stay the night." Ruth chuckles and shakes her head. "It'll probably mean more to him than our family party on Sunday."

"Well yeah," Amanda rolls her eyes. "I mean, who wants a load of relatives all over you on your eighteenth?"

"It isn't just his eighteenth is it!" Rachel snaps and it's the first time I've seen her fear and grief. It shocks me, which is ridiculous, but she has remained so calm about it up until now.

"I'm sorry Mum," Amanda says and she sounds it.

I leave the table and go upstairs, claiming a need for the bathroom.

What I need is Dominic's room.

It's typical, a lad's bedroom, messy but not out of control. There are posters on the wall, some of bands with names such as Muse and Kasabian and others, big glossy and depicting the "Machineries of War". Each of these bears the name of a red-top tabloid, so I guess they were some sort of free pull-out.

They show the equipment used by the British armed forces in its war against the EoD. One is covered with tanks and armoured cars, another with naval vessels and a third with aircraft. Among them are familiar shapes, Tornado, Jaguar, Eurofighter, but there are some unfamiliar ones too, including a dark, menacing arrowhead called the Panther. The legend states that this is the first of a new generation of fighting machines, fully automated and flown remotely, its pilot safe in a bomb-proof bunker hundreds of miles behind the lines.

Dominic's CDs are neatly stacked in a unit. It would have been big vinyl LPs in my day. I still have a few, stashed away in the Allmans' joint record collection. There are text books, and college work which is set out on the desk by the computer. I look at one some of his notes and calculations; the synchronous speeds and percentage slip of various three-phase induction motors. His hand is neat, the calculations meticulous, each formula written out, each stage shown.

Of course, today was his weekly college day.

Why is he bothering?

Because he's Dominic that's why and perhaps he's hoping to carry on with his trade in the army.

There's a letter on the desk.

I don't usually read his letters but this is on government-headed paper, Ministry of Defence to be precise.

"Dear Mr Dominic Allman

"Congratulations on your impending 18th Birthday. HM Majesty's Government sends you its best wishes and hopes you enjoy your celebrations on the 14th November.

"We would remind you that on reaching the age of 18 you are eligible for active service in the defence of the United Kingdom and are therefore required to report for duty with HM Army on Monday 15th November at Catterick Barracks by 15:00 at the latest. Please find map, free train pass and full registration instructions attached. Please bring a minimum of possessions with you. All clothing and personal equipment such as shaving tackle will be supplied to you on registration.

"If for any reason, such as illness or personal incident including close family member bereavement, you cannot attend on this date, please contact us immediately on the above telephone number. Failure to do so will be construed as absence without leave and is an offence under the War Emergency Act 2009. Valid reasons for non-attendance are listed in the instruction sheet. Please note that NO other situation is considered valid.

"Please note that your army identification number is 8754292. Please memorise this number as soon as possible and use it in any further correspondence or communication.

"Yours sincerely etc."

I stare at the letter.

Monday…

The words blur. I'm crying, I'm fucking crying. I sit on the bed, fists clenched, the letter discarded. I pound my fists onto my thighs, trying to bite back the tears. If I let it go I won't be able to hold it back and that will be of no use to anyone.

I struggle to get myself under control.

Monday. We have four more days.

Four is better than none.

Four.

I look around the room again.

I mutter his name. Then I go downstairs.

Something is nagging at me as I take my place in the lounge, something about the letter, a thorn pricking at the flesh of my subconscious.

Soaps and the usual cooking and decorating shows come and go then its time for "Officer Quest" and that's when I can't bear anymore and get up and walk out. I grab my coat from the peg and open the front door.

Ruth is behind me. "What are you dong?"

"I need some air," I snap. I'm not angry with her but she's getting the brunt of all this.

"Pete, you can't –"

But I can and I'm outside and walking and its bloody cold.

The wind is strong and laden with moisture which gives it a brutal, raw edge. The street is completely deserted and dark. Most of the lamps are switched off and those that are on have been fitted with some sort of cowling that directs the light straight downward.

I hear footsteps hurrying behind me and turn to see a coat-bundled figure, face obscured by a fur-edged hood.

"Pete," Ruth shouts at me. "Wait."

I do and she catches up and takes my arm.

"What the hell is wrong with you?" she demands. "There's a curfew, you'll get yourself arrested."

"Who by?" I say and indicate the empty street. "Who cares what goes on in Northwood for God's sake?"

Ruth studies me for a moment, her face mostly invisible, but her regard is intense. She sighs, resigned. "Okay, but we have to keep off the main street."

"We?"

"You don't think I trust you out here on your own do you?"

I laugh and put my arm round her and we walk.

"I was in Dominic's room."

"I know." Of course she knows. She knows everything. "I sit up there sometimes and cry."

"*I* cried," I say.

She looks at me. "Good."

"How do you bear it?" I ask her.

"By making myself bear it. What else can I do?" She stops walking, moves round to confront me. "We both have to bear it. Storming off upstairs or out here doesn't help anyone. You can do that during the day, but not at night, not when you have a family to keep together. At night you have to pretend. We're all pretending. Do you really think Amanda and Rachel are just breezing through this? They're on the verge of cracking up. I've heard them in their rooms, sobbing their hearts out.

"And we're not the only ones are we. These houses here, how many of those families have given someone up?"

Ruth is right of course, she always is. Oh I can repair the car and plumb and drill and fix and saw and pack suitcases into a boot and carry heavy loads and do the shopping and even cook sometimes. But I'm not the wise one, the pillar, the brains, the ideas-maker, the anchor of this relationship. That's Ruth.

It starts to rain again. The rain is cold and stings my face. Ruth pulls the hood more firmly over her head and her face completely disappears. She holds my arm. The air, and her presence, clears my head.

"Perhaps we should go back," I say.

She nods.

We stop at the end of the side street and I take her in my arms, or at least the package that contains her.

There's light, blinding, white, then an engine, brakes, shouts and footsteps. I stumble back, disorientated and confused and frightened. I reach for Ruth but someone shouts at me to stand still, fucking stand STILL.

I obey. I'm shaking, hands on my head because someone yelled at me to do it. Then I kneel because someone is shoving a gun into my back, then I'm face down on the road and it's cold and wet and hard. My arms are wrenched up behind me, I feel the bite of handcuffs. I hear Ruth cry out, protest, someone tells her to shut up and that makes me angry but I can do nothing.

I can't see if our attackers are police or soldiers. They wear black, they wear helmets with visors, everything is shouted. I'm disoriented by their aggression and the relentless, dazzling light. After I moment I'm dragged to my feet, I see Ruth in front of me, stumbling, one of the uniforms gripping her right arm. The handcuffs make me feel claustrophobic. I can't move properly, can't defend myself. If I fall I won't be able to break the impact.

A vehicle looms, an indistinct hulking ugliness. We're hauled and shoved inside, once more face down, now on cold, hard metal. My weight bears down on my chest and very quickly it's hard to breathe. I hear Ruth gasp for air. She twists her head to look at me, her hood is down now. I glimpse her briefly in the dim, yellow of the courtesy light – courtesy now there's a joke – and she looks frightened and angry. Then the door slams with a metallic crash and the light is extinguished. Two guards seat themselves on either side of us.

My arms ache, I'm sure Ruth's do as well. I feel humiliated and helpless. My claustrophobia grows more intense. Ruth sounds as if she is panting now. I tell her it's going to be okay. One of the guards tells me to shut up. I want to tell him to fuck himself but I can't fight back and he has a rifle and big boots and I don't want Ruth hurt.

The van is driven fast and roughly. The journey is endless and made terrifying by our blindness. I have no idea where we are or where we are going.

"My children," Ruth days at last.

"Should've thought of that," the shut-up guard snaps back at her.

"I have to call them –"

"I told you to shut up."

The journey ends abruptly

The doors are open again and we're dragged out. We're in a bright-lit garage of some sort, our armoured van one of three similar, bestial-looking monsters. There are metal stairs, a long, bland corridor lined, on either side, with doors that look like cell doors. I hear shouts for help, of protest and anger, but, thank God, no screams.

I wonder how small the cells are because I won't be able to take anything too small. I'll go crazy very quickly.

Then I remember what is in my pocket and my legs almost give way under me.

The memory stick.

Christ oh Christ, the memory stick, the one on which I made the copy of the Mason's guard-it-with-your-life database entries.

They will search us, of course they will. Clothes first then rubber gloves and Vaseline. Suddenly I don't care about that, it's the first part that debilitates me, that drives the air from my lungs.

I want to panic, to break down, but Ruth needs me and *I* need me. A babbling wreck is no good. I have to bear it.

She is innocent, I'll hang onto that fact, clutch at it and fill my head with it. Ruth knows nothing about the stolen data.

There's another door at the end. It's opened for us and we're pushed through then onto our knees. The room is completely empty, the walls, white-painted brick, the light provided by three fluorescent fittings, one of which flashes every so often. The ends of its tube are black.

"My God Pete, you really are one for trouble, aren't you."

I turn to see Mason enter. He's wearing his suit but now his shirt is open-necked. He looks unshaven, yet somehow, remains an example of sartorial elegance. At this moment, he is the most terrifying person I know.

"We weren't doing anything wrong," Ruth says. She is not pleading but making a statement. Her courage is returning and she is angry. "And I need to contact my children."

"Don't worry about that," Mason says kindly. "A wPC is already there, taking care of them."

The news is chilling. Arrangements have been made, we are free to stay in whatever official hell hole this place is for as long as Mason wants us to.

But first, before they lock us away, will come the search.

"You can let my wife go," I say and am amazed at the steadiness of my voice. "This is my fault."

"I am not leaving without my husband."

"I am impressed by the love and loyalty you two share. There isn't enough of it around these days. Everyone thinks only of themselves, what they can get out of a situation, not about how they can help others." Mason's smile fades. "You have both broken the law. We would be within our rights to detain you indefinitely."

"Ruth came out to get me home," I say. "It was me who walked out. I was angry, not thinking…"

"An easy mistake to make in the heat of the moment." He nods to one of the guards, who strides into the room and hauls Ruth to her feet. He spins her round and drags her to the door. She shouts, struggles, threatens. I try to get up but another guard pushes me down.

"What are you going to do with her?"

"What's wrong with you Pete?" Mason asks. "Why are you causing me so many problems and worries?"

"Where is Ruth?"

"Why can't you just get on with your job and live life the way you are required to, as a loyal citizen, as a law abider. Why do you have to be so awkward?"

"Where is *Ruth*?"

"You're good at your trade, you've done a remarkable job with the database – "

If only you knew how remarkable Mason.

" – and very quickly too, yet you kick and scratch and struggle like a badly behaved child."

"Where the fuck is Ruth?" Anger is good. It gives release to my fear and disguises it as defiance.

"Grow up Pete, this isn't about you. This is about the survival of our democracy, of our way of life, of our Country. The whole is so much greater then the sum of its wretched little parts. Do you understand me Allman, do you?"

"Where is Ruth?"

"I'm worried and disappointed. I should have you locked up. But we need your talent. So I'm letting you go, but believe you me Pete, your next transgression will be dealt with severely. Do you understand?"

"Where is Ruth?"

"Do you understand? Answer me!"

"Where is Ruth?"

Mason shakes his head, all regret and sorrow for this wayward child whose bad behaviour has dragged him from his home and hearth. And kin? Does a man like that have anything resembling a family? He nods at the guards and I'm on my feet and out of the door before I can protest anymore.

If Ruth is not in the van, waiting for me, I'll tell them about the stick. Bargain with them to let her go.

I'm quickly back in the garage, bundled downstairs and trying not to lose my footing because I'm still cuffed and vulnerable to falls. The van doors are opened.

And Ruth is in the back, rubbing her wrists and glaring out, white-faced, angry and afraid.

Once free, I put my arms around her and murmur that I'm sorry, so sorry…

She shakes her head and when she's able to speak and we are on our way home she kisses me and tells me it wasn't' my fault or hers and that she has seen a side of all this she was blind to before.

"They can do what they want. Do you see Pete, they could've killed us and no one would have known. And they would have, if it served their purpose they would have put bullets in our heads. It's because of the war. They can make the rules up because of the war."

When we get home she screams at the wPC to get out of our house and gathers our daughters to herself and cries. Dominic has been brought home by the police who burst into his party and dragged him out with a minimum of ceremony and absence of explanation. He thought he was being arrested. He's worried and pissed off. They obviously wanted all of us together where they could find us.

We sit in our lounge, drinking coffee and hot chocolate, pale and drawn and quiet because for the first time we are afraid. We feel vulnerable, watched, violated. We hardly dare speak, in case we say the wrong thing and the authorities come back for us.

So we huddle around the television and shiver and eventually pluck up the courage to go to bed.

I don't sleep though. Shock keeps me awake. The realisation at just how close I have come to being incarcerated and worse. I'm thinking too hard, my mind a whirl –

D Miller 33A – KB4 7KT, 4765325.

4765325

8754292, the number on Dominic's call-up letter.

4765325, 8754292…

I disentangle myself from Ruth and walk as quietly as I can downstairs into the lounge.

4765325, 8754292…

I pick up the cordless phone and slump down into the armchair. I start to punch in Dave Miller's number. I have to know –

I drop the phone onto the floor. What the hell am I thinking of? What if the phone is bugged? I lean forward and cover my face with my hands, trying to remember, the start of the war, why we are at war, I try to prise apart my memories of a normal life where aircraft do not drop bombs on our cities and our sons a not torn away from us and thrown into hell. I try to glimpse the real images buried in there. But I can't. There's nothing but family and work, the normal, the mundane.

I make the phone call in the morning, from a call box on Moorgate Street. I'm uneasy, glancing around, my burgeoning paranoia showing me shadowy, coat-clad figures watching from sand-bag muffled, shop doorways, following me through uniform-dotted, rush hour crowds. Every accidental collision is no accident at all, but yet another of Mason's agents, tracking me, observing me, making contact with the subject.

They've seen me enter this kiosk, noted its location, electronic surveillance is homing in –

No.

There's no one out there. No one is looking, following or even the slightest bit interested in Pete Allman.

I wait until my breathing is back to normal, until the shaking eases. I sweat despite the raw, damp wind funnelling down the street. I have to stop this, or I'll end up having a heart attack, I mean, I'm still not fully over the operation and illness.

I pick up the receiver, fumble money into the slot then stab in Dave Miller's number. He could, of course, have changed it, but according to The List, as I've come to call it, he's still at the same address.

The phone rings. I almost give up.

"Hello?" Hard, unfriendly, suspicious.

"It's me, Pete."

"Fuck off –"

"No, please, wait, I need to ask you something."

"What? Is the sun shining? What colour is the sky this morning?"

"Dave…look I'm sorry about your…your sight. I'm shocked and…"

"Not as fucking sorry as I am. Why the hell are you calling me? Feel guilty do you?"

"No…yes, I don't know. I don't understand any of this."

"You and me both." A pause. "I can't talk to you, I'm not supposed to talk to you and you shouldn't be phoning me, okay?"

"Don't hang up, I'll take a chance, just tell me something."

Another pause.

"Dave," I say. "Why shouldn't you be talking to me? We're mates, is it because I haven't been called up? I don't understand that either."

"No, I don't care about that, in fact I'm glad. The more people who don't have to go through what I did, the better…Look, was that your question?"

"Christ Dave, you're like a bloody genie, three wishes only."

He laughs, a gruff chuckle and I suddenly feel better.

"What was your army number?"

"What?"

"I said –"

"I heard, I heard. What the fuck do you want to know that for?"

"Something, I don't know, something odd, to do with my work."

Pause. Then; "4765325."

I'm not surprised, of course, but hearing the numbers reeled off freezes my blood.

"There's a list Dave," I say quickly. "My company's built a database for the SSU and it's full of names, addresses and army numbers. You're on it."

"Bastards." This, breathed, growled.

Dry mouthed, I say; "I've got a copy."

If *they're* listening *they* know now.

"Christ Almighty Pete. You have to give it to me, as soon as possible, but don't let anyone see you come to my flat."

"What's going on Dave?"

"You don't need to know, you mustn't know in fact. Just get that list into my hands and run."

"Dave."

"Yeah?"

"Dominic's eighteen on Sunday."

"Don't let him go Pete, keep him out the army. No one's coming home from what they're being sent into. They can't let too many of us come back. And no one comes back in one piece. No-fucking-one."

"Why? Dave just tell me what is going on –"

He's hung up and I sense that if I call back he won't answer this time.

I leave the phone box, once more glance round, see Mason's agents everywhere, feel the memory stick burning in my pocket. I could just dump it in the nearest waste bin, but it'll be found, and handed over and looked at and idiot that I am, I've left some of my own files on there as well, work documents with my name at the top.

And Dave wants it anyway.

I pull the hood of my coat over my head, shove my hands into my pockets and hurry down Moorgate towards London Wall.

My part in the great Database Extravaganza is complete, except of course for betraying my Country by giving Top Secret information to my best mate. I'm now officially in that twilight zone between projects, which means a day sitting at my desk carrying out admin work and completing some of the on-line courses and tests we're supposed to keep up with; health and safety, data security, equality and diversity. I seldom, if ever, bother with them, which drives Hendy to distraction.

Not that I mind, I enjoy driving the poor little bugger to distraction. We all do, especially Andy, who is much better at it than I am.

But then, so was Tommy…

I find myself staring at the computer screen, unable to move or actually do any of the work I'm supposed to be doing. My mind is filled with images of Ruth, manhandled, shoved and sworn at, of bright lights and vans and anonymous policemen.

I worry that my family has been arrested again, that they are not safe, at school, at work, I worry about air raids, about a million ways in which they can be harmed and how I can miss eighteen months of my life and wake up one morning and find myself in a war zone.

And Dominic, oh lets not forget Dominic, with his call-up letter and army number.

I reach for my list of things to do. I stare at it. I'm normally good with lists. I number the jobs in order of priority then carry them out strictly in that order, but this morning I can't be bothered, all the tasks seem insurmountable. I should go home, I should visit my family, each member, check that they're all right.

The siren goes off. As usual no one moves. I glance out of the window and look across the roofscape, waiting for the dark specks and the billowing explosions.

"Pete?" I look up to see Frances. "Are you all right? You look a bit pale. Do you want to go home? I'm sure Tony will understand."

"No, I'm okay, just lack of sleep that's all."

She nods, a surprising amount of what I'm sure is genuine understanding in her face.

"Okay, good, because there's a visitor for us in reception, someone about our next project. Can you pop downstairs and sign him in. He says he wants to speak to you specifically. He needs a database specialist and wants to find out if his project is actually feasible before he goes any further. Take him into the restaurant for a coffee, use the company catering card."

Why not? It'll break the monotony and take my mind off my fears and worries.

I get up, glance at the window again, still nothing, although I can see specks now. One, a small, black arrowhead which streaks from left to right then turns sharply.

One of ours I think.

I force some energy into my step and walk towards the exit. Something makes me pause, look back. I feel a sudden tension in the office, see people rising from their seats, looking towards the big window.

Then I see the aircraft, clear, dark, hunched and malevolent, seeming to hang in the sky, its nose pointed directly at us.

Bloody show-off pilot.

Its belly flashes, fire jets ahead of the machine. The image makes no sense. There's smoke and flame, then the aircraft is turning again, veering away now, showing us its underside. Its roar is deafening, the whole structure seems to shake.

The fireball it released is still racing towards the building.

Straight, fast, solid –

I see the glass shatter at the far end of the office. I see something come in, black, fire-spewing, man-sized. Rocket-shaped.

I hear one, solitary scream and it sounds like Katie.

The thing explodes.

The flash is shocking and bright-white. The concussion is like a sledge hammer to the head and chest that drives me back, down and onto my backside. It brings an abrupt and painful silence. The flame and smoke are terrible, an orange and black eruption that boils outwards at an astonishing rate, an engulfing, vaporising wave that breaks over and swallows the pens and their occupants. It pushes scorching air and whirling debris ahead of itself.

Then the floor seems to tilt and my hearing returns and I am in Hell.

I twist round, fling myself hard down onto the floor, grasping at the flat, carpet-tiled surface, clinging on to nothing. Things batter me, the air is hot and I can barely breathe.

I open my eyes and see feet, a tangle of legs. I'm kicked, something heavy falls on me and I realise it's a person, someone in a suit. I want to get up, I need to get up. I fucking have to get up.

I struggle and lash out and the weight rolls off. I scramble to my feet, using other human beings as handholds. People are jammed at the exit door. There is screaming and swearing, and smoke and heat and a noise.

Christ, jet roar. The bastard is coming back.

I get to the door, push a woman with scorched and smouldering clothes through the gap, then try to hold back, try to be brave and help people, but the press takes me with it and in a moment I am in the doorway itself.

And there, standing in the entrance to his office, mouth open, ashen, is Tony Henderson. He seems too shocked to move. I glimpse Frances, behind him. Then I'm through into the lift lobby.

People, astonishingly, unbelievably, stab lift call buttons. The alarms screech now. I am carried towards the stairs, I try to get back, try to claw my way toward the office. I can't leave Hendy in there, or Frances and Andy and Jamie. I can't...

The crowd drives me across the lobby, thins, I stumble, turn.

The office doors dissolve.

The world cracks open.

Flame boils and blasts into the lobby. I stumble back then run, my arms wrapped about my head as the concussion, the shock wave slams into me and sweeps my feet from under me.

It's dark now, the heat unimaginable. I cough, claw for air and inhale smoke and dust and stink. The air roars and rages, screams puncture the wall of sound.

This time I don't hesitate. I crash through the fire doors and onto the stairs. I'm alone, the main crowd just ahead, stumbling and shouting and sobbing and thrumming with raw, animal panic.

Down, down.

Ahead of me, people fall, the screaming is hysterical now. Above me, the upper levels of the stairwell disappear in smoke. The press of panicked flesh chokes off my breath.

A large woman in a light green vee-neck sweater falls in front of me, her cries are lost in the din. I grab her hand and drag her to her feet and suddenly keeping her hand tightly gripped in mine is the most important things in the world She has red hair. Her face and clothes are grubby, dusty, smudged.

We reach the bottom, where I claw and batter my way out into the ground floor reception area. I keep hold of the woman's hand though, I will not let go.

There's smoke down here, I cough, it's hard to breathe.

I run at the main doors, the women stumbles in my wake. She's shouting at me. I can't hear her words. There are too many people and too much noise. I see the security staff trying to keep order, they look shocked and frightened and helpless.

Out, oh God, *out*, onto the street where vehicles have slowed almost to a standstill. Drivers and passengers peer at us, at the building and upwards at the surging mass of flame and smoke that was once AlphaTech's floor. People have gathered and don't seem to know where to go or what to do. The pavement and road is a mass of glass and other debris. I force my way along the street, heading in the Moorgate direction. I no have plan or purpose other than to get away and take the red-head with me.

The road is smoke-fogged. There is utter chaos.

I see a flashing blue light.

I hear the jet again.

It rushes into a gap in the smoke. I don't like the way it's flying, nose dipped, the machine in a shallow dive. Its wings sparkle.

Chunks are blown out of the road further down the street, out of the cars and the people, who fall like scythed grass. The aircraft levels, and just before it disappears back into the smoke I see canisters fall from its wings. I throw myself against the wall of the nearest building and feel red head's hand slip from mine and then there is, once more, unutterable heat and light.

A searing wind blasts over and around me. I open my eyes, and see fire, a great liquid wave that rolls over the smashed and trapped cars and fallen struggling people. The wave breaks twenty or so feet away from me.

I cower back, clutching the concrete wall of my building. I can hear myself moaning like a frightened child but not feeling the sound leave my throat.

Napalm.

It clears, for a moment, a figure staggers out, a women, tatters hanging from her outstretched arms and naked torso. At first I think it's her clothes. As she comes closer I realise that it's flesh and that her body smokes and glows like embers in a fire. Her mouth is open her eyes wide and devoid of sanity.

She falls, silently.

The smoke hides her.

I get to my feet, more and more people are streaming out of the fire zone, many scorched, bloodied but shockingly whole, many more staggering, hurt, broken and burnt. Some go down, their slumped bodies merging with the debris and dust. I stand and watch them come, feel them brush past me, moaning, sobbing, but no one talking.

More blue lights flash, and sirens shriek.

Figures in dazzling yellow coats appear, they seem to have purpose, they shout and run and some drag hoses after them as they disappear into the choking, hot fog.

I stand. I look for the red-haired woman. I can't see her. I have to see her. I have to know she's still alive.

Then I realise that I have to go home, so I walk, just walk, with no idea how to get back to Northwood or where Northwood actually is. Perhaps I should go back to the building and help, but no, I can't because I have no strength and my mind feels as if it's closing down.

I saw the aircraft. I saw it clearly and now its image is burned into my brain and will never leave.

The aircraft.

The arrowhead.

My legs give way, Christ I'm tired. I sit down on the pavement and watch the emergency services rush past, hear the helicopters and try to remember what has just happened to me.

Someone speaks. I blink and look up to see a woman in one of those yellow coats. She has fair hair and is young and pretty.

"…all right sir? Were you in the building?"

I shake my head, open and close my mouth.

The woman crouches down beside me.

"Are you hurt?" she asks and her kindness makes me cry.

I shake my head.

She lifts a radio to her mouth. "Foxtrot Seven, I have a survivor by the entrance to Moorgate Underground, he seems unhurt but shocked. He's wearing an AlphaTech ID badge so he works in the building, uh, wait a minute." The wPC bends towards me, peers at my chest then returns to her radio. "Peter Allman. Yes, confirm, Peter Allman, Peru, Echo, Tango, Echo Romeo, Alpha, Lima, Lima, Mike Alpha, November. Please advise."

She waits, a distorted voice mushes out an answer I can't hear or understand. She turns to me again. "We have to wait here for a little while. There's an ambulance coming."

No, no that's bad.

For some reason I cannot ride in an ambulance, I cannot let this pretty young women take me anywhere. I try to remember why, something serious, dangerous, my pocket…

Panic claws through the fog, burning and shining and yelling at me to get away, now.

I make an attempt to get to my feet. The wPC looks alarmed and gently pushes me back down. "We have to wait for the ambulance Peter. It's very important, you're hurt."

I'm not. I'm confused and my head is aching and ringing and I keep coughing and crying but I'm not injured. I have to think of something, I have to act.

She glances round, I almost get up then, but she's still too close to me, too solid, all high-visibility yellow and assertive. The street is misted with smoke now, the traffic has slowed to a halt and I see blue and white tape going up everywhere. More bright yellow police are waving their arms and trying to clear the street. I see blue flashing lights, a fire engine, another, and behind that, an ambulance.

Oh no, no, no. I'm not going in there. Not with the dangerous thing in my pocket. The…the stick. Christ it pops into my mind, clear as day. The memory stick, the flash drive, The List.

An argument breaks out, a driver, trapped in the snarl and pandemonium, just as a fresh wave of tattered, charred and shocked survivors emerge from the smoke-mist.

The driver is out of his van, he pushes a police officer. The wPC breaks into a run, shouting into her radio as she goes.

I'm up, wavering and dizzy and unsure, but I'm up and staggering away down the street, back towards London Wall and the hell that lies there, because, the burning and shining panic-voice tells me that they will expect me to go the other way, to Liverpool Street perhaps.

The tide is against me, but I force my way through. The police and other emergency personnel ignore me, there is too much going on, the whole, the mass, the greater, has swamped any concern for the individual.

*

For a long time I don't know where I am. I've turned off into the maze of unfamiliar streets that seem to spiral in on Liverpool Street. I can't think anyway, my mind is fuzzed, I just need to walk. People begin to notice me and a few approach, offering help, asking if I was caught up in the bombing raid. I shrug them off. I'm probably rude to them. I don't mean to be. I just want to be left alone while my mind slowly melds together.

Eventually I head back to Liverpool Street. There are a lot of police but I'm one of hundreds who are battered, but walking and heading home.

There is a bloody war on after all.

My house is empty and I'm glad. It takes me a while to operate the door key and find my way in and when I do I go up to Dominic's room and sit down on his bed and all I can smell is smoke and scorched flesh and clothing. My skin itches from the coating of dust that is glued to my flesh, I cough. My throat is raw.

I can't move anymore, can barely breathe for the stink. I stare at the poster showing "The Machineries of War – Air Power" *Jaguar*, it says, *Tornado, EuroFighter, Panther*.

Panther.

The black arrowhead holds my attention.

Panther – the future of modern warfare, pilotless, remotely flown, deadly. It can be used as an air-to-air combat interceptor or a ground attack aircraft. A good platform for strafing and launching air-to-surface missiles, its under-wing pylons are suitable for both high explosive bombs and Napalm canisters.

Particularly useful for precision attack.

You see, "...it's no longer a matter of simply finding the target building, but deciding which window to punch your missiles through, which group of occupants to eliminate."

Eliminate, what a nice, clinical word.

Eliminate.

Burn, smash, maim, kill.

But it's one of ours. It's not an EoD aircraft, unless they've stolen some, or have their own version.

Yes, yes that must be it. They've stolen our design. Bastards.

My head drops, too heavy to keep up, too tired. I want to lie down but I can't. My body is locked in place. I have something in my hand, a piece of paper. Looking down I study it and realise that it is Dominic's conscription letter.

I read it without taking in any of the words. Almost know it by heart now anyway. One sentence snags my attention, I can't draw my eyes away from it.

"Please note that your army identification number is 875429. Please memorise this number as soon as possible and use it in any further communication."

Number. Number, Army identification number. Six digits.

"Bring it to me," Dave had said and he sounded frightened. What else did he say?

Something about Dominic.

"Don't let him go." That's it. "Keep him out the army. There's no coming home from what they're being sent into. They can't let too many of us come back. And no one comes back in one piece. No-fucking-one."

But how Dave, how do I save him?

I shake so violently my jaw locks in place and I can only groan though my clenched teeth. I crash back onto the bed, curl tightly, knees drawn up to my chest.

I close my eyes and see a woman stagger from a wall of flames, her clothes and flesh in tatters…

The front door opens, there are voices, loud, someone cries, almost hysterically. A louder voice intrudes, firm and calm, Ruth. God they're all home. Footsteps pummel the stairs, rapid, accompanied by loud sobs. Amanda, my eldest daughter. She swears at her mother. "Fuck the war, fuck it fuck it fuck it!"

"Amanda!" My rebuke is involuntary, instinct, reflex. No one swears in this house, it's one of Ruth's Rules and we all obey it (most of the time).

The sobbing stops abruptly. The silence is shocking, not even a breath can be heard.

"Dad?"

I nod, which is ridiculous because she can't see me.

"Dad?" Her voice rises towards tears again. Then she scrambles up onto the landing her footsteps irregular, she appears in the doorway, school coat hanging off her school uniform dishevelled, her bag dragged on the floor. Her pretty-too-young face is distorted and blotched.

She makes a sound, a strangled sort of "Ah…" Then she's in my arms and sobbing and I hold her tightly and I don't think I'll ever be able to let her go. A moment later, over her shoulder I see Ruth and Rachel. Ruth is also pale, and dishevelled, dusty, smudged. Which is odd, then frightening, was her school bombed as well? She tries to speak, but can't and in a moment she is holding me and Amanda and crying. Rachel hangs back, embarrassed, unsure. I smile at her, a weak smile but a smile. She comes in and I cram her into my armful of weeping women.

My eyes are dry.

My heart is empty.

Ruth untangles herself first,

"Why didn't you phone?" she shouts at me. "I thought you were dead. I thought your were bloody dead! Why didn't you call me?"

Amanda steps away. She looks uncomfortable now, sensing a row, the sort of emotional flare-up she is able to provoke, but can't handle in others.

"Ruth…" I shake my head. "Sorry…"

Ruth's face changes and she stares at me as if seeing me for the first time. "The Head called me into his office," she says. "He told me that London Wall had been bombed. That it was really bad. I went there to find you…They wouldn't let me past the tape but I saw…Oh God Pete, I saw…"

She stands there, hands by her side, her coat, all of her, dirty and dishevelled. My mouth opens but nothing comes out. And then she's back and we're alone holding each other so tightly neither of us can breathe.

I hear another voice, Dominic. Another thunder of footsteps on the stairs, then he's in the doorway, overalls and boots building site-dusty.

"Thank fuck," I hear him say but neither Ruth or I correct him.

We huddle together again, showered, cleansed, wearing dressing gowns and shut in. We've become a frightened pack, the dark outside our windows, sodden with threat.

The early evening news is extended. The air raid on London Wall is shouted at us, is wept and pontificated over. There is a computerised reconstruction showing my office building and a conventional looking silver aeroplane that passes then turns and sweeps in to launch two missiles into the fourth floor.

Tiny digital figures stream out of the smoking building only to be mowed down and Napalmed by the same little silver aeroplane

We see it again and again

Questions are asked. A minister speaks gravely to the cameras.

"This atrocity, this war crime cannot go unpunished. What we've seen today is both proof of the extent of the EoD threat and vindication of our decision to go to war against them and all they stand for. If they think they will cow us with this kind of brutal violence, they are mistaken, it only strengthens our resolve, increases our determination. And I also want to say this, to the Opposition who have been playing politics over this crisis, who have sought to gain political advantage out of the kind of human suffering and danger that we face each day as a Country and has been brought home to us in a very savage and bloody way this morning, *now* do you understand? Now do you see the truth of our cause?"

The Mayor of London follows, suitably dishevelled and shock-pale. "We Londoners have suffered a terrible blow today, but we'll carry on. Londoners always do. Tomorrow the tubes and buses will be filled with commuters, builders will be at work, banks and schools will be open. This isn't a defeat, this is a test and believe you me, we will pass it!"

Every day, one of them had said, the only truthful thing either of the pompous self-serving morons had actually uttered. Every bloody day. Like the raid I had witnessed out of the office's big east-facing window, the aircraft and flames and towering pillars of smoke, oh yes, it had earned a mention on the news, but why hadn't the mayor and the minister for whatever been in front of the cameras outraged and babbling about that atrocity?

Bombing the blue-collar masses in the East End, in Kilburn, Harlesden and Brixton is an acceptable consequence of war, it seems, but massacring the white collar elite, daring to damage the glass and steel temples of commerce in the City is a different matter altogether.

Bloody war.

"Officer Quest" blares into life.

EoD Bastards

The two remaining contestants are angry now, fired up.

We have no choice but to fight.

I hardly notice it, the flash ads, the momentary text that burns into my eyes and hooks itself into my brain. I should be worried about that but I'm too tired and sick.

The bombing raid has, the remaining "Officer Quest" contestants say, motivated them. The Bastards are going to pay for this and each of the contestants wants to extract revenge personally with their own, bare, office-soft hands.

I can't watch it, but I can't get out of the chair and I can't leave my family.

Until the doorbell rings.

No one moves. The ringing becomes persistent and increasingly angry.

In the end it's Ruth who gets up to answer it. Voices are heard, a mixture of male and female. Then she's back, with two police officers, one of each sex. They look young, harassed, bulked up with Kevlar vests and laden with radios and truncheons and other accessories of the trade.

"Mister Peter Allman?" the wPC asks and I realise that she is the same constable who Ruth threw out of the house last night.

"Yeah what?"

"We need to ask you some questions about the London Wall air raid and also to inform you that left the incident scene without permission or reporting your survival to the authorities, an offence under the Emergency Locations and Situations of Persons Act 2009."

"What the fuck are you talking about?"

"Pete." Ruth's warning voice shuts me up straight away.

"You are obliged to inform the police of your survival and whereabouts following direct involvement in any enemy action," the PC explains. He's polite, almost apologetic. The wPC glances at him. I see a trace of exasperation in her face.

"I did talk to the police as it happens," I say." One of your mates found me after I collapsed. Don't you lot ever speak to each other?"

"We are aware of that," the wPC says. "You were, in fact, instructed to wait for an ambulance and processing."

"Listen to me," Ruth says and suddenly she's face to face with the officer. "My husband was in shock, my husband is innocent of any crime whatsoever and if you don't get out of my house in ten seconds I am going to scream for a solicitor so loud you won't be able to hear anything for a week."

"Mrs Allman…" the PC begins.

"Fuck off," Ruth shouts. "Go and catch some bloody criminals and leave us alone."

I sense Dominic get to his feet and flash him a warning look.

"I think you had better calm down Mrs Allman," the wPC says, voice cold and eyes hard.

"And if I don't, are you going to arrest me as well?"

"If we consider you to be verbally abusing a police officer, yes we will."

"Don't you dare touch her," I say. I'm so angry I'm shaking, but I realise that we really do have to ease up because Ruth is not entirely accurate when she pleaded my innocence. There's the matter of the memory stick. "Ruth, it's okay. It's paperwork and bureaucracy, nothing else."

Ruth glances round at me and steps back so I can put my arm about her shoulders.

"No one is going to be arrested on this occasion," the PC says. "But we are going to issue a formal warning, both to yourself, Mr Allman and to you Mrs Allman because you also did not report your husband's survival and location."

"What I'd like to know is," Ruth says, quietly, calmly – and it's a deadly calm that I know well, and fear. "Who is the enemy here?"

"I'm sorry?" says the wPC. She seems genuinely puzzled.

"The enemy" Ruth repeats. "Is it the EoD or is it us, you know, the people who live in this Country and work for a living and mind their own business?"

"I understand." The wPC obviously doesn't, or doesn't care to. "But we *are* at war Mrs Allman"

"Bloody war," says Dominic and the PC in unison.

I almost tell them at that point. I almost tell them that I think the aircraft was a Panther, one of ours and that the raid may have been a friendly fire incident and not an EoD atrocity at all. But I don't. I don't know why. Too muddle-headed, too shocked and dazed, perhaps, too angry?

Or too frightened?

"Particularly useful for precision attack." Isn't that what the poster in Dominic's bedroom had said? "It's no longer a matter of simply finding the target building, but deciding which window to punch your missiles through, which group of occupants to eliminate."

I can't go to work next morning, even if I wanted to, because there is no work to go to. No AlphaTech, no Andy, Hendy or Frances, no brash Jamie or shy Katie. All of them are missing and very likely dead according to the PC who visited us last night. He told us this once everyone had calmed down.

So I stand at the front door and watch my family set off to their own jobs and their school. They are all pale and quiet. Ruth turns back to hold me one last time before she sets off towards the bus stop.

The crisp autumn air is, as usual, tainted with smoke. I can hear helicopters. The sky bears down on me, a heavy, lethal blue dome. I glance upwards, see nothing but a wisp of white cloud. I wonder if I will ever be able to trust the sky again.

A Land Rover races past, army green, radio antenna waving, another follows, then lorries, four, five of them. I glimpse soldiers crammed into the back of each one. After that, nothing but the helicopters and the ever present scent of burning.

Later, after clearing up the house, peeling some vegetables and other mundane acts intended more to stop me thinking than to actually achieve anything, I pull on my coat and leave for Northwood tube station. The memory stick is in my pocket and I'm taking it to Dave.

First, though, I have to go outside. That means, leaving the house, its four solid walls and a door I can lock to keep me safe inside. I don't like it out here, under that vast sky, I don't like the people I meet, I can't trust them, don't want to lock eyes with any of them, because they'll see, oh yes, they'll work it out, they'll know where I'm going and why.

The train doesn't stop between stations this time and I arrive at Wembley Park without incident or panic attack. I cross to the Jubilee Line platform, which is a mess, littered with what turns out to be sleeping bags and discarded food and packaging. There's a lingering stench of sweat and urine as well, all adding to my unease and claustrophobia. I'm glad when the train appears, for once finding refuge in its low-roofed confinement.

It doesn't take long to get to Kilburn.

I leave the station, take a couple of steps along the High Road and stop.

The place is wrecked, bomb-damaged I suppose. There are blackened gaps between other, scorched and broken buildings, shop fronts are boarded up, even those that are still in business. There is a huge crater in the middle of the road into which a JCB is tipping rubble. The air is heavy with smoke-scent.

Yet the street is still alive, is functioning, vehicles managing to negotiate the hazards, people walk, shop, drink and lounge in the café's and pubs. I'm glad to turn off, into a quieter residential street. There are some large town houses here, Victorian I suppose, most of them converted into flats and bedsitters. Dave lives here, in a second floor flat, cramped, ill-equipped and all he could afford after Terri left him.

Something is wrong. There are police here, one standing in the main doorway to the building, a patrol car parked half on the pavement outside. I see blue and white tape and the world begins to spiral in on me. The sky seems to lower itself, crushing me down into the earth.

This is the house where Dave lives. Dave Miller, my mate and someone who is on The List.

I back away, not wanting to bring any attention to myself. I feel someone behind me and spin round. There's an elderly lady there, her plastic carrier bag of shopping spilled on the pavement. I apologise, help her to pick it up.

"You ought to look where you're going," she snaps, then mellows. "Well, we're all a bit out of sorts today ain't we."

"What do you mean?" I ask.

"Don't you live round here then?"

"Yeah, yeah I do," I lie. "But I've been away for a couple of weeks. Something happened has it?"

"It's that poor blind fella, the one who lost his sight in the war. Shot himself, so they say. Poor bugger, it's happened to a lot of them by all accounts."

"What has?"

"Killing themselves, the Veterans, you know, can't take it, can't get over what they saw out there in the war." The last tin of powdered egg goes back into her carrier bag. "Seems a shame, surviving all those battles then doing yourself in once you get safely home."

"Yeah, it does." I can hardly speak.

"Well, thanks for helping, even if you did cause the accident." She's smiling, no harm done. She grabs my hand. "Look after yourself now."

I nod to her and watch her walk slowly up the path to the building next to Dave's.

Then I open the hand she had taken and see the note she slipped into my palm. Our collision was, it seems, no accident.

"Tricycle, 3pm."

I tear it up and deposit fragments into a number of different litter bins as I head back into the High Road.

I have no idea what "Tricycle" means. It must be something around here, a cafe, a bicycle shop. Or perhaps it's more cryptic than that. I hope not because I'm too numb for games. Dave is dead, another name added to that other list, the one that includes my colleagues at AlphaTech. I try to *feel* his death but I can't. There's a bleak, empty space but that's all.

It'll come though, the feeling, it'll slam into me when I least expect it and drive me to my knees and break me into a thousand pieces. Dave was like a brother, the one who would tell me the truth and stand up to me and shake me when I was a complete arse. He was also a good mate to have when the testosterone kicked in and the fists flew. He was a hell of a biker too, fearless on those ancient Triumphs and BSAs he would buy from ads he saw in the paper, then repair and polish and cherish.

The women loved Dave, it was his fair hair, the spark of mischief in his blue, blue eyes. Dave was sharp and intelligent and kind-hearted and so, so funny.

That was Dave, the slim, good-looking devil with tattoos and never-fading grin. That was my mate, not the angry, blind and broken ex-soldier, maimed in a war that appeared out of nowhere and shouldn't exist.

It's a theatre, both for plays and a cinema, trademarked by a stylised tricycle mounted over its entrance like a pub sign. At three pm there's a showing of the Directors Cut of "Picnic at Hanging Rock" I suppose that if you want to go the pictures or the theatre these days you have to go and get home before the curfew starts. Matinees must be big business.

The time is almost two pm. I find a cafe, across the road and take a seat by the window so I can watch for anyone familiar, or threatening, who might want to meet me there.

I order a mug of tea and a plate of egg and chips then pick up a newspaper from the counter, before returning to my table. There are lurid photographs of the raid on the tabloid's front page. The headline is simply "Bastards!" It goes on to say that the RAF is "gearing for revenge." Aircrew are queuing up to volunteer to bring Hell to the EoD cowards skulking in their hideouts.

I sling the rag aside in disgust and drink my tea. There's comfort in the feel of that big old warm mug in my hands, something old fashioned and solid. I watch the street. Life seems to go on despite the bomb damage. I close my eyes, hoping that when I open them again the hallucination will have passed. But it hasn't, the street is still there, the rubble and hole and that constant smoke tang that's even found its way into the café and mingled with the perfumes of grease and coffee.

A figure detaches itself from the steady to and fro of pedestrians. Dark coat, shaven head, one sleeve tucked into his pocket. He goes to the Tricycle's entrance and tries the door, which seems to be open now. I drain my tea, get to my feet and follow.

By the time I'm inside, Gary, Dave's self-appointed protector, has already bought his ticket and disappeared into the auditorium. I make to follow suit. And am startled by a hand that grabs the arm of my coat and yanks me into the gents' toilet,

"Dave's dead," Gary says, crossing to a urinal and working his fly.

I take my place beside him.

"Suicide."

That earns me a humourless, scornful chuckle.

"Yeah, suicide."

"So did the SSU kill him?"

"Dave told me you have something for us." He sighs. "In fact that was just about the last thing he did tell me. Last night, over the last beer we'll ever drink together. He told me you were going to come to see him and for me to keep an eye out for you, he wanted me to protect you. You must have been some good fucking mate of his."

I hesitate. "Who is *us*?"

"Friends."

"Whose friends?"

"Yours if you did but know it Allman. We can help you."

"Do I need help?"

"Your son does."

That stops me. I glance at him.

"Your son is eighteen in a couple of days. Yeah? They'll fucking take him Allman and he won't come back. No one does anymore. They let some of us back, just enough of us to con the public into believing people actually do make it home, but it was a mistake, and they're sorting it out right now. That's why Dave's dead, they have to make sure us Veterans keep our mouths shut. Those of us with enough brains and body parts left to be able to talk that is. That stick of yours is an SSU death list, if you hand it over to us it'll be our salvation, or the salvation of as many as we can contact and get out before the suicides really start."

"Out?"

"There's a…place. No fucker knows where it is except us Vets and I'm not telling you, not unless you give me that stick."

"How can you help my son?"

"Give me the stick and I'll tell you."

"Help my son and *then* I'll give you the stick. Take him to that *Place* of yours."

He steps back from the urinal, moves over the sink and looks back at me. He shakes his head as he washes his one remaining hand the best he can. "I'm not going to overpower you am I. I could have done, once. I didn't care how big the bastards were, I'd always have them. Are you serious about me helping your lad?"

"Depends what help means."

"There's only one way to stay out of the army, the Russians knew how to do it back in the days of the Czar."

"I don't want a history lesson."

"All second sons were eligible for military service, see, so families would cut off their second son's trigger finger."

"Christ —"

"It's simple, a botched mugging, a gun goes off and your son has a hole in his foot and he's no use to the army anymore."

No, no I can't do this.

But I don't walk away. Instead I close my eyes and try to think through the blood roar in my head.

"Think about it but hurry up, okay? I need that memory stick and fast, before more of us are murdered."

"Why do you have to keep your mouths shut?" I ask. "What's going on?"

He shakes his head. "I'm not going to be the one who tells you. If they arrest you and get you to talk, and they can, it's best if you know nothing. Just keep your son out of it. Look, you were Dave's friend, that makes you my friend. He trusted you, so do I. Sentimental, me. I believed him when he said you're all right. You can give me that thing now, walk away and spend a last few days with your lad or you can trust me. We can make a deal and I'll do the deed quick and neat and it'll be convincing and a' will be well."

"I…I don't know…"

"No, no I don't suppose you do. I'll give you till nine tonight, then I'm getting out of here."

He stares at me of for a long hard moment then tells me his number and leaves. I stand, already torn, already trying to push away the seed of terrible hope he's planted in my head.

I go in to the see the film. It's surreal, fey and shocking. The darkness of the cinema is a hiding place and that's what I want at the moment. I don't want daylight, I need to be concealed, invisible.

When the film finishes, a recorded voice warns the few of us who are in the building that the curfew starts in two hours and we should go home. Outside it's cold and darkening already. I pull up my hood, hunch my shoulders and hurry to the nearest bus stop. I no longer trust tube stations, the obvious mode of travel, if they're watching for me, or following me, that's where they'll be. Much harder to predict which bus stop I'll use and which bus even.

The journey is long and makes me feel slightly nauseous. The vehicle vibrates and rattles and is hot and stuffy. I should take off my coat but I may need to get out in a hurry. The seed is still there, lodged in the dark soil of my mind, a way out, a mugging gone wrong, one moment of violence and pain, but life and freedom given back to my son.

I see glimpses of yellow warm light from around badly fitted blackout curtains, I see the forced downward beams of street lighting, figures hurrying home, their worlds look simple to me, not fraught with the sort of life-destroying decision I'm facing right now.

Land Rovers charge along the streets, overtaking the bus, I see police, congregating on corners.

By the time *I* get home I feel sick, from the journey and from the decision I have to make. I know which decision is right. I can't allow my son to be injured, shot in cold blood, his body damaged, but what will happen to him if I say no? He'll be taken from us, and from what both Dave and Gary have said, I'll never see him again.

I walk quickly back towards my house, wondering what the hell sort of war we are fighting. Fear crawls through me, chills every part of my body, raw, cold, icy fear. I reach my home, still nauseous, my unease magnified by the sight of light around the edges of the blackout curtains.

Are their ARP Wardens in this war, does anyone rush around shouting "Put that light out!"? Shaking, cold, I open the front door and step inside. It's warm. I hear the television and voices. I hear a brief fierce squabble between Amanda and Rachel then a door slams. I find Ruth, in the kitchen, boiling a kettle.

"Thanks for preparing the dinner," she says. The vegetables I peeled are simmering on the cooker. "You okay? You look a bit pale Pete."

So does she. Her face, pinched from the cold, is also tight with tension. Friday. Dominic is due to leave us on Monday. This is our last weekend.

My last chance to stop it happening.

But it could also destroy my family. If Ruth finds out what I'm thinking of doing, she would never forgive, me, or would she? No, she would've hung onto the hope that Dominic would come back from the war and that the war is right.

Rachel appears. She smiles.

"You been winding up your sister again?" I ask her.

"She was being a total –"

"Rachel, leave her alone, okay?"

The front door opens and shuts again, Dominic's home. I glance at Ruth and she meets my brief stare. I see her bite her lip then a smile appears, too bright, too relaxed. Then her eyes shine and redden and she turns away. I take her, hold her and she buries her face in my shoulder and bites my coat to stifle her sobs. I hold her tight and almost, almost tell her.

There's a way Ruth, it involves a moment of violence, of pain and a lifetime of damage, but it will *be* a lifetime.

But I keep my mouth shut and feel her teeth clenched tight on the material covering my shoulder and her body shaking, holding her there until she relaxes, until she pulls away rubbing her face with the back of her hand and turns away quickly because someone is heading for the kitchen.

"Hiya Dad, Mum." Dominic throws the greeting in as he passes by on his way to the sitting room to watch television.

"You okay?" I ask Ruth. She nods, forces a smile.

I offer to finish working on the dinner but she wants to do it, activity, to take her mind off the imminent loss of her oldest child.

We make sure that dinner is a cheerful, noisy affair. Amanda and Rachel seem to have made up from their quarrel, everyone is on their best behaviour.

"You working tomorrow?" I ask Dominic. He works any weekend going, feathering his nest while he's single.

"No, not this weekend. They said there'll be a job waiting for me when I come home."

"Good," I say. "That's worth a lot" Then I say; "Do you want to come fishing tomorrow?"

The words almost tangle, nothing wrong with taking him on a fishing trip, a few hours with his Dad.

Last hours, a voice hammers in my skull, his last hours Allman. The voice is Gary's.

"Yeah, yeah why not. That'd be good."

"That okay with you love?" I ask Ruth.

"Of course it is, she says. "It'll get you two out from under my feet while I organise Sunday."

"We'll only be gone a few hours," I say. "We'll give you a hand when we get back."

"Pete, stay out all day, stay away, okay?"

Dominic and I swap glances. It's all an act, it's all fake, like a play where the conversation and laughter is constructed but not real, not felt.

"Harefield?"

Dominic looks at me as if I'm stupid.

"You know," I persist. "Harefield, the Grand Union Canal."

"No Dad, we can't go to Harefield, its out of bounds outside the barrier."

"What barrier?"

"Around London," Rachel says before Dominic can answer. "We're not allowed to leave London remember? No one is allowed to leave the town or city where they live."

Later, after the final episode of "Officer Quest" I make my excuses and go up into the bedroom. I sit on the edge of the bed and only realise that I am holding the telephone in my hand after a few moments.

There's a roar in my head, a scream, a noise so loud I can barely think.

I unfold the piece of paper on which I had scribbled Gary's number.

I put the phone down, close my eyes and there I see Ruth, sobbing, screaming and clawing at me to get to Dominic as he climbs into the Caterick train...

I see him dead, torn and burned...

I stab the numbers into the phone. I lift the receiver to my ear, I can't hear the ringing tone, I can't hear my own thoughts and I can barely hear my own voice.

It rings and rings, the sound muffled and distant. My heart thunders, the way it thundered when I asked Ruth for that first date. Only this time I feel sick and weak and I'm shaking. The ringing tone goes on and on. He's not going to answer. I feel relief.

"Yeah?"

Christ, it's him. Oh Christ...

"Who's there? Who? Come on."

"Pete Allman."

"When?"

He doesn't even ask me if I want to go through with it.

I can't answer, can't form words.

"When?" Harsher this time, demanding, impatient.

"Tuh....tomorrow, at Chalk...Chalk Lake. Fishing trip..."

"Okay. Bring it and we'll swap."

He cuts the call. I lay the phone down carefully because it is very important to do that and sit, staring and shaking.

Tomorrow.

We eat breakfast in silence; toast, cereal, powdered egg. It's still dark outside, but that doesn't matter because the curfew ended half an hour ago at 6:00 am. Our fishing tackle is in the hall, packed and ready to be shipped into the car, which has just enough petrol in the tank to get us to Chalk Lake and back. We don't have many fuel points remaining on our FuelAl Card. Al is a media generated nickname for allowance, apparently. The media seem to like inventing nicknames and forcing them on us. I remember adverts where computer applications were called Apps and Southern Comfort, SoCo. They all sound like shite to me but then who am I but a mutilator of my own children?

Dominic makes sandwiches while I wash-up then rob the cupboards of chocolate biscuits and crisps, neither of which appears to be rationed. I don't understand this rationing. Imported food, which must involve perilous sea voyages or flights over enemy territory, is plentiful. Home-grown food like meat, milk and eggs, which can surely be transported around the Country, isn't.

But then, the whole thing doesn't make sense.

I make two flasks of coffee and we're ready to go. One diversion is needed, to pick up some bait from an angling shop sited, strategically a mile from the Lake itself.

We drive in silence for a while. Dominic folds his arms and closes his eyes. I don't believe he's actually sleeping, I think it's a way of escaping the awkwardness. We've always been as easy together as a father and son can be. I make no pretence about being his best friend. I don't understand some of the things he says, some of his attitudes, clothes and music, but then my Dad, may God punish his vile old soul, didn't understand mine. The difference is that my dad expressed his confusion with his fists. He was a foul-mouthed, brainless fascist when I was a kid and I'll bet he still is. I haven't seen him in years, thank Christ. He wasn't a drunk, which made it worse somehow. He beat the shit out of me, my brother and our mum while he was sober, sane and sensible. He beat us because it was the only way he could control us and because, being a tinpot dictator and dominating our lives with his bloody opinions and orders and punishments, it was the only way he could communicate with us.

When he hit you he looked you in the eye, when he drove his fist into your belly or smacked his huge, garage mechanic hand into the side of your head, you understood that this was because you were a useless little piece of dog turd and he was only doing it for your own good.

I never stood up to him or beat him to the ground and made him beg forgiveness. That doesn't often happen in real life. I walked out. I packed a few records and clothes and a couple of paperbacks, climbed onto my Norton and roared away one wet Wednesday night. I was already trouble by then. I was already that arrogant little bastard Allman who go into fights and broke things and swaggered around and drank too much and smoked, swallowed and sniffed anything that blotted out the world and made him feel good.

I walked out and left my mum and my little brother and sister with Satan's favourite family man and I never went back. Dad's old and frail now and living in a council-run old people's home, according to the occasional letters I get from my sister. He never treated *her* badly. I'm not jealous about that, just glad she didn't have to put up with what the rest of us did. She wants me to visit him and make amends. I can't go because if I did I'd push a pillow over his face and put him down the way a vet puts down a dying animal.

As far as I'm concerned, the only good thing he ever did was to stop me hitting my own kids. On the rare occasions I did smack them it was a clinical act of discipline. If they made me angry I wouldn't so much as raise my hand but walk away until I cooled down.

So what is this act I'm planning for today? Clinical love, selfishness, abuse? Perhaps I'm no better than my own dad who thought pain was inflicted for the victim's own good. I glance at Dominic, still faking sleep, and hope he'll forgive me.

"I'm sorry," Dominic says and I'm startled. "You know, about all your workmates."

For a moment I'm puzzled, unsure what he's talking about. Then I understand.

"I don't know how to feel," I say. "I'm still numb. I keep thinking that I'll be going back to work on Monday and it'll all be there like it was on Thursday morning. I don't suppose I *have* a job anymore. No one's contacted me, perhaps there isn't anyone left."

"Don't worry," Dominic says. "I'll pay the bastards back once I'm in the Mob."

"Never mind paying anyone back, you just look out for yourself."

"I can't imagine it," Dominic says. "I mean all my workmates being killed. It could happen, I know that. We've been rebuilding the areas that have been blitzed, so I've seen what it's like when a place is hit by bombs."

I'm shocked, because he's never told me this before and I can't imagine my son being so closely involved with the effects of the war.

"I thought you were rewiring council houses."

"That's what you're supposed to think. The contracts we're working on are secret."

"You'd better not tell me then."

I want him to though.

"No, it's okay, as long as you don't tell anyone else."

"Of course I won't."

"We're building these huge tower blocks. They're horrible, like giant prisons. Everyone who loses their house in a raid is forced to live in them. That is a lot of people Dad, thousands and thousands. I wouldn't want to. The towers are claustrophobic enough to work in so God knows what they're like to live in. Every single flat is exactly the same. It doesn't matter if you're poor or rich. They block off an area after a raid then round up the survivors, give them food and medical treatment then allocate them a flat. Most people just do as they're told because they're too frightened and shocked to argue. They say it's temporary but they don't seem very temporary to me. A fuck…sorry, an atom bomb wouldn't knock one of those towers down."

"Who are *they*?"

"Huh?"

"You keep saying *they*, you know *they* make everyone move into the flats."

"Oh, yeah, the government I suppose. I mean the first people who turn up after a raid, before the fire brigade even, are the SSU, the uniformed branch. They look like the bloody SS if you ask me. We all hate them, arrogant little sods, shouting and giving out orders. Worst thing is you can't see their faces because they always wear dark visors. Some people manage to escape and live rough in the bomb sites. We sometimes leave food and stuff for them because anyone who pisses off the SSU is okay with us."

"So, if you're working in the bombed areas *you* must have been in air raids."

Dominic nods. "Never too close thank fuck."

I don't correct him. Suddenly the dark-haired, blue-eyed teenager beside me is a man. More than that, there's something old about him.

"Probably because the areas we're building in have already been flattened," he says. "It's odd." He chuckles to himself, shrugs. "Doesn't matter."

"Yes it does."

"I've already said too much dad."

"Then you might as well say the rest." Responsible father, me.

"Well, it's as if the EoD are working to a pattern, what's the word? Systematic, that's it, like they're concentrating on one area at a time and completely flattening it then moving their raids onto the next area. We're always joking that they're working for a demolition company with a government contract. But it is strange. I thought bombing raids were messy and not that accurate."

Except when a rocket needs to be fired into a particular floor of a building, through a particular window to kill – sorry, eliminate – particular people.

I nod to make it look as if I'm thinking deeply about what Dominic has just told me. I am thinking about it, but not trying to make any sense of it at that moment because there's too much confusion in my head for me to deal with yet another dose.

"At least I don't get to see any bodies. They're cleared out pretty quickly."

You would have seen plenty on a battlefield, I tell him silently, if I hadn't made a deal with a man with a gun. That's the name of a song by Steely Dan. *With a Gun* If this was a film, that would be the theme music.

Chalk Lake is deserted. Hardly surprising since it's not yet eight AM and most sensible people are having their Saturday morning lay-in. We park in the rough area marked for the purpose and struggle out of our nice, warm car into the cold. The utter and complete cold. I can taste it, it burns my throat and it makes Dominic swear. I should stop him before it becomes a habit and he does it in front of his mum. But not right now, at this moment we're pulling out our angling boxes, fold-up chairs and furled umbrella from the back of the car and I just need his living, breathing company and presence.

Laden and glad of the exertion because it warms us up, we trudge along a track that cuts through the thick, deliberately unkempt woods and down to the lake, which is artificial, a huge scar gouged into the earth so that its treasure horde of chalk could be uncovered and stolen. Thank God someone had the sense to fill the hole with water and let the area around it grow wild.

The woods stretch almost to the shoreline itself. A path, about twenty feet wide, is kept reasonably clear to allow walkers, anglers and bird watchers access to the water. It's so quiet here you could believe you're deep in the countryside, if it wasn't for the Wembley Stadium arch that rises above the trees on the far bank.

And the smoke, five dark columns staining the sky beyond and on either side of the arch.

We find our favourite peg and set up, which takes a few minutes of opening boxes, pulling out tackle then tying and baiting hooks. My hands shake so much I drop my first three maggots. The lucky survivors wriggle off into the undergrowth. At least they'll die of hypothermia (which, I am reliably informed, is a gentle death, like going to sleep, although I don't believe there is such a thing as gentle death) and not drowning or being swallowed alive.

Dominic catapults a handful of maggots out into the lake. The doomed larvae patter onto the water like rain. Then he casts, landing his hook neatly in the middle of the area he's seeded with bait.

The water must be unimaginably cold, chilling the blood of its inhabitants into a near comatose state. I doubt we'll catch much, but that isn't the point of this trip.

So what is the point?

For Dominic, a last day spent with his Dad before his new (and short, Christ how short it will be) life as a soldier.

For me, a calculated, cold and cynical ambush, sprung after an almost unbearable agony of waiting.

We settle into our fold-up chairs, warming ourselves as much by holding our coffee mugs as by drinking the stuff. We both wear the fingerless gloves beloved by anglers and television-cliché homeless and tramps. They prevent us from losing fingers and crying over the cold like the big, brave men we are, but it takes more than gloves to warm my soul.

It'll come soon, the hammer blow, the violent mugging that will leave us both injured but Dominic saved. I force my attention on the fishing, on the grey, breeze-troubled water.

I watch my float, an orange-and-black needle that pierces the water's skin. My concentration on that small plastic stick is fierce. A dog walker moves along the far shore, an elderly lady with a walking stick progressing at a brisk pace behind an animal that looks like a Labrador. Swans appear, wings extended as they make their final approach, then hit the water and settle into a sedate voyage across the lake surface. They swing near to investigate our floats then move on, apparently disappointed that they aren't edible.

Dominic mutters deprecatingly about the birds. They frighten the fish, get tangled in line, can be aggressive.

"It was their lake before it was ours," I tell him, although I'm not sure if that's true because the lake is manmade.

"Yes Dad." Dominic becomes serious, the awkwardness returns. "Do you feel bad about not being allowed to fight?"

The question is a shock. I haven't thought about it, because this year-and-a-half old war is new to me and devoid of any emotional resonance, other than the fact that I keep stumbling, like a newly walking toddler, into authority and falling flat on my face.

And the fact that I'm about to lose my son.

Whatever happens, I *will* lose him.

"I suppose the right answer is yes," I say. "But the truth is, I don't know because I don't know who we're fighting and who is right and wrong."

"The EoD, Enemies of Democracy, they have to be wrong Dad, it says it on the tin. *Enemies of Democracy.*"

I glance at my son, unnerved. He didn't even stumble over his response, even when I interrupted, despite his own dislike of the bomb site re-housing project and the thuggish SSU.

Bloody war…Bastards…We have no choice but to fight…

"Maybe I'll feel ashamed when this is all over," I say.

"You can't help being in a Reserved Occupation Dad."

"I could appeal."

"Yeah, you could. But I don't think you should."

"Why?"

"Well…you know…"

"You think I'd make such a bad soldier the army's better off without me."

"Yeah, absolutely." Dominic laughs and I think he probably does see me as the solider with two left feet. "I can't imagine you shooting anyone."

I'm having *you* shot Dominic.

"And you'd be telling everyone that the world belonged to the EoD before it belonged to us."

"It did."

"What?"

"Think about it. It was the troublemakers who gave us democracy in the first place. Enemies of the state, they were then, traitors, rebels, protesters, strikers. That all had to happen before democracy could be born."

"That's dangerous talk Dad." He's serious and I don't like it. I'm old fashioned enough not to appreciate being bollocked by my own son, but I keep my mouth shut. This isn't Dominic talking.

"We're a democracy *now* Dominic," I keep my tone light and clear of the irritation I feel at the way he's been brainwashed by all this crap. "I have a right to dangerous talk."

"It costs lives. People will be calling you cynical."

"And a radical and an intellectual?"

"What?"

"Supertramp."

Dominic shakes his head, face blank.

"Take a look in my record collection."

"Ah, right." Another of Dad's ancient and dusty old rock bands then, that's what he's thinking, as long dead as vinyl itself. "I think I know the song. It was sampled by –"

"Sampled? Why can't people write their own songs instead of stealing someone else's?"

"You're such an old…" He hesitates.

"Git? Fart?"

"Yeah."

My laughter dies. The wellbeing dissolves. I glance round, at the trees that hem us in.

There is so much peace here. Apart from the taint of smoke, it feels as if no bomb, rocket, bullet or hint of war can touch us in this place. But that's a lie, because darkness is coming.

Ruth will know.

She'll probably leave me because I arranged to have my own son maimed –

"Dad."

"Huh?"

"Are you okay? You're not in delayed shock or anything are you?"

"I don't think so…"

"I was telling you about the real reason I don't want you to go into the army."

"And?"

A pause.

"I don't want you to get killed."

It's obviously as hard for him to say this to me as it is for me to hear it from him. I don't answer but nod and give him a brief, hard hug.

*

Hours pass.

Dominic catches a couple of roach. I catch nothing, which doesn't matter. I'm increasingly restless and nervous. I wander into the trees, making excuses but needing to walk around. There is peace in the trees, in the dappling of winter sun.

Gary is nowhere in sight.

Come on…Come on…

I have to calm down. The shaking is bad now. I can't think, feel trapped and smothered. It's midday. This is wearing me out.

Perhaps *I* should do it instead. I feel my Swiss army knife in my coat pocket. Hamstrings would do the trick. Christ, I couldn't do that, even though there's no difference in the end. The bullet will be from someone else's gun but it's *my* finger on the trigger.

I lean against a tree, pounded by guilt and fear, and by the hell of Thursday and yesterday and the knowledge that everyone is dead, Hendy, Tony, Jamie, Katie, Francis, Dave…

I move slowly back to the river bank, scanning the woods nervously as I do so. No sign, no sound.

Gary isn't coming.

Something's happened to him. He wants the memory stick, it seems to be important to him. He would come if he could.

I emerge from the trees. Dominic looks round.

"You okay Dad?"

"Yeah, yeah," I say as I settle myself into my chair.

As if on cue the sky explodes. Two black shapes hurtle at us from the far side of the lake, ugly, malevolent and so, so loud. I yell and throw myself down onto the grass. The jet roar fills everything, beats at me, crushes me then fades, replaced by the hiss of breeze-rattled trees, the lap of water and squawk of startled birds.

I feel a weight on my back. Arms round me. Dominic.

"It's all right Dad, It's all right."

He's crying.

We pick ourselves up. Dominic stands, shoulders hunched, nose and eyes messy and wet. "Bloody war," he intones.

"Fucking war," I say.

Dominic looks at me sharply.

"I mean it." I turn to look out across the lake. "Tell you what, let's try for some pike. Have you got a lure?"

Dominic's smile is back. "Yeah, not my favourite though, lost that one."

He crouches by the box. I pull the knife from my coat pocket, open the blade.

Now.

While he's off balance.

One swift slice across the back of his knee.

Now –

"Got it." Dominic straightens, turns and his expression is suddenly one of puzzlement.

I close the knife and put it back into my pocket, unable to find an explanation. I'm no Abraham.

"Is that another Supertramp song?"

"What?"

"*I'm No Abraham*, is that Supertramp?"

I must have spoken that last sentence out loud. "No, not this time."

Dominic changes the reel and ties off the lure. It looks like a small fish, silver, hooked and jointed in the middle so it spins as it's dragged through the water. Dominic casts then hands the rod to me. Startled I fumble the changeover. I recover and begin to reel the lure back in. It flicks through the murk. Nothing. It looks as if I'm not going to break my duck.

I cast again, again. On my fourth cast I feel something, a weight, as if the lure has caught on some submarine obstacle. I release the reel. Line shoots out.

"Oh yeah!"

I reel in, stop and let the pike swim away a little. I reel in again, stop, again. No use trying to fight the bugger while it's angry and fresh. My shredded nerves are suddenly singing and I want that beast on the shore.

I force myself to play the game. Dominic is cheering, and shouting encouragement and laughing at me when I fumble. I see the pike's snout break the water, crocodilian, all teeth and long jaws. The line stretches from the left side of its mouth. It dives. I let it go for a few feet then reel it in again. I can feel the fight going out of it now.

This time I haul it in.

Dominic is on his knees, gag, long-nose pliers and towel all ready. The fish reaches the shoreline. A final tug and Dominic has it. It's not a monster, four or five pounds, but sleek and beautiful for all that. Dominic quickly wraps it in the towel, holds it carefully under his arm and forces the gag into its mouth to hold open its jaws and protect his fingers from the pike's endless rows of backward facing teeth. There are even teeth on its tongue. The pike is a predator, no doubt about that. Dominic works at the hook, and I admire the mix of delicacy and firmness he applies as he slides the hook out and free.

"Come on then Dad," he says and offers the fish to me.

He unwraps the beast and I hold it while he pulls a small digital camera from his pocket.

The fish is weakening, its mouth open, clawing for oxygen in this dry, alien universe into which it has been so rudely dragged. Picture taken, I lay the pike carefully in the shallow water by the shore. The fish twitches, its gills work. Then suddenly, with a small splash it shoots away into the lake, replaced by a slowly spreading cloud of disturbed mud.

Smoke.

Explosion.

We stay like that for a moment, me on my knees, Dominic standing. The sun is already low, its yellow glare tinted orange, the Wembley arch a graceful silhouette, the air colder than ever –

"Don't fucking move, either of you. Don't even turn round."

My breath fails.

"Gary."

"Shut up you stupid bastard. Just give me any money you've got and I'll leave you alone." He sounds out of breath, strained, every inch the desperate mugger.

"The deal is off," I say. "You can have the stick, but I don't want –"

"What the fuck are you talking about?"

"Gary it's okay. You can put away whatever weapon you've got. Please." I lift my hands. "The stick is in my left pocket. Take it and go."

A moment, his breathing is laboured, tremulous.

"Throw it to me."

"Can I turn round?"

"Slowly."

"Dad, what's going on?"

"Don't worry Dominic, let me deal with it."

I get to my feet, carefully, hands still raised. I turn, as slowly as I can. Gary is there, huddled in the same coat he wore yesterday. His right arm is crushed against his side. I see a dark stain.

Blood? Is that what it is?

"I haven't got much time," he says and the statement confirms my observation.

I slide my hands into my pocket. My fingers close round my wallet. The stick is in there, to make it more convincing because muggers normally steal wallets don't they? I take a deep breath and pull it free.

"Throw it."

I toss the wallet towards him. It lands at his feet. He lowers himself painfully, bends his knees and he reaches for it with his only hand, his gun hand. I watch his fingers scrabble in the grass.

"What happened to you?" I ask.

"Suicide," he answers. "The SSU, the plainclothes dirty tricks department, came to my flat. I heard them and went for the fire escape. One of them got a shot off. It's a flesh wound thank fuck, a bad one, but at least the bullet didn't hit anything important on its way through. So I feel great."

He has the wallet. He slips it into his pocket.

Now it's his turn to hand me something, a folded piece of paper. The manoeuvre is made awkward by the gun.

"Go there, when you need to. Friends, remember?"

He holds his hand out to me, the gun pointed, unwittingly I hope, at my chest. The paper is clenched between his two outer fingers. My heart pounds but I feel relieved. It's nearly over. My son is intact and whatever happens *I* haven't hurt him.

Except that, because of my cowardice, he'll go to war now.

Gary drops the paper on the grass, lowers the gun, turns away.

Someone shouts "Armed police!"

Gary spins back round.

"Put the weapon down! Armed police!"

And there's an explosion, a flash, smoke and a scream. Startled I stumble backwards, almost fall and actually see the bullet smash into Dominic's shin and erupt out of his calf in a shower of torn denim, flesh, blood and powdered bone.

Collateral Damage

Another shot and this time Gary is thrown into a bizarre pirouette. He recovers, staggers. A second shot and his head explodes. Just explodes, vaporised, gone. The rest of him melts to the ground, next to me, because I'm down as well; reflex, instinct, there are guns for Christ's sake, bullets.

Dominic shrieks.

I recover enough to scrabble for the paper then for the memory stick. Panic roars through me. I need to go to my son, now, *now*. But I have to retrieve the wallet. I shove my hand into Gary's pocket and find what I'm looking for. My fist catches. I struggle to free myself for a desperate, mind-howling moment. Out it comes and I slither away from the corpse then start to get up.

"Stay down!" No sympathy, just an order, hard, loud. I drop back onto my belly and twist my head to see a police officer, rifle raised and pointed at me. Another of them rushes to Dominic, who is moaning now, curled about his hurt, sounding weak. I should have gone to him first.

Another mistake. Too many bloody mistakes…

"My son…"

"What did you get from his pocket?" the armed officer snaps. "Tell me!"

"Wuh…Wuh…wallet…he stuh…stole my…"

"The boy's leg is smashed to buggery," the other officer calls out. His voice becomes gentle. "Okay son, it's all right, there's an ambulance on its way, it won't be long. It's okay."

That should be me, comforting my child, helping him. I try to get up again. "Don't move!"

"Fuck you" I shout back. He's got a gun and I'm not a hero but I need to get to Dominic. "We're the victims for God's sake."

The officer stiffens. He wants to hit me, to drive his rifle butt into my kidneys, but he's a police officer so he can't. Even in this insane new world the British police remain the British police; calm, sacrificing feelings to professionalism.

The SSU on the other hand, well, I doubt that restraint is in their rule book.

A siren throbs and wails, grows loud, the ambulance hopefully, probably in the car park. They aren't wasting any time, unless it was already on its way, following the armed police so it could be available to pick up Gary, dead or alive.

The light is fading now. It's fiercely cold. I hear Dominic's groaning and I can tell that he's shivering.

There are torches, more figures, the ambulance crew. They hurry over to my son and the police officer steps away. I can hear their voices, brusque and professional with each other, soothing and calm to Dominic. I hear him cry out and twist my head to see them lift him onto a stretcher. As they set off into the trees, other figures emerge. One of them is a woman in a dark coat.

She says something. There's a lot of talking, torches, movement. I'm finally helped up onto my feet. Someone wraps a blanket round my shoulders and leads me back into the woods. We reach the car park in time to see the ambulance race away, siren loud, lights splintering the near-dark.

There is a police minibus in the car park, its windscreen riot shield raised. There is also a large saloon. The woman stands by its open rear door.

"It's okay," she says as I'm brought to the car. "We'll take you to the hospital. You're in no fit state to drive, and you and I need to talk."

She makes it sound like an opportunity for a social chat.

"Is the Focus yours?"

I nod.

"If you give us the keys we'll make sure it's driven home for you."

She doesn't ask for an address. I hand over the keys after fumbling in my coat pocket. I almost bring out the wallet, complete with memory stick and the slip of paper giving details of those Gary called *Friends*.

Defeated, suddenly too tired to fight anymore, I slump into back seat of the saloon. It's clean in here and smells of leather. The woman gets in next to me and adds perfume to the mix. The courtesy light reveals long brown hair, an attractive strong featured face. Then it's dark again. The door shuts. Two men in plain clothes get into the front. The car starts, its engine luxuriously quiet.

"I'm Detective Inspector Williams," the woman says. "And you are Dominic Allman's father?"

I nod.

"Peter Allman?"

"How did you know?"

"Driving licence, it fell out of your wallet." She holds it out to me.

"Ah." Thank Christ that was the only thing that fell out. I take it from her.

"Did you know the man who shot your son Mr.Allman?"

"No….yes, yes I have met him." Careful, keep the lies shallow. And besides, Dominic might be questioned before I can get to him and straighten our stories. He'll tell the police I spoke to Gary by name, that I seemed to know him. He wouldn't do it to hurt me but he's frightened, in pain.

"Where?"

"In… In the Hammer and Nails pub, one lunch time during the week. He was a nuisance. He wanted to fight me. Look, I know he's – *was* – a Veteran, so he was probably shell-shocked, disturbed. I met him again, yesterday, in town. He's been bothering me ever since, threatening me."

The car drones quietly. This is almost a moment of peace.

"Which town?"

Careful. "Kilburn. I went to the Tricycle Theatre, to see a film. He must have followed me there."

"Why would he do that?"

"Like I said, he seemed disturbed. He latched onto me for some reason."

"He certainly latched onto you Mr. Allman, he followed you all the way to Chalk Lake, even though he had been wounded in a shooting incident."

"How do I know what he was thinking?"

"True. Did you realise he was already wounded?"

"Yes."

"What did he tell you about that?"

"Someone…" Oh, for Christ's sake just tell her. "The SSU came for him. He tried to run…"

"The SSU?" Williams chuckles humourlessly. "Everyone blames the SSU. We believe Gary Marshall was involved in some criminal activities, drug trafficking to be precise. A lot of Veterans have got themselves mixed up in crime. Life is hard for them. They can't get jobs, people are afraid of them. Unfortunately a lot of them are getting hurt."

Like Dave.

I think she believes this. I almost drag my wallet from my pocket and hand her the memory stick. Here it is Inspector, proof the SSU are hunting down and assassinating the Veterans because there is something the government wants to hide about this war.

But I don't because the fact she believes their crap about the Veterans means that she'll hand the stick straight over to the SSU.

"We were called to Marshall's flat by neighbours who heard shooting. He was making his escape when we arrived. We managed to follow him. The rest, you know." She shrugs. "We don't make a habit of shooting people Mr. Allman, but Gary Marshall was armed and he fired at your son first."

"I know."

"Your son is eighteen tomorrow isn't he?"

"You seem to know a lot about me Inspector."

"It's amazing what you can find out from a dropped driving license."

Bull shit.

"And no doubt he's received his call-up papers."

I don't need to answer.

"He won't be going now will he."

No, no he won't. For a moment I'm elated. It's over, he's safe.

"Very convenient that the desperate, pain-maddened Gary Marshall shot your son in the leg and not the heart."

"Are you saying that I arranged this?" I'm surprised at how outraged I manage to sound.

"Well, did you?"

"Look, Gary; Marshall was obsessed about the war, about cover-ups and conspiracies. He was also obsessed with stopping my son from being called up –"

"He knew you had a son? Were you on good enough terms to discuss your family with him?"

No answer. I pull the blanket more tightly about myself and realise I'm cornered.

"Listen," Williams almost sounds gentle. "I've seen this a thousand times since the war started. I don't blame you and quite frankly, I'm not interested in a case of foot-shooting, not today. I can be made to believe that your son was shot during a robbery. To do that, however, I need the truth about your relationship with Gary Marshall. Why did you have any relationship at all? He's a Veteran, they don't make friends easily, especially with someone who has been excused boots because they're in a reserved occupation."

"Okay, I met Marshall in a pub and he agreed to do the foot-shooting for me. I don't know any more about him than that."

"I don't believe you." It's a simple, plain statement and the very neutrality of its delivery chills me to my soul. "As soon as your name was called in an alarm went off, Mr Allman, and I was given this." Williams holds up a file. "The SSU arrested you for curfew-breaking a few nights ago. That's normally police-work, not something the SSU would get involved with. They must have been watching you, so what have you done to make them so interested?"

My "nothing" is cut off by a wave of her gloved hand.

"You also failed to report your survival of the London Wall air raid and now you're suspected of arranging a foot shooting. And as for your past…" She shakes her head. "Quite an accumulation of sins Mr.Allman. Now, what can you tell me about Gary Marshall?"

We're passing through an area of ruin, worse than I saw in Kilburn. Most of the houses and shops look like facades, their empty windows, pools of shadow carved out by the subdued street lighting. A bomb site then. Dominic was right. It does look like systematic demolition.

"Ask the SSU," I say. "You're all on the same side aren't you?"

I sense tension. Perhaps I've hit a raw nerve.

We whisper out of the desolation and suddenly we're at a hospital I recognise as the Central Middlesex.

"Look," I say as the car slides to a halt outside the entrance to A&E. "I don't care what you do to me. My son's life isn't going to be wasted in this fucking war and that makes me very happy. Yeah, I'm selfish and unpatriotic. But I'm also a father and I love my son and my family and that is all that matters."

"For God's sake Allman, I'm trying to help you," Williams hisses through gritted teeth. "Give me what I want to know and suddenly there's nothing I can charge you with. I won't be able to prove any foot-shooting, do you understand? It was a mugging, the man was an obsessive, turned psychotic by the war. All the SSU want to know is what Gary Marshall's game was, what he wanted from you. I can protect you, but damned if I will if you don't bloody tell me what I bloody well need to know."

I can give her the memory stick now, hand it over. I can walk away, back to my family. I can escape the nightmare.

But what about Dave, my best friend? He was murdered. The SSU killed him, I'm convinced of it. And who is to say they won't come for me and my family anyway. Better for me to be isolated, I'm the one they want.

I take a deep breath, a shaky one and say. "I'm sorry but no."

She sighs then opens her door.

"Come on, you have to go in and comfort your family. Oh yes, we've told them already. I'm afraid I'll have to come in with you."

We walk through the doorway into A&E and Ruth crashes into my arms. She is shaking. Rachel and Amanda hover nearby looking pale and frightened.

"He's all right," I say. "It was his leg. He's okay…" How do I know? He could have bled to death, could've died of shock.

"They've taken him to the operating theatre," Ruth says at last. She glances past me.

"Detective Inspector Williams."

A jet roars overhead. I flinch.

The sound fades.

An air raid siren wails. People look up, some move towards the exit.

The staff are nervous but carry on as best they can.

Ruth sits down again and gathers Rachel under her arm. Amanda looks childlike and lost. I sit down, hug her and whisper all the right words.

I hear another jet.

The siren goes off again. This time I sense a ripple of panic.

"We have to get out," Williams says.

"I can't," Ruth answers, there's an odd calm in her voice, one I haven't heard before. "I can't leave him –"

"He's being looked after," I say. Because Dominic or no Dominic, I can't stay in this building. I want to stay, I should stay but I can't.

Oh come on you cowardly bastard, this is a hospital, and surely lightning never strikes twice…

"It'll only be for a moment, until the all-clear." Do they still call it that? "Ruth, please, it'll be okay."

Oh those words, so easy to say and probably the least reassuring phrase in the world.

The waiting room is filling up as staff, patients and relatives use it for an escape route. There's tension, a controlled urgency, but no panic. This is routine, isn't it? NHS policy? Air raid siren means that the walking wounded and the well have to get out, like a fire drill. Leave your possessions, close all windows and doors, make your way to the nearest exit etc etc. It doesn't mean any bombs are actually going to be dropped on the building.

Not a hospital.

"Ruth, it'll only be for a few minutes." I have to shout now, the waiting room is uncomfortably packed and escape is becoming difficult. Too many people, too closely packed. I'm sweating, nails gouging my palms, legs shaking.

Security have arrived. Order is being imposed.

The siren wails though my skull, loud and abrasive.

Ruth is looking back, towards the corridor that leads to the main A&E ward. I grab her arm and shout her name. She isn't listening.

Williams' phone warbles, she pulls it out of her pocket, glances at me, finishes the call then says something to the plain clothes officer who has accompanied us into the waiting room.

He takes a step towards me.

SSU then, requesting that Inspector Williams delivers one Peter Allman, believed to be in police custody, into their tender care. Now. No excuses, because Mr Mason needs a quiet word.

The exodus from the hospital is gathering momentum, people are beginning to push and shove. The sound level cranks up a notch. I'm almost glad when the detective grabs my arm and begins to haul me towards the doors, using his bulk to carve a path through the crowd.

Except that my family is still in here, my wife, my daughters and my son. I struggle, his grip tightens. He's a big bastard, shorter than me but built like the proverbial brick shithouse.

There's a lull and Ruth suddenly breaks into a run, the wrong way, *into* the hospital. I shout after her, attempt another escape, but this time the detective wrenches my arm up behind me and the pain is unspeakable. I don't care. I have to stop Ruth. A glimpse of her, a beautiful, fair haired women, soft in one of those big grey, woollen things that's more coat than cardigan, and she's gone.

"I'll get her," Williams shouts "Take him to the car."

Another wave of people surges into the room and Williams disappears into the crowd, swimming against the tide, flailing her arms like a panicked swimmer, clawing and shoving.

I glimpse Amanda and Rachel, confused, torn, buffeted but not moving in either direction. I call to them to come with me. I shout, I yell, I shriek.

The crowd closes over them. I can't see them. Christ oh Christ, where are they?

The siren stops and is replaced by a scratch that cuts through the hubbub of voices.

I'm still screaming and ranting, ripping out my throat, trying to contact my daughters, my lovely, beautiful, frightened daughters.

Scratch becomes whine becomes roar.

And I'm out, sucked through the doors by the crowd.

I have to get back inside. I have to.

But that bastard has me and now his mate has joined in and I can't move my arms or control my legs because which ever way I try to run I'm being dragged towards the big, classy car I arrived in.

Roar.

Loud and louder and drowning everything.

We're almost at the car. I yank my head around again, a final brief look into the crowd as they stream out of the building and rush past.

Amanda…Rachel…Ruth…

Christ where are they?

The hospital explodes.

It's almost light when I get home. I'm exhausted, barely cogent of where I am or who I am or what is happening inside and around me, unable, in fact, to grasp much at all. Except that this is my house, a too-expensive four-up, two-down, pre-war semi. Pre *that* war, the one I understand. The front door is tight shut, the curtains open. The windows are lightless, black rectangles. Everything is closed and cold, waiting for us all to come back.

I'm here, I tell it silently.

It doesn't want me. The blackness inside that place wants the others, the warm and the loving. I'm too full of darkness, I will only add to the desolation.

Yet, even through the swirling confusion and burgeoning despair, a sane, angry voice hammers at me.

Idiot, wanker, stupid bastard. They'll *be watching the house, they're expecting you to come here.*

Or maybe not, perhaps they think I'm dead.

My family is.

My family is dead.

My family is dead my family is dead dead dead fucking *dead…*

I'm screaming but I can't hear anything, waves of concussion slam me onto my back, scorching heat burns my throat, my chest. Everywhere is light and noise, deafening, incomprehensible noise.

I scrabble at the tarmac, at air, until I'm sitting up, trying to breathe. There's nothing but fire, a vast boiling mass of flame and a blinding fog of smoke. I see bodies, crumpled heaps in the glare, an overturned wheelchair, a shattered drip bottle. One of the detectives is staggering back towards the inferno, arm over his face. The other simply stands, stares, mouth open. Smoke stings my eyes, my ears roar.

I am dead, switched off, shrunk back into a dark corner of myself and carried in a body that's driven by some spark that has survived the flame and screams and destruction of its family.

It's cold.

I frown. Cold. This is the first time I've noticed. And there's fog hugging the ground. I've been walking all night and I haven't felt any cold or been aware of any fog.

On my feet, the transition from sitting to standing unnoticed. I take a step towards the fire. A wave of heat drives me back. I'm still shouting and screaming. Names now, howling them over and over again, trying to force my way through the smoke and through the heat. Glass crunches under my feet, I stumble up against other living dead, trip over the real dead.

I try again, but I can't.

Again, again...

Get out, *shouts a voice, hard and relentless.* Fucking get out of here. Now, now!

I stagger back, lost in my shock, unable to feel anything else, unable to run back into the fire and unable to run away. The voice confuses me. I don't understand what it wants me to do. Surely they'll all come out in a moment; Ruth with Amanda and Rachel, and Dominic, mustn't forget Dominic.

A sound slices though my numbness; sirens, two-tone, the emergency services. There'll be a pretty young wPC who will tell me sit on the ground and ask me my name and make me cry with her sympathetic tone and tell me that I have to wait for an ambulance even though I don't want to because something bad will happen to me if I do.

Flickering blue light melds with the writhing glare of the fire.

Now I understand the voice.

I turn away and force myself to move, as the heat pummels my back and the first of the fire engines shrieks past me. Its sheer weight and energy carries a shockwave that almost tips me off my feet. I manage to stay upright however, my only thought, my only instinct, is the one compelling me to move, away, into the nearest pool of shadow. Behind me glass shatters, something collapses. I hear shouts and screams.

No one follows me. I'm utterly alone, staggering out into the smoke-drenched darkness. I cross a car park. There are people here, getting out of their cars, getting in. Some stand, staring, others sob uncontrollably. I ignore them and walk on, unable to speak or connect.

More fire engines. Police cars now. And a big, dark armoured van, no lights, or insignia. I recognise it because Ruth and I were taken for a ride in one of those last week.

Only last week.

SSU, here at a bomb site.

They round people up after a raid, lock them in giant tower blocks.

Somebody told me that, I can't remember who, I should, I need to, the frustration forces tears into my eyes.

Or are they looking for me?

Why? Who am I?

The van hurtles across the car park, towards the inferno. I plunge on into the dark.

My car is missing. I feel something I understand to be anger. Some shit, some fucker, has stolen my car. That makes me move, drags me through the gateway and into the concrete apron I call the front garden.

The police.

That's who. They drove it away. They said they were going to take it home for me. They lied. Everyone is lying.

The police.

I stop, right there in the middle of the front garden with its potted conifers and low brick walls. I glance round, peer into the fog-blurred grey. The police must be here, somewhere. They want me. I remember one of them dragging me out of the hospital just before…

Come on then you bastards, come on.

Nothing, only the stink of smoke and a distant drone of some vehicle about its legitimate, curfew-breaking business.

My anger fades and the numbness creeps back.

Who cares about my fucking car?

I move to the front door. There's darkness behind the frosted glass. I don't like it, I can't go in.

You have to, there's something in there you need.

I cough. I can taste smoke and fire.

I'm walking and walking and it's night but the dark is torn and unsettled. I'm on the side of a wide road, I know this road, it leads somewhere I need to go. You shouldn't walk on this road, I have to get off it, but I don't know how. To my left there are flashes, thunder, deafening. Things screech over my head, dark shapes in the night sky, loud and malevolent.

Smoke rolls over the road. It makes me cough and choke. It stings my eyes. I feel more heat, the fire is following me, because Ruth and my family are living in the fire now and they want me and they're coming for me and I'm frightened. I break into a run and the ground shakes and night turns to day and the air is hot and stinking.

I see more terrible flowers blooming ahead and to my right, silhouetting the Wembley Arch the way the setting sun had silhouetted it…when? A millions years ago? When?

The keys are in my hand and I'm at the front door.

I hesitate because the house is resisting me, pushing at me.

It doesn't want me, it wants the others.

They're in there.

Yes, yes, they're in the house, together in the cold shadows, huddled and frightened and waiting for me. Hand shaking I fumble the key into the lock and twist and push and pull. The door opens and the icy darkness spills out.

It becomes terrible.

I can't go in.

But I have to, I must.

I step over the threshold, switch on the light, the dark shatters, and the smells and objects and reminders and feelings, and the *truth* penetrate and tear at me so savagely I can't breathe or move. Coats and scarves are on their hooks, shoes in the rack, on the telephone table is the notebook with flowers on the cover that Ruth uses to record numbers and messages. On the wall is the paper she chose. Here are the doors I painted, the light fitting Ruth hates but has never got round to changing, the framed impressionist print, a memento from our visit to Monet's garden in Givenchy. All of it crashes over me and I'm drowning.

There's Ruth's scarf, and her quilted coat with the fur-edged hood –

What was she wearing last night? What was it? I can't remember, not this coat, she hasn't worn it since we were arrested for curfew-breaking. She was wearing something else. What was she wearing, what did she look like? I can't remember, I can't fucking remember what she looks like –

I collapse, fall forward, clawing for oxygen. A vast animal groan escapes my lips. It becomes a roar then a long howl of pain and grief. I sob and sob, the violence of it convulses me, rips out my strength until I'm on my hands and knees, tears and snot pouring out of me. My arms collapse and I curl on the floor and shudder out my grief until there is nothing left and every part of me aches.

As the sobs ease I realise I'm holding the coat, clenching it tight against myself. I bury my face in the fur and I smell her there, perfumes, shampoos and that sweetness that is only Ruth.

Dangerous.

The concept crawls into my brain.

Dangerous, here, dangerous.

I don't care. Come and kill me as well.

Dangerous. It's fucking dangerous!

The voice, that spark, cuts through the spinning, roaring grey, forces me to unfold myself, to sit up, arms round my knees, shivering and choking on those final, lingering sobs that manage to force their way through even as your crying stops. There is something I should do, though I'm not sure what exactly. I let myself calm then open my eyes again. Once more the familiarity and memories rush in to smother me but this time I manage to control their effect. I have to, there isn't much time.

The memory stick.

Christ, the memory stick and …and what?

I put my hand in my pocket and feel my wallet, and a slip of paper. I draw it out, unfold it.

OS TM423496

Another code, another meaningless puzzle for me to work out. I stare at it, my thoughts moving through sludge. OS. OS, OS…

It doesn't make sense.

It should, it absolutely should.

Friends are there. People who will help me, and would have helped Dominic, but he's dead now.

"Dominic is dead." I have to say it. There is a cruelty in the words, as much an act of self-harm as opening my arms with a razor blade. I want to repeat it and grind it into myself until I bleed, but I can't, not at this moment. I have something I need to do, a mission, a job, a task.

Friends are there.

There.

There.

A place then. OS TM423496 is a place.

The spark glows more brightly, although the flare is brief.

OS. O-bloody-S.

I get to my feet and shakily, carefully, move into the lounge, past the bookcase, which is laden with paperbacks and big, glossy hardbacks that are mostly Ruth's cookery books and my motorcycle books. There are DVDs and some CDs, though not mine. Mine are stacked by themselves in another corner of the room, rock and more rock, mostly 60s and 70s.

Ah, what the hell do they matter now?

I look for an atlas of the British Isles.

Just road atlases though, the grid references don't match, don't connect with the code.

Don't care…

Come on, think, think.

I don't want to think because the truth lurks in thought and I don't want the truth anymore…

OS, OS, OS, map, reference, OS map…Ordnance Survey. Ordnance-bloody-Survey. Those big, boring white maps my long-dead geography teacher used to force us to look at.

We don't own any, why should we? We drive to clearly marked footpaths, using SatNav and signposts. When we arrive there are visitor centres and simple, brightly coloured little tourist maps. We don't need to use real maps that show tumuli (whatever they are) and ditches and triangulation points.

Why am I remembering all this now?

And it's walk*ed, drove, went, didn't.* There is no more present tense.

Internet. There must be Ordnance Survey maps on the World Wide Web.

That means going upstairs.

I look up, at the carpeted treads, at the gloom-hidden landing. I can't.

I have to. It's that or curl up and die and let the names on the list die with me. Up then, onto my feet, wavering dizzily because I haven't slept or smoked since…

Since my family were wiped out.

Hanging onto the stair rail like a *Titanic* survivor clinging to wreckage, I haul myself up to the shadowed and cold landing. First door on the right, Rachel's room, next to Amanda's. The doors are both tight shut. Privacy privacy privacy, *my* space, *my* world. How the hell would they have survived in days when families slept ten a-bed?

They haven't survived these days.

To my left, the bathroom, I'll need that soon, then Dominic's room.

They are all in their rooms. I can hear them breathing, the sound wet and laboured through lungs that are fire-wrecked and fluid-filled. Every so often one of them wheezes out my name and they sound angry because I escaped and they didn't.

It isn't my fault. I need to tell them that I called for them to follow me. I tried to go back.

I'm sorry. Christ I'm so sorry.

My hand is on Rachel's door handle, pushing down –

No.

I mustn't go in, I must never, ever step though that doorway again, not Rachel's or Amanda's or Dominic's. My children are sleeping. My children must not be disturbed.

I close the cracked-open door once more and step away from it.

I hear a sob, my name, whispered.

Daddy…

Ahead is the main bedroom, our place Ruth, our world and shelter. The door is ajar and reveals a sliver of duvet and carpet. That's where I have to go. We don't have a study or an office. We have a bedroom corner set-up, complete with desk and laptop where Ruth can – could, could, *could* – prepare lessons and write reports. Not ideal, but she never complained. Me, I hardly ever use the thing. Working with them kills the novelty and the fun –

I stand at the door, shoulders hunched, fists clenched.

Come in darling…

I can't hesitate, I mustn't. Shivering I press my fingertips against the door's white-glossed wood. My hands are dirty, smoke-stained, bruised and cut. My face must be the same. I push.

The room swings into view, our bed, the fitted wardrobe…

When I step inside I do it quickly and coldly. I'm business and purpose and make straight for the computer. The curtains are open, those heavy black curtains that started all this. I don't look through the X-taped window this time but bend down to switch on the socket that feeds the computer. Ruth never leaves – left – anything switched on. No red standby lights ever glow in this house.

I love her…

I switch on the computer itself.

Then remember that there is no internet.

Andy told me that, gone-to-seed-and-not caring Andy Taylor, colleague, foil and friend. Dead Andy.

"What do you mean where's your internet?" He's shaking his head and frowning and at the same time giving me that half-smile he reserves for the fools he won't gladly suffer. "You know where your internet is. It's been closed down…There is a bloody war on, in case you hadn't noticed…Come on Pete, wake up."

I step back from the computer and my heel bumps into something. I turn and see the toolbox; pristine, red metal, cantilever. It sits on a huge sheet of downward facing gift paper. The box is open, the bottom section already filled with gleaming new tools. More screwdrivers and pliers and spanners lay beside it, still in their packets and boxes.

Dominic's birthday present.

My idea. The first time I'd ever made a successful present suggestion in my life.

No doubt Ruth, Rachel, and possibly even Amanda had been preparing it when the police arrived. They were going to wrap it then wait for me to come home from our fishing trip because once full of tools it would be too heavy for them to carry to its wardrobe hiding place.

Rachel would be the fussy one, making sure that all the spanners went together in this compartment, and the screwdrivers in that compartment and so on and on. Amanda would become impatient because any tools you couldn't use to improve your own, already perfect, body were incomprehensible lumps of metal to her and so, like, utterly boring. Bless her wonderful, confused, teenaged little heart.

I force myself to stand over the box and paper, and stare, to face it hard and let it hurt me until I can bear it no longer.

I don't leave the room though, but go to the wardrobe, open the door and reach up to a bundle of clothes on the top shelf. I pull them down and throw them onto the bed. Leathers and boots, worn, battered but usable. I tear off my coat and jeans and leave them on the floor by the tool box. For a moment I feel guilty, Ruth hates strewn clothes.

She's not here. She'll never be here again. I could piss on the carpet and nothing will happen. Ruth is dead.

I drag on the one-piece, which is tight over my heavy sweater. I don't care. I'll be warm that's all that matters. The boots go on last. Boots on the carpet, another unforgivable sin. Sorry Ruth, really I am.

I stuff the grid reference in my wallet, my wallet into one of my zip-up pockets, then open my bedside drawer and pull out one last item. A set of keys.

There is no last look round when I leave. I simply walk out and know that I will not be coming back. My clothes stay draped over the tool box, the computer stays on and the wardrobe door remains open. Like the junk the Americans left on the moon, never moving, never used again.

That's my footprint, my last moments in this place. Mingled and melded with those of my wife, son and daughters. I run downstairs and hurry through the house to the back door. The kitchen is a terrible place because there is food here, party food, still in its packets, piled on the kitchen worktops. There's a cake too, in its box. I know that a photograph of Dominic has been printed in icing on its top. I don't look. His face is gone from my memory too and looking at an image won't help.

I unhook the garage keys from their place by the back door and go out into the garden. Not much of a garden; a lawn, borders, a patio and garden furniture, all neat and pleasant, but no work of art. There's smoke beyond the fence, huge, dense columns six, seven of them. The air is thick with its scent. There were a lot of raids last night, it seems, a veritable blitz.

A lot of dead families then.

I open the garage doors and go in. This is my place. It's reasonably tidy, smells of oil and grease and is full of tools and shelves piled with tobacco tins, each one containing screws, bolts, nuts and other small items indispensible to the modern male.

There is also a motorbike.

Hidden under a sheet, dusty, used only for occasional summer jaunts, and usually with Ruth riding pillion. Out for the hell of it, racing down main streets and country lanes looking for pubs and cafes and secret places where we could make love in the open air and behave like teenagers. My helmet sits with hers on one of the shelves. Ruth didn't like her helmet being out here and always checked it for spiders before pulling it on.

There never were any.

I pick up her helmet, turn it over and search its padded interior for arachnids. No, its okay. Then I hurl the helmet across the garage as hard as I can and it hits the far wall and ricochets onto the hard, dusty concrete floor. I'm breathing hard, so fucking angry I could kill.

I've felt this anger before, a long time ago, pre-Ruth, before I clawed my way out of the shit and tried to make something of my worthless little life. I rip the sheet from my Suzuki and rock it off its stand then wheel it towards the doorway.

The closer I get to Ruislip, the thicker the smoke, until I can barely see my leather-gloved hands curled about the Suzuki's handlebars. A few vehicles loom out of the stinking fog, headlights on. I see people walking, dark shapes in the swirl, zombie-like, dazed and blank. I slow, down and the Suzuki's engine-noise changes from roar to growled heartbeat.

Flame writhes out of the murk to my left, I glimpse flashing blue light. There are sirens, distant, relentless. The tarmac becomes debris-strewn and hazardous.

Then blocked.

By a pair of dark, hulking and ominously familiar vans that have been parked across the road. I stop the moment I see them, not wanting to draw attention to myself or to be caught up in any SSU post-raid round-up.

I turn about, head back the way I've come, trying to calculate an alternative route down onto the A40 and into Central London. My plans are vague. I need an Ordnance Survey map, not something you can buy from your local corner shop. There's a W H Smiths in Oxford Street, which will be open (if it hasn't been bombed to rubble that is) even though it's the Sabbath. The shop will be big, I will be anonymous.

After that I have to get out of London.

Even though the city is sealed up, or so my family told me when I had suggested Harefield for that fishing trip. No one is allowed to leave. That's a future bridge to cross. I need to know where I have to get *to* before I can work out how to get there.

The raid seems to have been tightly localised and I'm soon travelling through streets and lanes unscathed by war, apart, of course, from those white X's taped over every window I see.

How much longer though? If the raiding is systematic as Dominic and others seem to think, then these rows of Sunday-sleeping house aren't long for this world.

Pinner, Harrow, they all seem untouched. Sandbagged and dotted with anti-aircraft guns, yes, but not a window broken or roof tile out of place. Northolt, though smoke-fogged by its proximity to Ruislip and despite the presence of an RAF aerodrome, is also relatively pristine, There is a lot of soldiery here, extra gun emplacements and a lorry that seems to be a mobile missile platform.

People are out, in groups, talking, I sense tension, not surprising when your neighbours have been flattened by bombs and you're probably next.

I wonder if moving house is allowed during these troubled times, because if not, all you can do is mow your lawn, creosote your fence and wait for the bombs to fall.

A police car and a pair of vans are parked outside a row of red brick semis. Uniformed officers are remonstrating with a group of angry residents. No one so much as glances at me. Thank God for modern motorcycle helmets and opaque visors.

The smoke thickens again, but there are no more road blocks and I've managed to reach the Target Roundabout unchallenged. I take the slip road down onto the A40 and that's when I see the wall.

It runs along the entire south border of the trunk road, a twenty foot high, barb-wire-topped, metal barrier. Is this considered to be the edge of London then? I almost lose control of my bike as I try to comprehend the sheer scale of the thing, which disappears into the distance ahead of me. My claustrophobia flares bright. Okay, London is huge, but a wall is a wall, a cage, a cage. Suddenly I want to know what's on the other side. I want to get *out*.

And I will, once I find a map. I'm going to break free and roar off into those open, open spaces beyond as fast as this machine will take me.

Or, at least, as far as its not very full petrol tank will get me.

Another panic, I can't remember how much fuel I have.

I open up anyway, the acceleration and speed-rush swamps my terrors and tears away my grief. There are a few vehicles out, military or commercial as usual, but some ordinary cars. People with fuel rations to burn.

The wall dips away to my right, following, I suppose the ragged edges of the great city. It disappears from view and my claustrophobia fades with it.

I chain my Suzuki to the motorbike parking racks by Regent's park, lock my helmet in the back box and head off down Baker Street. The area is perfect, not a scratch or cracked window. No bombs have fallen here, in fact, apart from the tape and the tang of smoke it is hard to remember that there is a war on at all.

This is a familiar place to me, part of a city I've lived in, and around, all my life, yet, on this bitterly cold, smoke-scented morning it feels as alien and disconnected from me as Mars. Nothing is home anymore, nothing throws the switch that lights up a My Place sign in my head. It no longer smells or sounds or tastes like Pete Allman's London. I'm lost, an automaton, one part of my mind and soul alert, alive, sharp and angry, the other, closed down and filled with jagged shards of emotional glass. One wrong thought or word and I'll bleed grief until I collapse. The lid is on, tight, but keeping it that way is sapping my strength.

It's still early so the shops won't be open yet. I have time to kill, me, a big tall bastard, conspicuous with his long hair, motorcycle leathers and murder in his eyes. I must try to hide and wait out the hours in some dark corner where I won't be noticed.

They must be looking for me, *they*, the police, the SSU, the authorities, unless they believe I was killed in the raid. Unless they've found the burned and broken remains of some other poor, tall, big, long-haired old bugger in the smouldering ruins and believed it to be me.

I find a café and slip inside to discover that it isn't Formica, plastic and friendly, but corner-café chic. I order tea and a breakfast and even in my state, baulk at the cost. I don't complain or comment however. It would be remembered. Anything would be remembered.

The food is tasteless, a way to keep going rather than enjoyment. The tea is comforting. It comes in a light blue mug, a nod towards the real café. I order another. Money doesn't matter anymore. Ruth would have been annoyed. Rip off, she would have said and walked out. But Ruth's not here and she never will be again, so I drink my overpriced tea and force down my last mouthful of overpriced and calorie-lacking breakfast undisturbed.

I grab one of the café's complimentary newspapers and force myself to read. The hospital bombing is shrieked from the front page. There are pictures, lurid and brutal, of burning buildings, fire-fighters and shocked survivors.

No mention of me, no talk of desperate fugitives fleeing the scene.

Only tragedy and destruction and yet more anger at the EoD.

At last the big shutters begin to rise, lights go on, doors open. I get up, pay cash and leave the café as casually as I can manage. Oxford Street, like Baker Street, is untouched by the war. It holds that same invulnerability that London Wall held. An arrogant certainty that oozes from its very, brick, glass and steel pores that no enemy would dare drop a bomb on its hallowed rooftops.

London Wall burned.

So can Oxford Street and Piccadilly and Leicester Square.

The realisation makes me scan the sky uneasily. Birds wheel against the winter grey, a helicopter dashes across the cloud-face.

I see a W H Smith's and cross the street.

The bookshop is cavernous and all but empty. I move down the aisles until I find a shelf packed with cerise-coloured Ordnance Survey maps as well as a massive book filled with them. I open the book.

OS TM423496.

How the hell do I use the reference? It's to do with reading one direction then the other. But which direction first, north-south or east-west? And which page? Which fucking page?

I make myself calm down and flick back to the beginning of the book. Ah, a map of Britain, divided into areas, SP, TL, TM. Okay, TM is East Anglia. I turn another page and there is an explanation of how to use the grid reference system.

I glance towards the door. A woman enters, smart coat, immaculate hair, then a couple, young and casually dressed. Next comes an old man, sprightly, dapper and whistling to himself. He peruses the newspapers. The couple pick up crisps and chocolate and move to the magazines. The immaculate woman heads my way. Her high heels clatter on the floor her clothes rustle.

She has a handbag on her shoulder and looks assured and brittle. She pauses at the main paperback section a few metres to my left. I glimpse a man enter, in his thirties, smart jeans, sweater, jacket. He's alert, glancing about, in a hurry. I freeze. He grabs a newspaper, a bar of chocolate and, like the woman, moves towards me then also browses the paperbacks. They are not together but they are close enough to block me when I head for the exit. The woman picks up a Patricia Cornwell, the man, a Stephen King, neither of them so much as glances at me. Their studious, almost deliberate disinterest makes me uncomfortable.

Back to the Ordnance Survey book. There are two types of reference, four figure and six figures. Mine is a six figure. The numbers run west to east and south to north. Read the eastwards figures first. The main squares are divided into tenths, so, the first number is the main square eastwards, in my case 42 East. The second number is the number of smaller, tenths squares that divide the main 42 square, that's three small squares. Same with the northwards squares, six small squares into the 49 square.Christ it's driving me crazy,

Next job, find the TM section of the book, which is big and conspicuous but better than unfolding maps and God knows how many I would have to unfold to find my grid reference. Page by page I go, slowly homing in. I trace the grid lines, my finger moving along the coast until it reaches a village called Chillingford and a town called Leiston. Nearby is Sizewell, famous for its nuclear power station. Finally the lines converge on a strip of land separated from the mainland, for most of its length, by a stretch of water. I read the name. Orfordness. The letters NT are printed beside it. The key reveals this to be National Trust. A footnote tells me it is only accessible by boat from the quay in Orford village.

I put the book down then run my finger over the other map books and pick out a road atlas. I can't buy it. If I do people will be suspicious.

"Yes officer," the lad on the till will say. "I remember, the long-haired man in the motorcycle gear bought a road atlas, I thought it was weird, I mean, no one can leave London at the moment, so why buy a map book? It's pointless…"

I glance left and right, my attempts at discretion probably a ludicrous pantomime to anyone who is watching, then open the atlas at its gazetteer. O…Orford, the village adjacent to the island. I read the page number and grid reference then turn to it. The main route is the A12, which starts as a branch off the A13 in Limehouse and heads north-east past Brentwood, Chelmsford, Colchester and Ipswich. I'll need to turn off, at a place called Woodbridge, a small town, on a river by the look of it. I peer closer, the river is the Deben. Okay, seems easy enough, fuel tank-willing of course. I just have to get out of London.

I look up. The Immaculate Woman is still peering at paperbacks, Roddy Doyle now. Sweater Man has moved towards the shop's doors. He's back at the newspapers, even though he has one tucked under his arm. There are a few scattered customers, but no one who unsettles me as much as these two.

He glances back and holds my eye for a moment too long.

It's Sweater Man. If anyone is in here looking for me, it's him.

I glance around. No one is watching. I look for cameras but none seem to be pointing in this direction. Not the most popular section for shoplifters I suppose. I tear the page. The noise is deafening, but no one hears it except me. I need this last segment of the map, the one that shows the country lanes and by-ways that will lead me from the A12 to Orford itself.

Another tear, still no alarms or cries of Stop Thief!

One last tear, a long one that frees the page, a loud rip. I close my eyes, wait for the hue and cry.

Nothing. I quickly fold the paper and pull out my wallet and act as if I'm counting money. My performance is atrocious, more suited to some silent movie melodrama than I-don't-want-to-be-noticed method acting. I shut the book and return it to its slot on the shelf then pull out another to cover my crime. I take a quick look then return that one as well.

One more item needed. My mouth is dry, my heart racing. My final trick will be getting past Sweater Man because now I'm convinced he is either a police officer or plainclothes SSU.

I walk carefully away from the maps, down a different aisle to the Immaculate Woman and make for the stairs. I approach Sweater Man who glances at me but makes no move. He's studying a magazine although I can't see which one it is. Then I'm bounding up the stairs to the games and hobbies department.

There, I steal a compass.

Slight of hand, smoke and mirrors, the thing, neat in a small green plastic case is in my pocket and I'm carrying a box of water-colour paints and an artist's pad to the till. I'm pleased with this touch.

Couldn't have been our man, because what the hell would a dangerous fugitive want with a painting set?

Carrier bag in hand I set off back down the stairs. The exit is in front of me and Sweater Man is still there, leafing through magazines. He turns towards me as I close in. Our eyes lock. The doors are only a few feet behind him.

This time he holds my stare and a shy smile alters his face and the stare becomes a hopeful look. Oh Christ, I've pulled. It must be all this leather. Avoiding any more eye contact I walk past him. I feel his tension, which, in turn, stretches my own nerves towards breaking point.

Someone shouts.

The voice is feminine. I turn to see The Immaculate Woman, running towards me, lifting a radio to her mouth. I break into a run. She zeroes in, throws herself between me and the door. I keep running. I hear sirens, distant, but approaching fast.

The woman is in front of me, shouting, at me this time, and reaching into her coat pocket.

I crash into her and she is hurled against the door which opens to let her fall backwards onto the pavement outside. I stumble and dance over her but I don't go down.

Thanks be to every god in the universe.

I run.

Through herds of pedestrians, onto the road in front of buses, lorries and a police car, which jerks to a sudden halt, two-tone blaring and lights flashing. It freezes me, rabbit in the headlights. I can't move. I sense the woman getting to her feet. The doors of the police car are opening. There's another behind it. A van races past this second car and swerves, as if its driver is panicked by the sight of police. I hear a crunch, glass breaking, the sound, sharp and shocking. Then there is that moment, that brief stillness that follows a crash, everybody stunned.

Long enough for me to cross the other side and *run*.

I barge and crash, people fall and stumble. I am the fugitive, the big, hairy, leather-clad beast, the hunted animal, hounds baying at my back. I smash my way through any obstacle because I am scared and angry and desperate. Something batters my right thigh as I run, irritating, annoying, fucking enraging me. The watercolours and art pad, I'm still carrying my shopping. I drop it, just open my fist and let it go.

Underground Station. I plunge into its entrance, wallet torn from my pocket. Praise the Lord for Oyster Cards. I'm in, driving my bulk and desperation through the burgeoning crowds, dodging, darting, swearing. Central Line, where is the bloody Central Line? I make the escalator and as I weave my way downwards, not relying on mechanicals to get me to the bottom, I realise that I have trapped myself.

I don't look back. They're coming. I can feel them, pounding through the station, spreading out, taking the escalators behind me.

At the bottom I turn right, not interested if this is the correct platform. I follow the passageway, see the platform ahead. There's an alcove, "Staff Only", about ten feet deep and ending in a closed sets of gates. Beyond the gates is a murky, unlit staircase. I dart into the niche, and squeeze myself into the corner where the gates meet the grim, cold wall. It's shadowed, dim, it stinks of urine, it is a pathetic hiding place and as soon as I'm in there I know I've made another huge mistake.

People hurry past, no one looks in my direction. There's just enough shadow I suppose. Voices echo. I hear a train rumble into the nearby platform.

Two constables run past, bulky in their Kevlar, one of them speaking breathlessly into a radio. Their attention is straight ahead, neither looks my way. They're making for the train, the one they think I'm boarding. There'll be more Law on the other platforms, radioing the Transport Police to intercept me further on.

Another officer jogs by then stops. He looks round. I press myself further back, mouth so dry I can't swallow, heart thundering so loud he must be able to hear. I hold my breath, turn my head away so I'm looking straight ahead, at the filthy wall opposite, concentrating on the stained white tiles.

A radio squawks, I hear a reply. Then heavy footsteps go back the way they came, away from the platform. I breathe again. The train drones then pulls away. Another arrives at a more distant platform. I start to shake, reaction, my legs almost give way but I stay upright, pressed into my ridiculous little piece of gloom.

I almost walk away then, I need to get on a train and head east. I can't wait any longer but the sensible, the awake and alive Pete Allman, yells at me to stay where I am. The police are all over the station. This is a poor hiding place but it's all I've got.

So I wait. I grow tired and sit, knees pulled up, eyes closed, head against the cold hard wall. I probably look like one of the homeless, a scruffy dirty bundle of humanity sleeping it off in the shadows.

They'll find me, oh yes, they'll find me all right, once the real search begins.

Two officers pass by slowly, searching the faces of the passengers around them, the same two as before I think. One shakes his head. The other laughs. They disappear from view, perhaps they're hiding as well, waiting for me to stick my head out then, boo, you're nicked!

Minutes crawl by, hours, days. I'm cold now and tired. My head aches. My eyes grow heavy. I force them open, mustn't sleep, dangerous to sleep. My eyes close again –

I jerk awake, dazed, yes, and confused. I don't know where I am…but remember quickly. People pass by. Footsteps. A train rumbles. There is music, an acoustic guitar and a voice. I recognise *Pinball Wizard*. The busker is good. I struggle to my feet, body heavy and stiff. I take a deep breath and carefully move to the entrance to the alcove. I glance up and down the corridor. No police. I step out. A few people look at me, puzzled, some with expressions of distaste. I run my hand through my hair, yawn and set off towards the platform. I feel vulnerable, exposed. But I can't stay in that place any longer.

The platform is moderately crowded. There are no police that I can see. Tense, jumpy, I note that the next east bound train arrives in two minutes. A long, long two minutes. I move to the far end of the platform, read the advertising posters on the opposing wall. Jack Daniels is there as always, that good ol' boy and his slow, slow matured bourbon.

A warm breeze swirls along the platform. Flashes of electric blue smear the wall, then comes the rumble and clank as the train bursts out of the tunnel mouth. Come on, stop, stop. I wait for the doors to open, come on, open. *Open.* Hiss, I'm in, sitting down, huddled into myself, leaning forward, trying not to catch anyone's eye. The shaking is back.

Shouting, running feet, police hundreds of them, pouring onto the platform, through the carriage door –

A gang of youths male and female erupt into the carriage amid curses of relief and squeals of laughter. The doors shut. The train jerks into motion.

Liverpool Street is closed.

The British Rail terminal is deserted, the big Arrival and Departures board blank, the shops all shuttered. There are police, but they seem interested only in making sure that the Underground passengers leave the station and not stray onto the main concourse.

It looks as if it has been shut for some while. None of my fellow passengers seem surprised or perturbed but quietly move towards the exit, past the Upper Crust bakery and Costa Coffee, all with their blinds closed. I had no idea. I worked, what half a mile away and arrive for work at Moorgate Station every morning and I didn't know that all railway routes easterly out of the capital are closed.

Because no one is allowed out, which means that it's probably the same at Euston and Kings Cross and St Pancras and all the rest. Once in London you stay in London. Again the claustrophobia wells up. I want to get out and it's not just that I need to find those Friends and deliver the memory stick, it's because I cannot be closed in, I cannot be walled and buried and forbidden. It brings on the sweating and panic. It makes the shaking worse.

I step outside and rub my face with trembling hands.

So much for simply streaking Ipswich-wards on an Intercity express, so much for roaring up the A12 on my motorbike. I take some deep breaths then pull out my stolen compass and start walking north east.

No one follows. No one seems to care.

The air is heavy with stale smoke and burning. Office blocks, concrete and glass give way to housing, row upon row of tiny terraced dwellings, squat, two and three storey flats. Washing hangs over balconies, the streets are lined with parked cars, many of them rusting and unused looking. Fuel is rationed. Cars are a liability. Kids play. People walk. I see tower blocks, I feel tension and depression. I have no idea of the time but the wind is cold and the sky grey.

There's grime and smoke-filth here, everything smudged and smelling of fire. I check the compass regularly. Reach the end of a street and stop dead. No mans land, scorched earth. Two hundred metres of nothing, every house shop, pub and streetlamp demolished and crushed into a hard packed urban desert.

Beyond this, a wall stretches as far as I can see left and right. Twenty, perhaps thirty feet high and, inevitably, barbed wire topped. Rearing up from the other side is a tower, a huge, brutalist, concrete column, dotted with windows and as solid and sealed as a coffin.

There's noise coming from beyond the wall, engines, metallic scrapes and crashes, the occasional shout. Building site noise. Sunday or no Sunday, the work must go on. That means there must be a gate somewhere because supplies have to get in and the work force need to get out to go home.

Dominic worked on one of these sites...

I hear police cars. Distant, not necessarily coming for me but I can't take that chance. I set off across the no man's land towards the wall. The ground is rough and uneven, rubble moves and rolls under my feet, there are ankle traps and tripping hazards. My motorcycle boots help but if I'm not careful I'm going to end up on my face with something sprained or broken.

I half run, half walk, looking back, seeing only the fenced-off back gardens of the last row of houses. There's a railway viaduct to my left but I don't suppose many trains actually race over it these days. I reach the wall, the sirens are growing louder.

A domestic, a break-in, must be, nothing to do with me, no one has seen me or knows where I am.

Please.

Breathless I stumble along the base of the steel barrier. There's dust, fumes and then the groan and drone of lorries. I run faster, taking another risk with my ankles and bones, following the wall round a sharp left hand bend until I blunder to a halt a few hundred metres from a convoy of trucks and vans, shunting towards, and through, a huge set of double gates. A pair of security guards stop each vehicle but seem more interested in checking documents than searching for stowaways.

Sirens, close.

I parallel the line of trucks back into the streets that border no man's land then work my way past the downbeat terraces and rows of abandoned cars to the building site approach road, I find a junction, its traffic lights dead and useless. Apart from construction transport, few vehicles seem to venture into this area.

The convoy crosses the junction.

I wait, catching my breath, which is difficult seeing as I'm bathed in diesel fumes. There's a gap. The lorry that precedes it is carrying what looks like sand, its trailer open-topped. Accessible.

Thank you God.

I glance over my shoulder and see two police vans racing down the street towards me. I reach the lorry and duck round to its rear. There isn't much in the way of handholds but I grab what I can and begin to haul myself up.

My arms ache, my feet scrabble for purchase, exhaust fumes sear my throat. The lorry shakes and rolls as it hits the rubble surface of no man's land. I haul myself up over the back to collapse into its load of wet sand. Finished, I lay, sinking, arms and legs akimbo, staring up at the bleak, grey sky. The sand is cold, icy air rushes over me as the lorry moves on another few yards towards the gates. I can hear the sirens, close, perhaps they saw me. Too bad I guess, I've done my best.

The lorry stops. I hear voices, abrupt, gruff. A moment, then the lorry moves again and I see the top of the gateway slide over my view of the sky. I'm in and I need to get out of this lorry in a hurry because when it tips out its load I'm likely to be buried alive.

I roll over and crawl to the back of the trailer then peer over the edge. I can see one of the police vans blocking the gateway. Two officers are out, talking to the security guard. My lorry swings right and bumps its way down a street formed out of Portakabins and construction machinery. At the end of the street there is the beginning of a tower, a huge dull square wall about six feet high, set into a soaring network of steel girders. I glimpse another lorry behind us. Obviously the police have cleared the gate now and are either in the building site or have decided not to bother. The other lorry is still a long way off. I take a deep breath and scramble onto my haunches then clamber over the back. I hang painfully by my arms, then let go. I hit the ground hard and roll, the violence of the impact shocking and unexpected.

No time to lick any wounds though. I get to my feet and run into a gap between two Portakabins and crouch in the cramped space and catch my breath. I pull out my compass to see that east is back across the temporary street. I wait for the next lorry to pass, roaring and groaning and splashing through huge puddles.

The police vans are behind it.

They are the same type that came to Chalk Lake yesterday, windscreens protected by riot cages. I give them a few more moments to get well clear then make a run for it, scrambling across the "street" and throwing myself into another Portakabin gap. This time I keep moving, squeezing through, until I emerge on the far side.

Where there is desolation.

Miles and miles of ruin, of shattered, burned houses, of mountains of rubble, of debris such as television sets, wrecked furniture and clothes. The ground itself is ripped apart by craters, most filled with muddy brown water.

And looming over the ruin are the towers, scores of them, hundreds, a forest of concrete set in straight uniform lines that march away into the distance like the identical headstones in a military cemetery. The image is surreal, oppressive and devastating. I recognise nothing, no street or corner. I was never an East Ender, but I know my city. *Knew* my city.

I set off into the ruins, careful to avoid those which are being eaten away by bulldozers and diggers. Engines rev and grumble, masonry crashes in billowing explosions of dust. I wonder how many bodies are still buried in the rubble.

I also wonder who the hell the EoD actually are because this is not the work of some terrorist gang. This is all-out war, total, strategic, global-type war.

There is a garden, potted plants set against a brick wall, a child's swing and a small toddler's tricycle. The sodden, dank grass is bright green, long, scruffy and weed-rich. The garden ends at a patio door, glass intact, door closed, and all set into a fragment of brick wall not much bigger than the door itself. Behind is an immense pile of broken masonry and burned wood that was once a house. The neighbouring home is still standing, although there are no tiles on its now skeletal roof or glass in any of its windows. This garden is strewn with debris however. Where the third house once stood there is now an immense, rain-bogged hole its sides banked up with rubble.

I pass by and reach a junction where a set of traffic lights stand forlorn, their coloured eyes smashed and vacant. Directly across from where I stand is a row of shops. No plate glass remains, the street outside is littered with packaging, cartons, rotting magazines and newspapers. Everywhere there are smashed, burnt cars and vans. One road is blocked by an overturned lorry. It looks like the corpse of a gigantic insect.

The sky boils, smoke-coloured, now heavy with rain.

It all ends a hundred yards or so to my left where the ruin gives way to a to open space and beyond that the concrete giants that rear out of the torn earth to shelter, or is it imprison, the homeless and shell-shocked. Squat, single storey blocks are clustered about the towers' skirts. Coloured logos decorate their walls. Supermarket brands, clothes and furnishing stores. The living dead have to eat, stay warm and be comfortable I suppose. Each tower and shopping complex is surrounded by a barbed-wire fence.

The light is fading. I'm weak and dizzy for lack of food and water and I'm cold. My mood is darkening with the day. Memories and sorrows are beginning to break through.

They couldn't have felt anything. It was too quick, blam-blam-blam, a white hot blast and devastating shockwave then nothing. And Dominic was unconscious anyway, on the operating table, his leg under repair –

I need to rest, before I collapse from hunger and exhaustion. Some of the ruins have walls and semblance of a roof, enough for a little shelter. Tomorrow I'll be able to think, to plan, to get some food perhaps.

Right now I must sleep.

I start the hunt for a reasonable hiding place. I can't decide, can't think. I walk and walk and all the time I see fire and smoke and my dead wife and children, each one a charred corpse, unrecognisable.

I can smell them, burned meat, scorched hair and clothes.

Daddy…why did you leave us Daddy?

I can't turn round, Christ I must *not* turn round.

Darling...don't walk away from me...darling I need you... please...

Get him!

Dominic?

"Fucking get him!"

I stop, turn.

"Dominic? Is that you? Dom –"

Four, no five figures are racing down the street towards me, expertly dodging debris and craters. They look young, scruffy. Each one wears an armband, blue I think, hard to tell in the gloom. They're all armed, with clubs, lengths of wood and steel bars.

They're not my family.

I run.

I don't know where the energy comes from but I pound down that cracked, bomb-cratered street like an athlete. Desperate as I am I won't be able to keep this up for long. One of my pursuers laughs. I'm running for my life and my family have been killed and someone is laughing at me.

Fuck it. *Fuck it…*

I see something laying in the road, to my left. I stop and snatch it up. It's a length of iron pipe, about three feet long, heavy. Perfect. I spin round and charge back at the little bastards.

They stumble to a halt. This shouldn't happen. They don't normally have to fight someone their own fucking size. One of them is way ahead of the rest. He looks as if he's panicking, unable to decide whether to stand or run. I make the decision for him swinging the pipe round towards his ugly little head.

I see a lot in that moment. His pasty, gaunt, vicious face, his close-cropped hair, his clothes, modern, not cheap, and fashionable, the blue armband and the ID badge hanging round his neck. Official, all official.

He flinches, jumps aside as some survival instinct kicks in, and the pipe cracks not against his skull but against his left side. Who cares, I've hurt him, the little bastard is writhing and howling on the ground and I'm charging the rest of them.

Their shock has passed, they see safety in numbers and they're come straight back towards me. Most are sixteen or seventeen but there are one or two adults. All wear the armbands and sport the ID badges.

Anger drives me at them, red-brained, mind-screaming rage. But the sane part is yelling again, telling me I'm stupid, that I'm going to get myself beaten to death.

I slip, almost fall. I feel a brutal impact and my right arm is numb, I can't lift the pipe. Shit, now I'm finished. I use my left arm to protect my face. I see them closing in, hate-filled and sensing blood.

A brick arcs though the air and crashes onto the road in the middle of the gang, another, another, until there is a rain of rubble thudding and cracking on the road. The gang back away, look round wildly but see no enemy to fight. A fireball arcs from the upstairs window of one of the derelict houses to my right. It hits the road, glass shatters and flames flare bright. Molotov cocktail. I feel a wave of heat and it paralyses me.

...I'm screaming but I can't hear anything, waves of concussion slam me onto my back, scorching heat burns my throat, my chest. Everywhere is light and noise, deafening, incomprehensible noise.

I scrabble at the tarmac, at air, until I'm sitting up, trying to breathe. There's nothing but fire, a vast boiling mass of flame and a blinding fog of smoke. I see bodies, crumpled heaps in the glare, an overturned wheelchair, a shattered drip bottle...

The gang finally scatter, scrambling back down the street. One or two pick up rubble and hurl it back but another Molotov finally sends them into retreat. None of them stops to help the one who I knocked down. I can still hear him groaning and swearing behind me.

I get to my feet carefully, all the time trying to rub some sensation back into my shoulder. I look up towards the empty, shadow-dark window from which the missiles had been thrown. I can hear voices. Friends or foes? It doesn't matter. I'm too exhausted to run anymore, so I wait.

Figures emerge from ruined, ever-open doorways and from behind walls. They turn out to be a mixed group, led by a short, stocky woman with sensible grey-hair, who stops a few feet from me, suddenly cautious, as if I'm some sort of wild animal. She wears an anorak-style coat and cords, all grubby and worn. Her face is dirt-smudged and heavily lined.

"Why were they chasing you?" she asks. Her accent is clipped, middle class.

"Fucked if I know," is all I can say in return.

The woman holds a length of wood at the ready. It has nails driven through it at one end.

"Well, by the look of your clothes, you're new to the ruins." She appears to make a decision. "You'd better come with us." There's hardness in her voice and in her expression. There seems to be little compassion for the stranger about her, rather a resignation to the fact that they have to help me and that they may as well get on with it. "The Specials will be back with reinforcements," she says. "We've disrespected them no doubt, their honour is at stake."

I don't have a choice. I'm alone, hunted, tired and hungry and these people have saved me from a bloody hard beating, possibly even saved my life.

I follow the group back across the street, through an alleyway between two of the derelict houses from which they had launched their ambush and into a jungle of ruin and rubble, scrambling and clambering until we reach a narrow side street where everyone takes a rest.

They're an assortment of ages and sexes. There's a tall, emaciated man blessed with a broad grin who introduces himself as Charles. His accent is strong possibly German. We shake hands. There's an older man, dapper, even in his worn-looking and dusty-looking coat and trousers and another, sullen-looking character, badly cut hair, glasses, about thirty. He glares at me, but doesn't seem to want to catch anyone else's eye. Slumped against the wall is a young man with a pale face and long black hair, dead straight and parted in the middle. He seems to have trouble breathing. A girl stays close to him, her hair the same colour but wild, unkempt. Her face is pierced, lip, eyebrows, cheek. I realise that the pair of them are probably about Dominic's age. Not much of a band of terrorists or resistance fighters, but they saved me and they seem to be on my side.

All of them look hungry, their skin is weather-beaten but sallow, their eyes red-rimmed, bloodshot, and they smell, perfumed with the ripe odour of the unwashed, and something else, something stale and chemical.

Alcohol.

These people are living rough.

The tang of booze gives me a craving for a beer, two beers, as many as it takes to blot out the memories and the cold. If they smell of it, then they've got it and I mean to partake of their treasure trove.

A water bottle does the rounds and at last I get to drink. I'm thirsty, I want to gulp it down but this is an act of hospitality and I'm not going to abuse it. I need these people. So I sip and pass it on to the angry man in glasses. He nods but its more good manners than warmth. There seems little connection between them, virtually no communication or fellowship. Each one appears sunk into his or her world, reluctant to look outwards. Even Charles, friendly as he is towards me, seldom speaks.

I don't ask where they got the water from. I see a supermarket logo on the bottle.

"Pete," I say to the sullen man and offer him my hand.

He doesn't answer me. The old man speaks up. "Geoff," he says and there's another hand to shake. His grip is firm. "At least you did them some damage," he says. "Little buggers."

"I'm Margot by the way," says the stocky woman. Another handshake. "I look after these people. We're Survivors."

The Survivors, Dominic mentioned them, people who live rough and evade being rounded up and imprisoned in the towers. Well, to be honest, they don't look as if they're doing too well.

"I suppose I'm a survivor now," I say.

"Welcome to the club," says Geoff. He waves his makeshift weapon in my face and I laugh politely at his pun.

The young girl is looking at me, staring. It makes me uncomfortable.

"Who were they?" I ask, "You know, that gang."

"Specials they call themselves. Paid by the police or government or someone to hunt us down and get us into those bloody lumps of concrete. Kids and army rejects. Vicious bunch."

"Yes and they'll catch us napping if we don't get a move on." Margot straightens and without a further word or backward glance, starts walking.

We enter some sort of industrial park, a small one that consists of a couple of bombed-out warehouses and a handful of industrial units. All have their windows shattered and doors blown in, but some still have a roof. More Survivors are gathered round an old style brazier outside one of the units, warming their hands against the fire and drinking something hot from assorted mugs and cups.

Coffee, I smell coffee. This then is heaven.

There are children among them, and the very old as well as a bunch of middle-aged men and women. They wear mixed and matched clothing, are quiet, withdrawn, and regard me with outright hostility as I follow Margot's group into the unit. Can't say I blame them. Another mouth to feed.

The place is full of old blankets and sleeping bags, mattresses and cushions. Boxes are piled in the corners, many bear labels announcing them to be foodstuffs. I've no idea where it all comes from and I don't much care. Margot picks up a sleeping bag and an armful of grubby looking blankets and throws them to me. "You'll have to go out and find yourself a mattress or a cushion." she says. "There's plenty lying around out there in the ruins."

I pull a blanket about myself and close my eyes, just happy to have something to keep me warm and a soft bundle to sit on. A moment later I become aware of a presence and open them again to see Margot. She's holding two mugs of what I see is tomato soup. I take one gratefully.

"Are you the boss around here?" I ask her.

She shrugs. "Suppose so. I'm more like a mother. Someone has to keep order and impose boundaries, and give them some sort of purpose."

"Did you live round here, before it was bombed?"

"Well, sort of. My house, in fact my whole street is buried under one of those towers now. Nice street, it was. There was a church at one end, my church. I went every Sunday, without fail."

And ran half of its committees no doubt.

"Why do you live like this? Why not give up and get an apartment in the towers?"

"Get thee behind me Satan," she says. "I will die before they lock me up in one of those."

"But they can't be that bad. There are shops –"

"What have shops got to do with it?"

Nothing much of course.

"Tower dwellers have got shops, true. And they have jobs, or jobs that are imposed on them from above. Most of them are working on site clearance at the moment, and in the shops of course. They're not allowed to leave the ruins. Emergency measures apparently."

It sounds like a giant labour camp to me. I sip tomato soup and find Nirvana.

"You can turn yourself in if you want to," she says.

"But this lady's not for turning," I answer.

She smiles, briefly, reluctantly. "Coffee?"

What do you think? I would kill for coffee at this moment.

"Yes please," I say politely. "No sugar."

"This isn't a café," Margot says sharply as she leaves. "Once you've had a rest you can get your own food and drink."

It isn't Margot who brings the coffee but the face-pierced girl.

"I'm Laura," she says. "Were you bombed?"

"Yeah."

"Were did you come from?"

I sip coffee, and it's as glorious as the soup. "I don't want to talk about it," I say. "Sorry."

"It's okay." She sits down opposite me, uninvited but I don't mind. She's a kid, lonely, tired and scared.

"Thanks for this."

"It's a long time since someone new joined us. Most people like you join the gangs."

"The Specials you mean."

"No, the gangs, the ones who get us food and stuff. They rule the bomb sites. The police are trying to fight them but the gangs are well armed and the police are scared of them. One day they'll send in the army and that'll be that. Except some of the gangsters are soldiers, you know, who ran away from the war."

"Deserters you mean."

"Yeah, that's it, deserters."

"So why do they look after you? What's in it for them?"

She looks away. Shrugs. "I dunno, they just do."

She's lying, of course. Robin Hood never existed. Criminals don't give food and other essentials of life away to the poor, not for free. But I'm not going to get any deeper into this right now. There's food and drink and that's all that matters.

The Ruins as these people call this gigantic bomb site, is like some kind of badlands, full of tribes, Specials, Survivors, Gangsters. And judging by the accents, the bombs have levelled more than just houses. People like Margot would never have even acknowledged the existence of people like Laura before the war, other than the object of some Good Cause or other. Now they are lodged in the same burned out warehouse, unwashed, smelling of booze and fighting in what's left of the streets.

"Are you staying with us?" Laura asks suddenly.

No, I'm getting out of London, escaping the asylum. "I don't know."

"If you go Out, will you take me with you?" She sounds desperate.

"Out?"

"Yeah, you know, out of the city."

Ruins, *Out*, I'm living in some post-apocalypse science fiction story.

"Like I said, I don't know what I'm going to do, but if I do decide to go Out, I can't promise to take you. I'm sorry."

I want to.

Because she's the same age as my son, or perhaps even as young as Amanda. And already I'm starting to believe that helping her will atone for leaving them to die. I have to stop thinking that way. Laura is a stranger, a being from another world. Laura is a mess, a liability and possibly dangerous. She's pale and emaciated and she's shaking. She smells and she's been drinking or maybe worse. Laura is not my daughter.

She is not my fucking daughter.

"I know how to get you Out," she says.

I don't look at her but hunch myself over the coffee and concentrate on the hot, hot drink.

"I said I'll think about it Laura, okay?"

She gives me a quick, shy smile then scuttles back to her introverted, glowering boyfriend. I know that if I do get out of London I'm not taking *him*. I lie down, hands behind my head and stare up at the remains of the metal roof. I can see the gathering dark through holes, I can hear talk and laughter. Coughs, chest rattle. A child starts to cry.

Christ, why doesn't someone help these people?

But they are. They're rounding them up and cramming them into the towers, where it's dry and warm and there's a bed and food. And work.

I'm exhausted and I'm content just to lay here. Voices are raised, swearing, and argument, possibly a fight. A squabble in the herd. I hear Margot's voice, sharp and authoritative. The argument stops. God knows how much longer that woman is going to be able to hold this band of the desperate together.

People come and go, each one rummaging in one of the boxes piled against the far wall, and pulling out tins and packets as well as cans and bottles of booze. In the end I can't resist it and wander over there myself. I find a loaf of bread, some processed cheese, and some cans of Special Brew.

So the gangs provide this. Without them the Survivor community would quickly fall apart and die.

Again, as I close my eyes, I wonder what's in it for them.

It doesn't matter, just relax.

... Inspector Williams disappears into the crowd, swimming against the tide, flailing her arms like a panicked swimmer, clawing and shoving.

I glimpse Amanda and Rachel, confused, torn, buffeted but not moving in either direction. I call to them to come with me. I shout, I yell, I shriek.

The crowd closes over them. I can't see them. Christ oh Christ, where are they?

"Pete. Pete, wake up."

I start, scrabble at the blanket, cry out –

It's Margot, leaning over me. "Time to go."

"Where?" My heart sinks. I can't walk anymore.

"We don't sleep here, it's too dangerous. We have to sleep in the Underground, with other Survivors. The gangs can protect us there, so come on, hurry up. Safety in numbers."

For a moment I'm tempted to tell her that I'll take my chances out here, but it would be pretty stupid. The Specials will no doubt be out looking for revenge. So I get up, take up my meagre bed and follow the rest out and down yet another derelict street.

*

I don't know which station it is that we eventually enter. The front is open, the ticket barrier defunct. We converge with a stinking, battered, quietly shuffling crowd and shamble through the main ticket hall and onto the long-dead escalators. Even though I can't see them now, I hear Laura and the Happy Boyfriend arguing, harsh whispers and occasional shouted insults about being stupid and crazy. Then it's dark, terrifyingly close, confined and crowded. A few people shine powerful torches around and I glimpse the dark shapes behind them. Men mostly, faces shadowed and invisible, yet somehow I sense toughness, authority and barely restrained violence.

The charitable, caring gangsters then.

For a moment I feel as if I'm part of a cattle herd, kept by armed and dangerous farmers, but for what?

I cling tightly to my self-control and try to keep my new found friends in sight, even though the torch light is sporadic and constantly on the move and because the Survivors don't possess good manners down here. There's a lot of pushing and shoving, bodies squeezing themselves through in their hurry to get down the platform first.

When I reach the platform myself, I see why. There are bodies everywhere, glimpsed in the torchlight, with very little floor space to spare. I give up trying to find those I already consider my own and bunk down in the first piece of bare concrete I can find. Beams of light sweep the platform. I hear voices, gruff and threatening, ordering the Survivors to settle down and shut-the-fuck-up. I do as I'm told. These people are dangerous.

I lie down, and try to forget that I'm deep beneath the city, that I am literally under ground with several million tons of earth bearing down on me. I can't get enough oxygen.

Christ I have to breathe.

I slow down, force myself to take deep, slow, steady breaths.

It quietens and the murmur of conversation is replaced by the usual coughs, snores and wheezing lungs. I roll onto my side and, after a while, see the torchlight moving over the crowd. The guards are on patrol. Every so often one of them whispers something and a bundle of humanity and blanket either gets up and allows itself to be led away, or is dragged to its feet by force. I think that each bundle is female. I hear sobs. I hear a slap.

Now I know how the gangsters are paid.

The uncertain, dancing torchlight gives glimpses of a skinny bastard, shaved head, goatee beard, bulked up in some sort of parka. I watch him prowl among the sleepers and possum-players. He shines his own torch hard into faces, hauls people over to inspect them then, mutters and moves on.

He's close now. I can hear him breathing. He snaps at whichever lucky person he's chosen.

"Sit up, fucking sit up."

She does so.

It's Laura.

He grabs her arm and starts to haul her to her feet.

Christ knows what possesses me at that moment, what stupid, crazed fucking demon wrenches me upright and throws me across the few feet between me, Laura and that vicious, miserable streak of turd who has her. Whatever it is, it colours the world red and fills my head with murder.

He doesn't even see me coming and when my thick, hairy skull buries itself in his scrawny belly he merely grunts and folds without so much as a word. His torch goes flying with a stroboscopic splintering of light that dances over the lying-down and standing up.

I hit him again, this time with my fist. I don't need to see him because my hand is round his throat and I'm squeezing so hard he can't move his head. Something cracks and crumples under my knuckles. His nose probably, which means I've messed up his film-star looks. That's good enough for me. I draw back my arm again.

And there's light and shouting and swearing and a rising tide of voices.

His mates are coming, wading awkwardly through the suddenly shifting, heaving sand of bodies, throwing light in all directions, knowing that something is wrong but unable to work out what it is.

"Pete, Pete for fuck's sake."

Something is tugging at my arm, grabbing my hair. It annoys me. There's screaming in my ear too, my name.

Laura. Laura is pulling at me, begging me to come with her.

The redness clears, and somewhere in the deafening roar of hate and bloody need that fills my head I realise that we have to get away from here, while there is still noise and chaos, while the Turd Streak's mates are still bogged down and confused.

We slither, scratch and bite our way through the stinking mass of flesh and blankets, spreading our own little waves of panic and confusion. Laura is ahead of me, her breath loud and tremulous. I can't see her, then I can, then I can't. Torchlight freezes us, darkness frees us as we crawl on towards the edge of the platform.

I realise Laura has our sleeping bags.

I guess we're not coming back.

The hubbub is growing louder. No one knows what the hell is going on. I can hear the curses and shouts of the gangsters, closer now, and I'm scared and angry and breathing too fast because the claustrophobia is rolling over me in giant, debilitating waves.

The concrete runs out. My hand gropes into space. I roll over and lower myself down. My boots touch the ground and I let go. Immediately I fold myself into a crouch, pressed hard against the face of the platform. Laura? I can't sense her or hear here. I've lost her.

I start as a hand touches my chest. Small hand, girl's hand. It grabs the open top of my leathers and tugs at me. I let her lead me along the platform edge, towards the mouth of the tunnel.

The noise above us is reaching fever pitch.

Then the station is lit by a brief flash followed by a shocking, head-cracking detonation.

Someone's fired a gun.

Christ, shit, a *gun*.

I've no idea where the bullet went or who or what the shot was intended for but a silence descends. I realise that Laura and I have frozen again, hunched beside the concrete cliff face of the platform.

"Will every body keep fucking still and shut up!"

The voice is male and loud and not to be argued with. Except by us. I move, grabbing at Laura and creeping towards that precious tunnel, my boots pounding the gravel, my heart announcing to the world that I'm down here, my eyes aching from the darkness that presses into them like grit-impregnated fists.

I touch the rails, it's impossible not to. No shock. They must be dead. Or is it only the middle rail that is electrified and lethal. I can't remember, and does it matter? We've just got to get to the tunnel.

I hear a groan, torchlight sweeps the crowd. A name is shouted.

"What the fuck happened to you?"

That probably means that the Streak is conscious again, all bloody and dazed. And in pain I hope, lots of pain.

Every move I make feels like an explosion of noise. Progress is a slow agony. A part of me wishes they'd get on with it and find us so I can go down fighting. No God, I don't mean it. If they find me they find Laura and I will *not* let her go. My defiance is rooted in fear, terrible paralysing limb-stiffening fear for this girl who is suddenly my wife, son and daughters incarnate.

On we go, crawling through the dark toward that tunnel mouth, only a few more yards. I can feel it, all but see it, a refuge, a hiding place, a mouth to swallow us whole.

Beams of light punch open the dark above us. The gangsters are making for the platform edge now, no doubt kicking and stamping their way through their charges, weapons ready. An example has to be made, no one fucking slaps one of theirs and gets away with it.

I feel brick, then cables. We're in the tunnel. Now we straighten, move more quickly. We're noisy, panting and stumbling. The quiet from the platform is a terrifying, silent running, the savage, well-armed submariners listening for a telltale crunch or gasp.

We freeze again, breath held.

They know we're down here somewhere, in either the *in* or the *out* tunnel. Unsure which. Not wanting to spare too many of their number because their human cattle herd is restless and in need of control.

As for Laura and me, we're trapped in here now, committed. There's only one direction to go in. But not yet, we have to hide, to stay motionless, silent and invisible until some chance, some distraction, gives us the opportunity to run –

"No," Laura whispers suddenly and it's more sob than word. And she breaks away and I hear her blunder off into the dark.

Shit. I hesitate then follow. I try to run quietly, but I can't see – there are obstacles, the rails, the cable frame that runs down the tunnel edge. I tense, waiting for the shout, the light, the shot.

The light comes first, a beam of it that pierces the tunnel, but, thank Christ, not far enough in to reach us. The shout comes after the light, followed by footsteps and curses. They're running, but carefully, unsure, tripping and stumbling over the cluttered tunnel floor.

I blunder into Laura and grab her arm. "We're trapped," I pant. "You keep running, I'll wait here for them. They probably don't know who's gone, at least you'll have a chance –"

"No, no don't do that Pete. You don't have to." She sounds terrified by the prospect of going on alone. "They won't follow us, not all the way. The different stations are run by different gangs. We just have to get near enough to the next one and we'll be safe."

I admire her confidence.

"Then we can wait until morning and get out after everyone's gone."

A flash of torchlight and clatter of footsteps startles us into motion again.

Get to the next station, good idea, but exactly how far away is this station? I smoke, I don't exercise regularly, I've only been out of hospital after an operation and infection for only a few weeks. I'm already so out of breath it hurts and I'm stuck in the dark with only one way to run and that is taking me into an even deeper, walled-in blackness.

Like the grave, like the blackness my family have gone to. Christ how dark that must be, what a cloying and impossible and inescapable night death is. And they're all there, my children and my Ruth. Oh God, my Ruth. I want her, now, I want her to be here with me. I want to hold her hand and to smell her perfume and taste her sweetness and for her to hold me tight and tell me that the dark won't hurt me and to stop being so bloody childish and pull myself together –

A series of explosions rip the tunnel to pieces. Flash, flash flash, bang, bang bang. Things crack past me, something slams into the wall near my head and stings my face with fragments of brick.

They're shooting again and this time, they're shooting in our direction, if not directly at us. I don't know if they've seen us or if the shooting is wild, and literally scattergun.

Which ever it is, it kicks us into a headlong, equally wild and hazardous sprint. I hear Laura moan each time she breathes. Then my own head is filled with that familiar white roar and I'm plunging on into a featureless, endless dark and I don't care where it goes or how far.

Now it's my friend.

They must be close now, sighting their weapons onto my back, taking aim.

Not Laura, please God, don't let them shoot Laura, let me it be me, send me to Ruth, but save the girl.

Light, up ahead, not bright but something that breaks the complete and utter nothingness. It spurs me on, a thirsty man, throwing his last reserves of energy into a mad dash for water.

Or mirage.

The light changes from a vague grey mistiness to something more defined, until, at last, it coalesces into a coin-sized disc. The tunnel mouth then, the next station, where the friendly, local gangsters must have set up some illumination that's more stable and permanent than handheld torches.

Laura stops running, a silhouette, bent double, hands on knees.

This is it then, the neutral zone, our refuge for the rest of the night.

Hopefully.

What if the same gang runs both stations?

What if, what if, what if? I can't run any further and nor can Laura. If they come for us then they come for us.

We move to the tunnel wall and hunker down, the sleeping bags wrapped around ourselves. It's uncomfortable but I can put up with that. There's light. There are no footsteps or torch beams. As the seconds slide past I dare to believe that our pursuers have reached the border and turned back.

"Thanks," Laura says. "For, you know, like, saving me. I think they were going to take me this time."

"Take you?" Come on Pete, you know what she means.

"Anything with a cunt is fair game."

I'm startled by her coarseness, but then, her life is too hard and rough for niceties.

"They use us for fucking each night and then they take some, the best looking ones, and pimp them out. There are plenty of people in the real world who get a kick out of humping bomb-site girls."

Presumably the real world is the city outside the ruins.

A pause, then Laura says. "I thought I was too ugly and messed up and that no one would pay for a dog like me. I thought I wasn't any good for anything more than a night's fucking. Seems like I've turned into a swan."

I want to say something positive to her, but there's nothing forthcoming. She *is* messed up, and she's dirty and downbeat and battered by life. But all that can be put right. I slide my arm around her and hold her tight. She burrows in. I can feel her shaking.

"What the hell is in it for them?" I say. The question is rhetorical. "Okay, they get some sex and pick up women they can traffic, but is that all?"

No, I answer myself. That isn't all.

Out there, in the so-called real world they're the bottom of the ladder, thugs and crooks who rule over their filthy little empires and eventually get themselves arrested and imprisoned. Here they are the scum who have risen to the top. They have power and authority in the ruins. Yes, they make a living out of trafficking, but they also have life and death in their hands, they have a kingdom and they have loyal subjects. They can be beneficent and they can terrorise.

Christ, what is happening to this bloody country of ours? It was bad enough before the nightmare, now it's turning into some sort of Hell.

"It's all right," I murmur, voice soothing and calm, holding Laura the shivering child tight. I rock her and she quietens and in the dark I'm rocking Amanda and Rachel and Dominic.

It's the morning exodus that wakes us. Murmuring, shuffling and shouted orders to fucking hurry up. We stir ourselves and crawl to the tunnel mouth, bleary-eyed and cautious. Peering round the edge I see that the light in this station is provided by a handful of gas-fired Tilley lamps, the type Dominic and me used to use when we went out fishing at night. The Survivors who haunt this station are getting to their feet, struggling blankets and sleeping bags out through the exits. The guards stand over them, with all the arrogance of the well-armed and ignorant. In the unsteady light I see a group of women and girls huddled at one end of the platform. Their hands are bound behind their backs with cable ties and when the torches play over them I see fear in their eyes.

Bastards, utter, fucking bastards.

I know that launching any sort of rescue attempt would be suicide.

But I can't leave those women to be farmed out as whores, I can't.

So how do I save them?

The decision is made for me anyway because once the main body of Survivors have left, the women are hauled, kicked and cursed to their feet then shoved toward the exit, some crying, some silent, one of them begging to be released, offering money, her body, anything.

I can still hear her, even when the lamps are extinguished, the platform finally empty and the utter darkness returned.

We wait for a few more minutes before venturing out ourselves, groping along the platform wall then clambering up off the rails. We feel our way to the exit, following the echoes of the departing gangsters and their harvest of flesh.

It's raining when we finally emerge from the station. The early morning grey is darkened and slicked by an icy downpour that fills the craters and cracks in the road and paints the ruins with dank murk. A few Survivors are making off down the street, heads down, bundled and clumsy in the blankets and bedding they've wrapped about themselves.

We find some rope strewn over the back of a burned-out lorry and tie our own sleeping bags onto our backs.

I look back to see that the station we've just left is Bow Road, so the first station was probably Stepney Green. Disappointing. I haven't travelled far in my wanderings through the ruins.

I'm hungry and thirsty, my head thudding from lack of caffeine. My body is aching and bruised from my night sleeping rough, and my shoulder is stiff from the blow I received from the Specials. I look at my compass. We're heading north, we need to veer to the east, make for Stratford.

"No," Laura says when I tell her. "We have to follow these survivors and see if we can buy some food off them."

I'm too hungry to argue and anyway, it seems like a good idea, so we set off in the stragglers' wake, careful to stay well back and, hopefully, unnoticed.

We move past lines of abandoned, rusted and sometimes burned-out vehicles. The houses are shattered facades.

"I know how to get us out," Laura says as we walk. "We need, like, a demolition site where they're still tearing down the bombed-out houses. They use a lot of the rubble for rebuilding, but there's so much a lot of it is driven away and dumped Outside. Some of the lorry drivers will take people with them, if you pay."

"How much?" Stupid question, but then I'm starving and thirsty and still recovering from my night in the dark.

Laura looks at me but doesn't answer.

Christ.

My head is pounding so hard its making me dizzy and sick. I have no idea of the time or where we are. Ahead and behind and on either side of me are ruins, and they're beginning to agitate me, beginning to close in. I want to see something else. I want to turn a corner and see buildings that aren't rain-dark and burned and smashed. Worse still, are the towers, rearing over the shattered rooftops, already grey and dulled, hundreds of them, thousands, millions.

Are they what the city is going to be once the EoD have finished their work?

The survivors we're trailing suddenly dart to the left, down a narrow alleyway and out of sight.

"Their camp must be down there," Laura says "I'll follow them, you find somewhere dry for us."

"No, it's dangerous, I'll come –"

"Jesus Pete, don't be so bloody stupid. They'll take one look at you and chase you away. And if anyone is likely to get into trouble around here it's you. I've been living here for a year, I know how it works. You don't."

"How do I know I can trust you?" What the hell am I saying? My head is spinning, I can't think.

Laura turns and looks at me, angry, close to tears. "So what do you think I'm going to do, like sell you to the Specials of something?"

"I'm sorry. I…I'm sorry Laura. I trust you."

It's just that you're going to buy us food and drink with your flesh and you're too young to do that. That makes me a pimp doesn't it? My God whoever it was that started this war should be burning in Hell right now.

Laura's pale, metal-studded face softens. "Lets find somewhere to crash then I'll see what I can scrounge."

We poke around for a bit and eventually settle on a ruin that looks as if it was once a corner shop. I slump to the floor and sit with my arms around my knees. Laura tells me that she'll be about an hour. I don't want her to go. But who am I? She's the expert around here.

The shop has part of a roof and a couple of walls which provide a bit of shelter from the rain and icy wind. I try to sleep. Not easy. Every time I close my eyes I see her, lying on the filthy ground while some faceless, filthy Survivor drunk paws and gropes her. Then her face becomes Amanda's and I open my eyes and pace and lean on the wall, palms against the dank plaster, head down. I look for a weapon and find a piece of wood about three feet long. Not brilliant but it's better than nothing.

After a while I sit, study the torn page from the road atlas, fiddle with the compass then close my eyes and start again. I try to fill my head with good things. Fuck it's hard.

Ruth.

It's Ruth, screaming, tears streaming down her cheeks, face contorted. Her hand crushes mine so hard I think she's going to break some bone. I'm exhausted, about ready to cry myself except I don't. She needs me calm and strong. I realise that I'm shouting something to her. "Push," that's it. "Push! Push!"

The room is bright-lit, full of people in disposable-looking uniforms and masks. Machines bleep, a doctor sits at the end of the bed, staring at a point between Ruth's legs that has been mine to stare at and mine alone for a long time now.

The room is hot, I want to sleep and I want to gather Ruth up in my arms but she keeps swearing at me whenever I get too close then at the doctors then at the pain and then she screams and groans and pants and gasps.

And crushes my hand, Christ she has a strong grip.

"Come on, come on," I pant.

"I'm trying!" she snaps back. "Shut up, oh God!"

Another yell-howl-scream then a different sound, a cry, a strange little-but-loud voice in the mechanical and human din. Ruth seems to collapse, a nurse lays a scrawny wriggling wet creature gently onto her chest. The thing makes a squalling noise that grows louder by the second.

"A boy," someone, a nurse or doctor or cleaner for all I know, exclaims. "It's a boy. Healthy and bouncy and wise."

I open my mouth and nothing comes out. Steve, the name flashes into my head, We'll call him Steve. Steve Allman, yeah, good. Solid.

The thing is wrapped in a blanket and presented back to us. Ruth murmurs and reaches out for him. I just stare.

"You can touch him," someone tells me, so I reach out with a big clumsy hand and pull the blanket down a little to see a head, an eye and then the complete, screwed-up, Winston Churchill face and it is the ugliest most beautiful thing I've ever seen.

"Dominic," Ruth murmurs.

No, Steve, his name is Steve…

Ruth holds him tight and cries.

"Dominic," I agree and bend over to kiss my wife and whisper into my son's tiny ear. "I'm going to kill you."

I jerk awake, sweating, crying out. There's someone across from me, propped up against the wall. Laura, she's back, but something's wrong. Her eyes are open but dull, her jaw slack. She's dead. Oh Christ…

Then I see her chest rise and fall, and the lighter, the spoon and hypodermic spilled onto the floor beside her.

She's *on the nod*, post-heroin flush; mental function clouded due to depression of the central nervous system, slowed and slurred speech, constricted pupils, vomiting and constipation.

Expert, me.

No, I never did the stuff myself, but some of my mates did.

Some of my mates did it and didn't live to be *old* mates.

I move across the ruin, sit beside Laura and hold her tight and again, for the millionth time since I woke up to this hell, I want to cry. I feel her shaking, hear her stertorous breaths. Her skin is clammy, her bared left arm bruised and needle-scarred. I should have known. I should have fucking known.

I let the tears come. I rock her and stroke her lank, dirt thickened hair and sob over what she is and what she represents. Christ, my family only died a couple of days ago. I'm entitled to grieve aren't I?

A thin stream of bile, or vomit bubbles from the corner of her mouth. The bubbles become line then a stream. She groans wetly. The mess fills our corner of the ruined shop with a sharp, sour stink.

I rock and murmur and even sing some lullaby I used to croon to my own children. Outside, rain hisses and thuds on the scorched and rusting car roofs. The clouds are so dense now it might as well be night.

A jet streaks overhead. I flinch but I don't run for cover. In the distance I hear the heavy, muffled slamming of bombs.

*

After a while I notice that Laura has brought two old-looking supermarket carrier bags. I hook one with my feet and draw it to myself, untie the knot and find food. It's mostly packs of sandwiches, tubes of processed cheese and some fruit, a bit rough-looking, but edible. There are tins as well, soup and beans mostly, the type with a convenient ring-pull on the top. We've got nothing to heat them with but you can't have everything.

I pull out a sandwich carton. It's too gloomy for me to read the sell-by date and I have a feeling that it's just as well. A bite reveals the filling to be tuna and sweetcorn, mixed, no doubt, with enough preservatives to grant the diner everlasting life. It smells and tastes okay though. I find a bottle of water and use a little to wash Laura's vomit-stained cheek. I eat as much as I can force down into my stomach because I have feeling that I may not be able to eat again for a while. Fat and full, I close my eyes and let myself drift. I'm uncomfortable and cold but I'm not letting go of Laura.

I'm not sure when I become aware of the voices. I suppose they've been there for a while but in my semi-comatose state I'd allowed them to merge into the general mush.

Laura seems to be asleep so I carefully disentangle myself, get to my feet as quietly as I can and move towards what was once was the shop window but is now a huge hole in the scorched and battered wall. There's a big pile of dusty, rotting wood just this side of the window and I drop to my hands and knees and crawl over to hide behind it. I peer over the top at the street outside.

Nothing but the rusting hulks of cars and vans, the craters and the ruins.

Then I hear the voices again; a shout, laughter, mostly male although I think I can hear a woman as well.

A moment later three, no four people wander into view.

One of them has long hair and is clambering over the roofs of the derelict vehicles. He's the laughing one. He wears a long coat, which looks expensive and surprisingly clean for this place. Then I see the blue armband.

Specials.

The woman appears, ironically she has short hair. She's casually dressed, jeans, leather jacket and roll neck sweater, and, like the car walker, she wears a blue armband. Two more Specials follow her, close, one in sports wear, head obscured by a hood, the other a shaven-headed brute decorated with a tattoo-dragon that crawls out of the top of his tracksuit top and up his neck.

Each one carries a club, shiny wood, a baseball bat perhaps.

The gangs rule the night, the Specials own the daylight. Is that how it works? Is there a difference between the two because they all look like a bunch of violent fascists to me?

The big bastard is eating a sandwich, shoving the bread into his tireless jaws, not closing his mouth as he chews.

"Jammer!" the woman shouts at Long-Hair. "Jesus, grow up won't you?"

Jammer just laughs and jumps up and down on the roof of a van, making monkey noises and scratching his armpits. I hate him because he reminds me of another obnoxious little teenage pratt called Pete Allman.

"Fuck him," the woman says. "Right, Yan, take the left side of the street, Craig, you take the right."

Yan, it seems, is the hooded one, Craig, the brick shithouse, and the one who angles across the craters and debris towards the shop. I see his ID badge now, swinging from its chain as he lumbers towards me. He carries his club with the nonchalance of someone used to bearing arms. He rams the last of his sandwich into his mouth then wipes his lips with the back of his hand.

He sniffs.

Keeps coming.

I drop down, gripping my own makeshift club tight, holding my breath. Silent running again –

"Pete."

Fuck. Laura's come back to the land of the living.

She calls my name again. Craig stops, frowns, hefts his club into a more warlike position. I draw back then scramble as quietly as I can across the floor to Laura, who is looking around now, wide eyed, afraid.

Before she can say my name again I clamp my hand over her mouth and grab her tight. I shush her, then nod in the direction of the broken window.

She stiffens, eyes wide. I look round carefully and see Craig, pushing his way past the broken wood. He still seems to be alone. There is a way out, the wall to our left, broken down enough for us to scramble through. But if we try to get out now he'll see us and call in his friends.

It's only as I get slowly to my feet that I realise that not only am I still holding my own makeshift club but also a brick. Light breaks through as Craig finally rips away enough of the pile to struggle his bulk inside.

Frowning, he looks around but doesn't see us. Maybe it's because the gloom is heavy enough to require adjustment of his eyesight.

That's when I hit him with my own club, as hard as I can. I bring it round and against the side of his head and the contact is sickening. He grunts in surprise and staggers away from me, but he doesn't go down.

Any moment now he'll shout –

He seems stunned confused. He sees me and his now bleeding face twists into a mask of hate. I dart in, club raised, but the bastard is quick for his size and suddenly I'm doubled over, gasping for breath as he slaps his own club across my stomach. Christ it hurt.

I sense him move in, club raised again.

Then he's down, suddenly, clumsily.

Laura is crawling onto his back as he tries to push himself onto his hands and knees. He cries out, twists and struggles. Laura's arm rises and falls and I realise she's holding the empty syringe, stabbing over and over again into his back, his neck.

He's going to yell. His mouth is open.

I smash the brick down on his head. I feel something break. I hit him again and again and again. I beat and beat at the red mess that was once his scalp. I can't stop. I *need* to hit him. I need to I need to…

Laura's tugging at me and pulling my hair and slapping me around the head. I look round, breathing hard, angry at her. She backs away. I can see fear in her eyes and realise that she's scared of me.

And of herself.

There's blood on her hands, literally, staining her pale and grubby skin.

Some sense returns. I look down at Craig and realise that I've probably killed him. I see the mess, I see an eye, open and sightless, I see blood. I try to work out if he's breathing but I can't.

No time though, not now. We have to get out.

The beast is out. I killed him. I beat a man to death. I couldn't stop, it was a need, a hunger and it has left me shaking and dazed...

Jammer.

Strange word but one that is bright in my head and associated with trouble.

Jammer, Jammer.

One of the other members of the patrol, gang, whatever this unit call themselves. He and the woman and Yan, the hooded one, are somewhere, close. They're going to miss Craig and come looking for him. So we have to go, now. Laura seems confused, bewildered and weak. I snatch up the sleeping bags and the food then grab her hand and drag her to the rear of the building and out.

The cold rain is a miserable shock. I shiver, I'm tired and, I realise, covered with gore. There's the remains of a backyard, a segment of brick wall, a knocked over dustbin, now rusty and burned. We clamber over rubble and into a service road that runs between the shop and a row of burned terrace housing. We swerve right and as we do so, Jammer appears a couple of hundred years away. He looks around, casual, not expecting to see anyone. Just another derelict to search before the unit can go back to the wherever it is they fill their bellies and heat their bones.

He looks in our direction and I see him stop, dead, then lift a mobile phone to his ear. Calling, no doubt, for reinforcements.

We head for a cluster of towers that loom over the shattered rooftops. Laura claims to know the whereabouts of the nearest demolition site. She says that the Survivors she bought the food from told her how to get there. I'm going along with it, what choice do I have? Anyway, there must be a demolition site somewhere on the borderline of the ruins.

I'm nervous, looking around the whole time, expecting trouble. We've lost Jammer and the Specials for now, but they're out there somewhere, hunting for us, up for revenge and probably just one of several packs called in and sniffing for blood.

I carry Craig's club and the bags of food. My sleeping bag is once more strapped to my back. I try to keep the image of Craig's broken head with its torn scraps of flesh and cracked white bone, pushed down into my own brain as deeply as it will go. Knowing his name makes it worse. It's a link, a personal connection.

Reaction is making me shake almost as hard as Laura. Guilt tears at me, he was only doing his job, one of life's losers now in gainful employment, one of a bunch of pre-conscription youngsters earning their living and only following orders.

The rain has eased, but the street is a quagmire. I hear noises, voices, footsteps. I don't know if they're real, if they're Specials, Survivors, or me, talking to myself. Who knows? Laura is almost unconscious. She needs to rest. *I* need to rest, but the hounds are closing in, crawling through the ruins like ants, thousands of them.

We reach the edge of no man's land. There's a huge plume of dust about a mile away, demolition site according to Laura. The problem is that it's to the west, back towards the city, a long walk, and if we find no willing lorry drivers there, a wasted trip.

Problem is, there's no dust cloud to the east.

It's almost dark when we finally stumble to a halt. The diggers and bulldozers are working under the glare of floodlights. The air is thick with grit.

At least there are plenty of lorries.

Now all we need is a driver willing to give us a lift Out.

We hunker down into yet another pile of scorched rubble and catch our breath. Laura has hardly spoken. I offer her some food but she refuses it. At least she drinks a bit of water. She says she would eat ice cream, but raspberry ripple is in short supply here.

She sits with her eyes closed for a while and I'm just beginning to resign myself to one more night in the ruins when she seems to gather herself together and gets wearily to her feet.

"Better do it before they all go home," she says. Her tone is old and world-weary.

"There must be some other way," I protest weakly. "And you're not up to it anyway."

"Fuck you," she answers and before I can say anything else, sets off towards the row of lorries waiting to be fed with rubble.

Something catches my eye and I glance back the way we've come. Light, a white pinprick that bobs about between the ruin and the no mans land. A torch. I stare hard, and eventually three figures separate themselves from the gloom.

The Specials?

As I watch, another handful, complete with a second torch, emerge from the ruins. The two groups pause and mingle. Then resume the trek along the borderline towards my hiding place. They don't seem to be in a hurry. They're searching that's why.

I turn my attention back to Laura and see her, a tiny, frail silhouette in the glare. She's at the closest of the lorries, looking up at the cab. The door is open, the driver talking to her. A moment, then the door shuts and the engine revs.

Thanks, but no thanks luv.

She disappears round the rear of the lorry, merging with the complexities of bright light and deep shadow.

Back to the Specials then. Their numbers seem to have swelled considerably, many of them strung out into no man's land, others weaving in and out of the ruins. They've probably worked it all out, but they need to check that we haven't gone to ground short of our destination.

Come on Laura, please, dear God, come on.

Come on what? Suck a big hairy lorry driver's cock for me? Let him paw and grope and eventually ram himself into you? I try to shut out this new wave of images, but they burn clear and merge with the others; the fire and smoke and blood.

The Specials draw closer, closer. Torches sweep the gathering dark.

Lorries, rev and growl and roar away with their loads, diggers and bulldozers gorge on rubble under the white hot glare, but for how much longer? What time do they close down for the day? What time is it now?

A figure emerges from the wash and dazzle. It waves, furiously.

I glance back at the Specials. Can they see her? Shit.

I get to my feet, stiff and cramped and break into a shambolic run through the shoreline of the ruins. Laura is all but jumping up and down, her arm an urgent semaphore

A cloud of dust billows over me. I cough and almost go down. When I emerge, fisting the grit from my eyes, I see that I'm close. I look back but the dust obscures everything –

No, here they come, torch beams, figures, walking, stopping, pointing.

I run faster and at last Laura's hand closes on mine and she leads me back along the rear of the lorries. Our chauffeur is waiting impatiently by his vehicle. He's tall and raw-boned with long, rock musician hair. The tailgate is open. We clamber onto the empty truck. I see the Specials, following our route, torches probing into each trailer.

Laura grabs me and shouts, but the engine and demolition din is too loud. She curls up about her bundled sleeping bag in the middle of the trailer, foetus-like. She looks up and waves for me to do the same. I hesitate, confused, wondering if we're simply hiding or about to be crushed to death by rubble.

I join her, she pulls me in close.

A crane revs, and I look up in time to see a metal water tank being lowered towards us, upside down. Its open top is a black mouth, come to feed. It settles over us and we're trapped in steel-lined, premature burial.

Before I can move or protest or panic, there is a deafening, skull-fracturing roar, like a wave, a torrent of titanic hail. Rubble. They're burying our steel coffin under tons and tons of rubble.

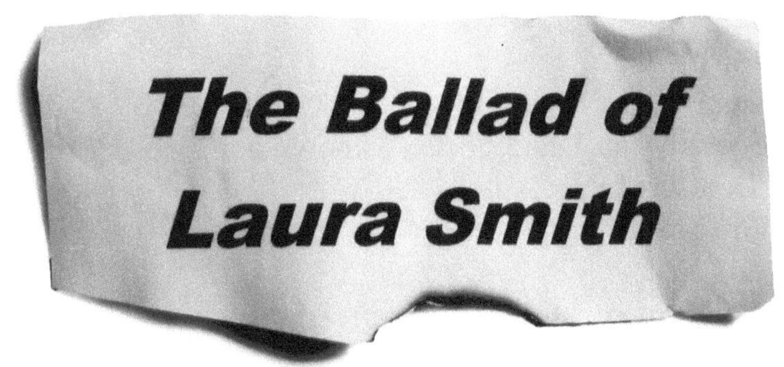

I moan like a frightened child and it's Laura who pulls me tight to her this time. The lorry revs, lurches into motion. The journey's only just started and I'm already on the verge of insanity.

"Are you okay?" I ask Laura. *I'm not. I want to scream and rant and pound my fists against these steel walls until they bleed.*

My voice is muffled, devoid of echo, its flatness emphasising the lack of space around me, the lack of room, the sheer proximity of the walls and the roof of this steel box.

"Yeah, I'm okay. Why shouldn't I be?" Laura sounds edgy. "Jesus."

It was only a fuck after all, devoid of emotion or tenderness, an act of raw prostitution, but, in the end, only a fuck, which makes it all right.

The lorry bumps and grinds and I concentrate on breathing and not on the tons of rubble bearing down on us from all sides. I ache, my body is pressed in on itself and I remember Ruth and me, face down in the back of that van and it seems a million years ago.

Laura hugs me and I hug the food bags.

I *am* buried alive. This is unbearable, unendurable, I want to move but I can't. Christ, it's getting hard to breathe, the oxygen must be running out. They'll find us dead.

The lorry slows, stops. There is an everlasting wait. No one is unloading the boxes. Nothing is happening. They're going to leave us to die here.

Vibration. The lorry moves again.

"Who are you?" I ask.

"What?"

"Who are you Laura? I don't know your second name, where you come from, anything."

"Who cares?"

"I do."

Just talk to me, I need a voice in the dark.

"Laura Smith, okay?"

"Yeah okay, but where are you from? What did you do before… before the war."

"You really want to know don't you."

"Why else would I ask?"

There have only been strangers since my family died. I want something more, some depth, some substance.

"Before the war I was a student, at a college." She makes it sound as if it's the most obvious thing it the world and I'm stupid for asking. Amanda used to do that. "My parents were, well like, my dad was a professor of anthropology at Brunel, you know, in Uxbridge, and my mum wrote novels. Marion Smith, yeah?"

"No, never heard of her."

"I'm not surprised. They weren't bestsellers. They were women's books, I mean, not chick lit or anything, but they were about women and their feelings and relationships. The critics said that Mum could be the next Anita Brookner."

"Right."

"You don't know who she is either do you."

"Yeah I know Brooky, she used to buy her fish and chips from the same chippy as me and she drinks at the *Blue Dog*. You have to watch her when she's had a couple of pints though."

Laura chuckles and so do I, the sound is odd and out of place here in our premature grave.

"Idiot," Laura says.

"So? Where were *you* the day war broke out?"

Come on, tell me what happened, how it started.

"At a party," Laura says.

*

And at that party there was a girl called Ranna, real name Rhiannon but she hated her name and never let anyone use it in her hearing. Her parents were *Fleetwood Mac* fans apparently. Ranna was bad and that's why Laura let herself be drawn into her circle. She wanted to be bad herself. If you couldn't be as intelligent and capable as your brother and ended up at college on an art and design course while he was studying medicine at Warwick, if you didn't show the potential to achieve the greatness that your parents possessed, then the only thing left was to kick, and kick hard.

I am crap therefore I will act crap. Not a bad motto Laura decided, because it summed up everything she was feeling that night. The party was wild and noisy and already spiralling out of control even though it was only two hours old.

Ranna was fun and outrageous and dangerous and there were times she frightened Laura.

But what was life if you didn't allow yourself to be frightened now and then?

The party was in a flat. Laura didn't know the host but Ranna did and that was her ticket in. The lights were dim the music mind-numbingly loud and most people were either drunk, stoned, eating each other's faces or all three.

Laura was swigging her third bottle of Red Ice when she felt someone grab her hand and yank her away from the drinks table and out into the hallway. The lounge door slammed shut, dampening the music but not its hydraulic beat.

"What're you doing?" Laura asked and giggled. For a moment she thought Ranna was asking her to the bedroom, she'd always wondered about the girl because she had never seen her with any boyfriends. Her giggles covered unease and an odd excitement.

But then Ranna pushed open the bathroom door.

"Want to try something sweet?" she asked.

"Depends."

She pulled a small plastic bag from the pocket of the leather jacket she wore. It was full of white powder. She poured some onto the surface of the toilet seat. Laura's mouth dried. She had smoked plenty of grass and popped a few Es, but this…

"Coke, but no cola," Ranna said and carefully pushed the powder into two neat lines with a credit card.

"Maybe not," Laura said and hated the little-girl fear in her voice.

"Maybe *yeah*. Look its harmless right? Watch." Ranna rolled up a piece of white card into a short straw then snorted one of the lines in one, swift, neat movement.

She held the tube out to Laura. Ranna was grinning, face flushed, eyes shining.

Maybe *yeah*.

Laura snatched the tube and crouched down by the toilet bowl. "Coke yeah?

"Coke."

By that time the word was molten and meaningless. There was energy and good feeling and joy. Even when someone turned on the television in the lounge and switched off the music and people blinked and uncurled themselves to stare at the images on the screen.

The Houses of Parliament were on fire, MPs had been killed at a late night sitting. The Prime Minister had been in there. Canary Warf was burning too and half of Limehouse.

Everyone looked confused, presenters, journalists who had rushed to the scene, bystanders caught by the cameras. There was blue light and yellow hi viz and jammed cars. Then a shot of Big Ben, silhouetted against a wall of flame.

Something, a splinter, a crack in the haze warned Laura that this was serious. Very serious indeed.

She sat, transfixed by the screen, trying to comprehend, to swim through fug. Mobile phones began to go off. Parents phoning sons and daughters, are you okay, where are you? Come home.

It took years, centuries, for her to understand that her own phone was ringing. She didn't answer. Instead the fire and pandemonium and sirens heard now through the flat's windows faded into grey then sleep and after that, when she woke again in the grey small hours, cramped on the lounge floor, sickness, diarrhoea and utter weakness.

*

At home, later that day, there were recriminations, hard questioning. Where was she last night, why didn't she answer the phone? But the fury abated quickly.

No one went to work. The Country seemed to be standing still. There had been more explosions, in London, Birmingham, Manchester. Huge blasts, multiple eruptions of shattered masonry and splintered glass.

Outside the the Smiths' Pinner house, a gentle breeze ruffled the polite shrubs and the early evening sun soothed warmly. No hint of crisis. Inside, the television was on. The Prime Minister, Elastoplast on his neck, bruised cheek, arm in a sling, stood at the despatch box in the burned-out ruin of the House of Commons, surrounded by battered but brave survivors of the bomb.

"Last night and during the day a series of air strikes have been unleashed against our Country," the Prime Minister declared, his voice edged with just the right mix of anger and calm. "The bombing is indiscriminate, cowardly, levelling residential areas, killing civilians. Those responsible are craven and ruthless enemies of democracy." He paused, winced from some injury that was still fresh and raw. Then continued. "We have been watching them for a while, gathering intelligence from the shadows and desolate corners of the world from which they operate and considering our own action, but now we must be decisive. With immediate effect we will take the war back to them."

The House roared, MPs from both sides were on their feet. The dissenters were almost invisible as the camera pulled back to reveal the extent of the bomb damage to the House, and suddenly it was like the final scene of that sentimental old war film Laura remembered watching one rainy afternoon when she was ill and off school. *Mrs Miniver*, that was what it was called, and its last scene was a church service. As the camera pulled away it revealed that the church was a ruin, but the indomitable Brits wouldn't let something like a bomb or two dampen their spirit.

Watching from the doorway behind her Mum and Dad who were huddled on the sofa, Laura realised that this was a declaration of war. Yet it sounded so vague, so un-definite. Who were we fighting? Where were they?

Who were flying those aircraft?

Monsters? People?

The Enemies of Democracy.

Everything unnerved her. She was edgy, uncomfortable and afraid.

Next day she stayed in bed, too unwell to get up except for trips to the toilet. She wasn't hungry. She felt a vague need but was unsure what it was she needed. Sometime during the bright-lit morning, as the warm breeze billowed her curtains through a window her worried mum had opened to "let in some fresh air", she heard a series of deep thuds then distant sirens and the scratch of a jet.

The unease grew into something more tangible. Real fear. What if these enemies of democracy dropped their bombs on Pinner? On their house? She couldn't sleep, couldn't get out of bed. She was frightened, flinching at every unusual sound or loudly passing car. She drifted in and out of sleep and each time was woken in a panic by some noise, too loud, too sudden.

That afternoon, Dad came in. "Pack your case Laura," he said. He was not a formidable or particularly assertive man but there was a grimness in his long, bespectacled, soft-chinned face that alarmed her. She had never seen a look like this before. This wasn't a disaster movie or something that has happened to someone else. The threat was real and immediate.

Another explosion rocked the city as he spoke, a long way off, but loud and powerful enough to rattle the windows in their frames.

"We're going to the cottage." Dad told her. The cottage was in Derbyshire. She hated going there because it was lonely and boring and devoid of mobile phone signals or broadband and too far from anything that could possibly entertain her. And now it was frightening because there seemed to be comfort in the city, in the press of people, in the traffic and noise and safety-in-numbers crush. What if those enemies of democracy invaded while they're out there all alone?

But this was one of those occasions when Dad was not to be questioned. She threw clothes into a case without thought of season or practicality. The car was crammed, the back bulging with food, more clothes and bedding and countless other practical items. There had been word from Richard. "He's okay," Mum said. "Warwick hasn't been bombed. Coventry received a few hits, mostly in the rougher, residential areas."

So that was all right then.

Traffic was heavy. Cars packed and crammed like the Smiths' mingled with commuters and lorries and vans and people who seemed to be just driving. Then it stopped altogether in Edgware, on the road that led towards Apex Corner and the A1.

Blue light flashed. Police, yellow-coated and sweltering in the heat, walked along the rows of jammed, unmoving vehicles. They knocked on windows which were rolled down for the occupants to receive the same message.

"Sorry sir/madam but the road is closed we're not letting anyone out of the city at the moment."

It was the same at all exits. Everything from full road blocks to patrol vehicles parked across the road. Other uniforms appeared, lurking in the background; black body-armour topped with full and impenetrably visored helmets.

"Desperate times call for desperate measures," Dad said uneasily as he executed yet another, and their final, three-point turn in Hainault. It was almost dark, about ten pm, by now. Everyone was exhausted, defeated and the journey home long and arduous because the city was awash with traffic and confusion.

The bombs started to fall with the night. Staring out of the passenger window Laura watched the horrible dazzling blooms unfurl along the river, a long way from the roads the Smith family travelled but still within the sealed borders of their city.

The lorry shudders and rocks and I hear our rubble tomb shifting above and around us. How strong is the tank? Exactly how many tons are bearing in on its fragile-seeming flanks. The old terror is coming back and I struggle for breath. I really do have to get out, if only for a moment. I need some light and space. I need to *move* –

*

College re-opened, places of work and business resumed operation. London, indeed the rest of the Country, was, according to the media and the government, defiant. Life will go on, they declared, no one can destroy democracy and the will of the British with a few bombs.

Laura, however, found precious little defiance in the corners of Britain she frequented. Everyone she met, at college, in shops and in the pub, was scared. The air raids took place every night. The outskirts of the city suffered most although the bombing seemed to moving steadily inwards. It was the facelessness of the enemy, the lack of nation, skin colour or political belief that made it so terrifying.

The army was mobilised, troops shipped out to the front, wherever that was.

Conscription was announced after the first week of the war. Richard phoned to say that he had already volunteered. His parents were proud and worried and then seemed to sink into a state of living death. Suddenly Laura was a non-entity. Life was a grey, lonely, fear-sodden uncertainty. Night became a place of flaming, thundering malevolence that lit the clouds, and hurled fire and debris skywards. It surrounded and walled her in and crept ever closer.

Perhaps they weren't air raids at all but the advancing Enemies of Democracy. There were rumours, fearful and whispered. Talk of EoD parachute drops, followed by massacres, rape, torture.

Everything was confusion and ambiguity.

Suddenly she needed…something.

Ranna was there of course and Ranna knew what would help, even though the white powder cost money. Laura quickly found a ready income and was astounded that no one noticed. The cash card was best. She had found a slip with a PIN number scribbled on it in Mum's purse, careless. The card could be quietly slipped from Mum's handbag once she had settled down in the front of the television at night with Dad. Laura took out modest amounts here and there, all lost in the general ebb and flow out of her parents' accounts. Their puzzlement was brief as they frowned over their statements.

"I really can't remember withdrawing thirty pounds at Tesco's, I hardly ever go there," said Mum. They were, of course, Waitrose shoppers.

"Well *I* didn't," said Dad.

"Must have been me then," said Mum and with a bemused shake of the head, the matter would be dropped, the puzzle abandoned.

A curfew was declared ten days into the emergency. Leaflets were delivered. Every one to be indoors by eight pm.

People ignored it, the whole idea was outrageous. The young saw it as another set of rules to break. Ranna laughed the whole idea to scorn. It was like the law against using your phone while you were driving, something to be held in contempt. Who would enforce it? Who cared? Laura joined in, slipping out of the house to meet up with Ranna's gang as her parents resumed their nightly zombification.

Then, one night the police came, cars skidded to a halt at the end of the street, officers appeared from dark corners and doorways.

The group scattered, Laura among them. Coke crystals still glued to her upper lip, sweating and confused, she made it over a fence and into a garden where she crouched, silent and terrified. She heard Ranna's angry screams and curses.

Three days, no word, then stones at her bedroom window and a pale, shocked Ranna clambered into her room via Dad's ladder. She had been locked in a cell. No charge no interrogation. Just left there and then, when the questioning finally started, interrogated relentlessly by two hard and emotionless men in immaculate grey suits who were not police officers because the police quite obviously hated them.

Their ID cards said SSU.

So now the fear was not only of what the night skies would bring but of stepping out of line, of speaking too freely, of being watched.

Rationing began. Just a few items. Only temporary.

Towers were under construction to house the bombed-out homeless. Only temporary.

The cities were sealed, no one allowed out, ingress, strictly controlled. Only temporary.

Everything was confused and temporary and closing in like the ring of fire about the metropolis. The sky was always alive with flame, the smoke-scented air rumbling day and night with the sounds of war.

*

One night in September, before curfew-time, Laura came back home from meeting up with Ranna and they were waiting. Mum and Dad, grave and pale. For a moment Laura thought that there was news about Richard, the worst news.

"You've been stealing from us," Dad said regret painted onto a white hot fury he struggled to hold down under middle-class reasonableness and forced concern.

He wanted to hit her. Laura could feel it, could sense it in the air around him. This was the last straw, the final indignity.

Laura shook her head; deny, deny, deny. Prove it…

"You've been using my cash card and taking money out," Mum sounded close to tears. "Why Laura?"

Laura broke first, screamed obscenity, slammed the front door and ran.

She heard Mum shout at her to come back. The curfew…

Fuck the curfew. Fuck Mum and Dad –

As she reached the end of the street, Laura was frozen by a sudden flare of light. An instant later the light became noise and she was picked up and hurled through the air and dashed against the ground. Heat blasted over her. The world shook. Again and again and again.

When it was done and she could roll over and sit up she saw fire, the bottom of the cul de sac, straddled with blazing destruction. The trail of flame was speared across the next street and the next, the line of bomb blasts neat and ruler-straight.

She scrambled to her feet and ran but the heat drove her back.

Her house was at the bottom of the cul de sac.

Her house.

Mum.

Dad…

Sirens, blue light, then other, squat and malevolent vehicles and suddenly the night was not only filled with the yellow-jacketed heroes of the emergency services but also with dark, faceless uniforms.

Laura, now a creature of the dark let it take her as she shrank back then turned and ran and, eventually, found other survivors, instinctively afraid of the SSU and the towers. By then she needed more than a line of coke to soothe her soul.

*

She's crying and I try to hold her and murmur comfort.

The road becomes bumpy, gears work. I hear the rubble shifting around on top of us. I cling onto Laura more tightly and she protests because I'm hurting her. I try to relax, try to breathe evenly and steadily and not to think about the dark and the close, close walls of our coffin and the fact that I may as well be a hundred foot down in the earth.

The lorry stops, air brakes hiss. There is crunching and manoeuvring and then the world is tipped on its side and it is terrifying because there is a lurching drop, a moment of weightlessness and then a crash that jolts through every bone in my body. I yell in fear and hear Laura's scream cut off by the titanic roar of pouring rubble.

Finally the tank is lifted from us by yet another chuffing and grunting crane and light comes in. I blink and screw my eyes against it and let Laura struggle out first. The driver helps her. I hear her thank him. I climb out without any offer of aid being made to me.

The glare is from a set of large floodlights that illuminate a valley made entirely of rubble. There are mountains of it as far as I can see. Our driver lights up a cigarette, then nods towards a huge hill of broken masonary to our right.

"Climb over that and you'll be on your way. And good luck." He takes a deep drag then nods to me once and returns to his lorry, which roars into life then grinds away, the steel box the only thing left in its trailer.

There are other lorries, and battered looking cranes and bulldozers. No one pays us any heed whatsoever. Truck-delivered refugees must be a common sight here.

We climb, in the full glare of the floodlights, scrabbling and struggling over the lethal shifting side of the heap. It's about twenty feet, mostly brick and concrete but studded with wood and metalwork. The climb is exhausting, especially with the food packs under my arm and sleeping bag on my back, but it's also exhilarating. Because I'm moving and there is space all around me and I can breathe. The air is far from fresh though. The smoke stink is so strong it hurts my throat.

Laura reaches the top first. When she does so she simply kneels there staring. When I catch up with her I see why.

I look out across the fragment of countryside washed by the overspill from the floodlights, and see…

An apocalyptic nothing.

Devastation on such a scale that I can barely comprehend what I'm seeing. Laura cries beside me. She clutches my arm. We can't speak.

Any road that passed through here has long been pounded out of existence, any building vaporised into piles of scorched rubble, no semblance of structure or architecture remains. The ground is churned to mud, great holes ripped into its flesh. A mist that stinks of smoke and rot clings to the earth and fills its countless wounds. The horizon glows red, the light bright enough to cast a shifting, bloody pall over the landscape.

I pull the compass from my pocket, even though I know the direction in which we have to walk. Habit probably, or wishful thinking that perhaps we aren't facing north-east after all and that we need to head off down a more pleasant, meadow-strewn, brightly flowered path.

Nope, Armageddon it is, looking neither left nor right.

"No wonder they won't tell us." I'm thinking out loud, not expecting a response

"What?" Laura's says anyway, voice dismal and childlike.

"Where the war *is*? Where the battlefields are. What is actually happening. No wonder it's a secret."

"Big fucking secret."

I look at her. She's staring straight ahead, eyes wide, tears rolling down her grubby, emaciated, metal-studded cheeks,

She's right about that. But how the hell have they managed to keep it from us?

By walling in the cities and not letting anyone back from the front line, that's how. By imposing a curfew that forces us to hide in our homes and watch television every evening (what else can the modern, undead citizen do now that imagination and creativity have been effectively fucked by years of drip-fed inanity?), then burning the sense out of our brains with obfuscation and confusion all served up with a hefty dose of subliminal messaging. I bet they even drug our food. It seems as if they tried letting a few hundred wounded back home to add a little realism to the charade. I even have their names on an electronic list in my pocket. It was a mistake, one that they are seeking to rectify with bloody efficiency.

They, they *they*? The government? The authorities? The Shadows, Power and Glory that take upon themselves the right to run our lives? God? The Devil, the Freemasons, Tescos?

Whoever they are, they will deserve their eternity in the fires of Hell. I even want to be sent there with them so I can watch their torment. Hand me a pitchfork Satan…

Why didn't they tell us? The enemy is at the gates, the EoD are here, the invasion has taken place. Have we become such children we can't handle the Truth?

The soundtrack to this vision of ruin filters into my brain. A distant, heavy thunder, the scratch of jets, helicopters.

"Come on, we can't stay up here. Someone'll see us."

I take Laura's hand and we scramble clumsily down the side of the rubble hill, reaching the damaged earth in a minor avalanche of dust-billowing masonry. Mist swirls about our ankles like the fake fog in a Hammer Horror graveyard. If it's poisonous then it's already too late.

I feel alone and afraid. Laura's presence is suddenly more responsibility than comfort. I look at the compass again, a nervous tic. North-east then. We find a semblance of road (the A12?), fragments of tarmac, even a white line or two. It isn't much but it's better than the mud. The air is bitterly cold and laced with icy rain.

Blood-lit as it is, the ruin around us is short on detail and structure. We trip and stumble.

Then Laura cries out and her hand slips from mine. I grab at her and somehow catch her arm, but not in time to stop her from sliding away from me and down into a mist-filled hole. I teeter on the edge, then her weight drags me from solid to crumbling earth and down I go, arms windmilling, managing not to fall over and hitting solidity again in a sort of crazy, hopping dance.

The crater isn't deep, six or seven feet. Laura has fallen onto her bottom. There's a puddle, a dirty, freezing lake that separates the two of us. I work my way round it and sit own beside her. I offer her some food from our dwindling supply. She shakes her head.

"Eat," I say.

"I can't."

"You have to."

"I'll be sick."

... *"Being sick all over my desk was a bit thoughtless but, hey, what's a few diced carrots between friends?"*

"At least I didn't throw up over my own desk," I say.

"Very good point. Fuck me, you must be bored to come back here." ...

I chuckle.

"What's so funny?"

"I remembered something, a mate of mine…it doesn't matter."

"Is he dead?"

"Who?"

"Your mate."

"Yeah."

"Was he in the army?"

"No."

"Don't you want to talk about it?"

Do I? "We worked in an office, in London Wall."

"Oh." It doesn't seem to mean anything to her, but why should it? She's been living like an animal for the last six months. Survivors don't have television to watch or newspapers to read.

"It was bombed, everyone I worked with was killed, at least I think they were. Perhaps some of them got out."

"You worked in an office?"

"What's so strange about that?"

"You don't look like someone who sits at a desk all day."

"What do I look like then?"

"I dunno, a car mechanic or a builder."

"Strange, seeing as I used to be one of those, until I found a nice cushy desk to lay my head on every day."

"Which one?"

"Which what?"

"Mechanic or builder, which one?"

"Guess."

A moment, then, "Mechanic."

"How'd you work that out?"

"The leather gear, you must be a biker, bikers are always messing about with engines."

"Remarkable Holmes."

"What?"

"Holmes, you know Sherlock Holmes."

Her silence is all I need. "You don't know who he is do you."

"Dunno, there was a film about him but…"

"Don't they teach you anything at school?"

"I've left school, I'm at college…" Her voice trails off and with it the teenager I'd been teasing.

I hear her sniff and realise she's crying again.

"I want to go home." Her voice is almost too quiet for me to hear. "I want to go back to college."

"You will," I tell her as gently as I can. "The war won't go on forever."

Won't it?

"Where's *your* home?" Laura asks suddenly.

"Not here."

"Have you got a family?"

"Yeah."

"I'm sorry. It's none of my business –"

"They're dead as well. Ruth, Dominic, Amanda and Rachel, that's their names and they're all dead. They were blown to pieces by bombs, in a hospital. They were smashed and burned and buried."

"Pete, don't talk about it."

It's odd to hear her use my name. I'd almost expected her to call me Dad.

"It was my fault," I say.

"No it isn't. The EoD killed them –"

"Who the fuck *is* the EoD? Why should they want to kill my family and my friends? It is my fault anyway. Dominic wouldn't have been at that hospital if I hadn't..."

Laura is quiet this time.

"It doesn't matter. I can't go back and change it."

"Tell me, you know, what happened?"

I shake my head.

"What were they like? Was Ruth your wife?"

"Yeah. She saved me." I shiver and Laura hugs me more tightly. God knows how we're going to survive the night. All we have are the clothes we're wearing and our mouldy old sleeping bags.

"And were Dominic and the others your children."

"Dominic is – was – the oldest. He's…Christ, he would've been eighteen now."

And in the army.

I talk. I tell her everything, about how I woke up one morning last week to find that we are at war. I tell her about the List, the memory stick and the Veterans and where I'm going. I tell her about Gary Marshall and foot-shooting and a burning hospital.

I tell her too much but once the lid is off I can't stop. I grind it out, unemotional, cold, angry and when I finish, I know that I've made a huge mistake because if we're captured and made to talk there are two tongues that can be loosened instead of just one.

But there is some relief in my confession, some easing of the pain, of the pressure building up inside me. It doesn't last long because I don't believe that talking about things always helps. There is some grief and agony that will never go away, no matter how many times we share or analyse them. Some pain is better buried as deeply as our minds will let us dig.

I don't think Laura heard the end of the tale anyway. She's quietened, her breathing is steady. I can't keep my eyes closed, so I lay still, trying not to feel the cold, staring up at the few stars visible through rends in the dense, no doubt poisonous, cloud.

I fumble her sleeping bag open and manage to wrap it round her. Once I've done the same with mine I hold hers in place with my arms. I eat before I finally settle down. Christ it's cold.

Sometime in the early grey, I become aware that Laura is sitting up beside me. I blink away the meagre sleep I've managed and say her name. She doesn't answer. Her mouth is open, her eyes wide, as if she's staring at something. Hallucination perhaps, some effect of her last heroin fix?

"Laura?"

She makes a noise, a sort of groan and sob.

I sit up, to offer some comfort, then I see it too.

Strewn all over the crater are…fragments. After a moment I understand that they are bones; skulls and scraps of clothing, and all burned. I see rifles, rusty and useless, helmets, their camouflage paint, heat blistered and peeling, full-face visors melted into surreal sculptures. The longer I look, the more I see, lining the walls of the pit, filling the stagnant pond and scattered about its shoreline.

Beside us, under us.

"Get me out," Laura says, her voice is ominously calm. "Getting me fucking out of here."

I wrestle free of my sleeping bag, feeling them now, crunching and grinding in the mud under my backside, under my hands as I crawl free. Breathing hard and fast, near to panic, Laura scrambles and struggles behind me. We've seen death, we've dealt it out for Christ's sake, yet this is far worse, far more terrible. Every other time we've walked away, left it behind us.

Now we're sleeping with it, standing on it, crawling over it.

I claw my way up the sides of the crater, earth comes free in my fists and I know that if the crater was any deeper I would never have got out. But I do and turn quickly to haul Laura up over its lip. She kicks and scrabbles at the mud, desperate, frantic.

We're out of the shell hole, but nothing is different.

The entire, brutal, landscape is seeded with human remains. Mostly scorched and blackened down to bone.

Mostly.

A thousand, a million people? Soldiers, civilians, it's hard to tell the difference.

*

We walk because we can do nothing else. We are exhausted, hungry but not able to eat. We've retrieved the sleeping bags, thick with mud and sodden and the remaining bag of food, now light and almost empty. There is nothing recognisable here. No landmarks or buildings. The road-fragments are becoming more sporadic, the bones more plentiful.

Something looms ahead of us. A hill, a ridge. It doesn't look as if it's part of the landscape. As we come closer I realise that we will have to climb because we're too tired to tramp around it, and anyway, we might be able to see something from its summit, about twenty feet up, a landmark, some buildings, anything.

Laura nods when I suggest it. She's barely spoken all day. Her face is pale and tight, as if she is pressing her jaws so tightly together she will never open them again. She clings to my hand, and only lets go when necessary. I don't mind. I need her hand too.

We climb, slowly and awkwardly, bone-filled soil rolling away under our feet, we slip and slide down and claw, we use lumps of road and other solid debris as hand holds. Finally, dizzy with hunger and exhaustion we reach the top.

It is a crater. An immense, titanic, unthinkable hole, perhaps half a mile across. The sheer magnitude of it is beyond comprehension. The ground inside it is ash into which is mixed torn, blackened metal and scraps of human beings. Surely only a nuclear explosion could cause this sort of damage. If so, the hole must be radioactive, and therefore, so are we.

So what are the symptoms, hair loss, sickness, weakness? I've been feeling most of those for a while, but that's because I'm tired, shocked and hungry. I spit into my hand, no blood.

Not yet.

"Look, Gary look!"

Laura's been so quiet, it's a few seconds before I understand that it's her voice shouting my name. I follow the direction of her outstretched arm. Tents. A cluster of them, and vehicles, dark, military-looking. There's a flag, Union Jack or whatever it's called these days. The tent canvas displays a white circle and red cross.

Laura lets go of my hand and before I can stop her, she sets off down the inside slope. I follow, shouting at her. It's too late now, we must have been spotted, two maniacs, running and yelling. At least this is a hospital, or welfare centre or something of the sort, Red Cross, safety and warmth and food and comfort. Aren't they supposed to help everyone? Don't they remain neutral? Fucked if I know. Laura is racing across the crater floor now, kicking up ash in tiny black explosions.

Like the mud stirred by the pike Dominic and me returned to the water on that icy bright Saturday afternoon a hundred years ago...

Laura reaches the first tent, slows then stops. It takes me a few moments to catch up.

The camp is very quiet.

Silent in fact.

Nothing moves except the swirl of cloud overhead and the wind ruffled surfaces of the many ponds and lakes that dot the crater floor.

I move past Laura to the entrance of the nearest tent.

I smell it even before I pull open the flap and I'm sick. There isn't much to come up and I'm soon dry-heaving into the ash.

These soldiers weren't burned. These were massacred in their sick beds along with their doctors and nurses and then left to rot.

As I straighten I see other bodies, most of them, splayed in the ash, all humanity hidden behind uniform and visored helmets. Friend or foe, attackers or defender, there is no way to tell.

"Perhaps there's some food and stuff," Laura says.

I look round, startled by her level-headedness in the face of such carnage, especially after the way she reacted to the burned remains we encountered earlier.

She's right about the food. But to get it we have to go inside these tents.

At first we wander, aimlessly between and round them, peering into the backs of the ambulances and lorries. We find nothing of any use of course and soon end up back where we started.

Christ the smell is unbearable.

"This is a waste of time," Laura says and wrenches back the flap of the largest tent and goes in.

I have to follow her. I can't let her go in on her own.

I find her bent double, hands on knees, groaning and fighting for breath. Dead soldiers lay on the floor, tangled with nurses and uniformed men sporting Red Cross armbands. All eyes are open, bodies punctured and torn. Others lay on their bunks, many still attached to their now empty drip bottles. Some are in plaster, a couple of them wear neck braces.

The stench is beyond anything I have ever experienced before. There are no flies. It's too cold, thank God, but there is movement, quick, scurrying, accompanied by the occasional glimpse of dark fur and long, fleshy tails.

We move through this hell until we pass into what looks like a kitchen area. There are crates, a portable gas stove. Some of the crates are open and we find ration packs, dried meat and fruit, bottles of water and tins, their lids conveniently fitted with ring-pulls. We find some backpacks and fill them until we can barely walk. Doesn't matter, they will lighten up quickly. There are also rolled sheets of padded metal foil and I have some vague idea that they are designed to keep you warm. I take two, one each.

There is medical store, watched over by an orderly who now lies on the floor, most of his face bullet-ripped. There are other wounds that look as if they have been *gnawed* into his flesh.

Somehow the bullet holes are more palatable.

I grab bandages and paracetomal. Laura snatches a handful of glass bottles and seal-packed syringes. I don't try to stop her. I'm tempted myself. My own chemical indulgence is a handful of Temazepan packs. I need to sleep, and not dream.

Swallowing bile, my stomach convulsing again, I lead the way back through the main ward. I almost make it to the exit before I'm sick again.

The rumble and thud of war is louder with each step. The entire horizon seems to be ablaze.

"We can't go round it," I say.

"Are you crazy? We can't go through that?"

"Look at it Laura, it goes on as far as we can see in both directions."

"But we can't." She's a little girl, stepping back from me, terrified.

"So what do you suggest we do? Huh? Come on, tell me." I'm getting angry.

"Wait until it stops. Until it's over."

"And how long is that going to be? Look at this place, there've been fighting here for months, a year even. Do you think it's suddenly going to stop just because we want to get past?"

"You told me it would end. You told me I'll go back to college. You did, you told me that."

"For Christ's sake Laura, I was…"

What? Offering comfort, patronising, lying?

"We have to go that way, there isn't a choice."

"Yes there is."

"No Laura, there is no choice."

"Don't shout at me."

"You're being bloody stupid that's why I'm shouting at you."

"You scare me when you shout."

Before I can say another word she turns round and runs, back the way we've come, over the shattered tarmac and mud, between the burned bodies. I call out to her but she doesn't turn round, she's like a frightened animal.

I set off after her, my pack heavy and banging against my back. I shout to her but it only makes me more breathless.

She disappears into the everlasting mist, straight into a thick bank of it. I plunge in after her and when it thins and I stagger to a halt in the middle of more chaos and desolation I can't see her anymore. Suddenly I'm scared, scared and frantic. I shout her name, shout until I'm hoarse. I wander aimlessly, everywhere is the same.

Where is she? I can't leave her out here in this fucking wasteland. It gets cold at night. She needs food and warmth and someone to look after her and I can't lose a child again. Please, no.

My panic is almost rage. I shout and yell at her and stumble and notice that the light is fading. Christ we've been walking all day.

Ahead is a crater ridge, small looking, she could be in there, cowering against the soil wall, shivering and crying and angry among the charred corpses. I head towards it, walking and half-running.

A figure rises above the ridge.

Thank God –

The figure is too big to be Laura, too bulky. It wears a helmet a visor, body armour. It has a rifle.

Another joins it, another.

"Stop! You, stop!"

I obey, momentarily confused then realise that the fog bank I've just emerged from combined with the bad light might give me a chance to get away. The backpack is army property, as is the food, the foil blanket. I'm a looter. They shoot looters don't they?

I make to turn and a shot rings out. I hear something hurtle by my right ear. A bullet.

I stop, out of breath.

A group of soldiers clamber out of the crater and move slowly and carefully towards me.

It takes me a few seconds to realise that they're not soldiers at all but SSU.

SSU. I feel my entire body and soul crumble to dust. As I watch them advance I wonder if I should just run, give them an excuse to shoot me and be done with it. But my nerve has failed, my will gone.

They form a loose arc around me, weapons raised. One of them speaks into a radio and a moment later I hear an engine whine and groan out of the gathering murk. A dark, lumbering mass appears, rocking over the shattered surface. It's an armoured truck of some kind, not like the usual hulking SSU vans but a huge box on a dozen big wheels. Its back doors crash open and I'm shoved around to the rear and shouted at to get in.

For a minute I hope that….but Laura isn't among the thirty or so, shivering individuals huddled in the back. I join them. No one speaks. They all look dirty, cold and hungry, men and women, many with backpacks and filthy sleeping bags. Pilgrims like me then, townies who have managed to get through the barriers and Out.

We glance at each other but no one holds eye-contact for long. What's the point anyway, the SSU have us and Christ knows what they intend to do with us. They could easily line us up and despatch us with a few bullets out here and no one would be any the wiser. In fact, the longer the sick-making journey lasts the more I'm convinced that this is what is going to happen.

I'm coming Ruth, I whisper.

It scares me though, that final moment, waiting for the explosion, the impact, the utter shock of it as the bullet tears into me and fills my head with white then red then nothing.

Someone pulls out a pack of cigarettes and lights up. The man has long hair, longer than mine, and a thick beard. He looks gaunt, skeletal almost. He catches my eye and offers the pack. I take a cigarette and share his lighter. I draw deep and thank him.

"Baz," he says.

"Pete."

"What do you think? Firing squad?"

I shrug, disappointed that he can't come up with anything better then me.

"I was in a rock band," he says. "Bass player. The glamorous job."

"Anyone famous?"

He grins through his beard. "Nah, bunch of middle-aged farts. Pub band, weddings, parties and corporates, that sort of thing, doing well though, making a bob or two. We called ourselves *The Warriors* would you believe. What prat calls a rock band *The Warriors*?"

"You I suppose."

He laughs, the sound becomes a racking chesty cough.

"Are you all right?" a woman asks. She is Indian, youngish, in her thirties perhaps. She is also thin and haggard,

Baz manages to nod then gets out a yeah between coughs.

"Too many cigarettes," the woman says.

We laugh, a quiet, embarrassed laugh.

"I'm Diya," she says.

I shake hands with her. Her hand feels small and delicate but her grip is strong.

"We live…lived in Wembley," Diya continues. She seems to need to talk. "It was being bombed, every night, sometimes during the day. I couldn't take it anymore. Aaman, my brother…He's gone. I lost him. We got separated somehow…He's tough, a policeman, he'll be okay. Worried about me probably."

We're a shattered, frightened, broken example of humanity but there's warmth between this little corner of the group, those of us who need to talk and hear each other's voices.

"There was a young girl, with me." I say. "She wandered off and…I was looking for her when I was picked up." I scan the faces around me. "I don't suppose any of you saw her; dark hair, piercings in her face?"

No one had, of course.

She's still out there and now she's alone and she doesn't want to go through the battle zone so she'll try to get back to London but she won't make it. She'll be hurt somehow, killed, by the war, by the cold, by fear.

I rub my face, feeling the roughness of my new beard, of my hands, and wonder what the hell I look like.

"Where were you going?" I ask. I have to be careful, they'll ask me but I'll lie.

"The coast," Diya says. "They say there are communities there, villages. But I don't think there are, everything is gone."

"Same thing," Baz says and lights up another cigarette.

"You won't have any left for the firing squad," I say.

He chuckles grimly. "They give them to you, so I've heard, generous to a fault."

The lorry stops. Air brakes hiss. The doors open and we are shouted out.

I was hoping that my prophecy of a lonely death out here in the wasteland was pessimistic nonsense, but the fact that we've been unloaded in the middle of a nowhere that looks like the rest of this hell-hole nowhere is not encouraging. There are mud and shell holes, that endless ground-hugging fog and the stink of smoke and rumble of war and, I realise that there are four other SSU lorries parked in a circle around us. Their headlights glare into our eyes from whichever direction we look.

Each vehicle disgorges its sorry load out into the night cold and we are all herded into the temporary, lorry-bounded parade ground. There must be over a hundred of us, all hopefuls who fled their cities and towns in search of paradise and now prisoners of the SSU.

We are formed up, first into groups, then shoved, prodded and sorted into straight lines

I look about and see young and some old and even two children. Everyone looks down, a few at each other. I look for my new found friends, glimpse Baz.

And Laura.

She's in another group on the other side of the "square". I raise my hand, try to get her attention, but I can't. Someone shouts at me and

I sense rifle butts and boots being readied so I lower my hand. At least she's still alive. She looks okay, scared of course but there's a young lad beside her, someone her age to look out for her.

I feel a pang of jealousy. Not sexual, but because she has found someone else to take this journey with. Stupid I know, but I can't help it. There isn't much else for me to hold onto.

At least no one looks as if they intend to shoot us. One of the SSU, more astronaut than a soldier in his armour and visor, starts to move through the ranks. He, or she, slaps a hand on prisoners' shoulders, seemingly at random. It appears to be some sort of signal for the selected one to be hurried away to one of the lorries.

I think of another selection, sixty odd years ago, the fit and healthy separated from the elderly, infirm and children, who were all marked for death in the gas chambers.

The SSU officer looks at Baz and passes him by. A few more then it's my turn. I feel the officer's visor-hidden stare.

He or she moves on. No tap.

The officer also passes Diya then moves on to the next group, Laura's group. I watch and pray to a god who owes me no favours. I watch as the officer moves closer to her. She holds the officer's stare and I am proud of her defiance and guts.

I wait for the decision, my prayers growing more desperate.

Let her come with us. Please, with us –

Tap.

We're loaded back into our lorry even more silent and grim than before. Even Baz is quiet, sharing cigarettes with me. Diya cries softly and at one point I take her hand and try to offer some sort of comfort. She lets me but it doesn't seem to help.

"They took my…" Daughter? Is that what I was about to say? "My stepdaughter."

Yeah, yeah that's what she is, my stepdaughter.

"What are they going to do with them, and with us?" Diya asks.

"Send us all back," I answer. "They'll probably set us up with a nice flat in one of those new tower blocks." The thought had just occurred to me and whether blind optimism or logic I don't know.

"I'd rather face a firing squad," Baz says and stubs out his last cigarette on the metal floor between his feet.

I glance at my compass. We're heading east. Towards the war.

Baz doesn't have to make the choice. There is no firing squad and we are not at the towers. The lorry delivers us to an army camp, a floodlit canvas town somewhere in the vicinity of the front. The place is all tents and barbed-wire, sandbags and uniforms. Groups of soldiers sit and stand around at one end of what I assume to be a parade ground. They watch us disembark and there is no contempt or pity, nothing but a hollow-eyed stare. They look tired, beaten and some vacant, as if lost in a narcotic haze.

The sergeant who greets us is far from an empty husk however.

"Good afternoon," he says cheerfully. He is slight-built and short, probably at the minimum height for a soldier, or doesn't that matter anymore? "My name is Sergeant White. Welcome to your new and exciting life here in Her Majesty's Armed Forces. We trust you'll enjoy your stay with us and if you have any complaints, any little thing that isn't to your liking just come and see me and I'll endeavour to put things right for you. Nothing is too much trouble. Blankets too rough, tent too cold, caviar ration too salty, just let me know." His charm turns to a roar. "Follow me and try to march. Left come on left-right-left-right."

We cross the square to a large tent furnished with two straight rows of identical canvas chairs. Men with electric razors wait at each one. When they've finished we are bald and thin and somehow fragile looking. Even the women are shaved. Diya seems not to care, but is sunk into herself, withdrawn from the world.

Next comes the uniform, a baggy, warm and heavy camouflaged overall. I transfer the memory stick and map page surreptitiously into my new deep pockets. Our masters don't seem to care what we keep or discard, as long as it isn't a weapon.

There's a backpack that contains shaving tackle, hair brush and a basic first aid kit. And it is only then my slow-moving brain comprehends that I am now in the army. No one has asked for my name, no one has questioned me or made me sign anything. I am one of about a hundred odds and ends who have suddenly become soldiers; men and women, shorn, uniformed and press-ganged.

It happens fast, we're disorientated, confused, exhausted and defeated. The sergeants and corporals shout and scream at us and shove us and we are marched here then there, we receive injections, we are probed and listened to and forms are completed and boxes ticked.

Finally we are herded into a large mess tent where we eat, basic but hot and filling food and drink copious mugs of tea. The food is so wonderful that I almost cry as it fills my mouth and slides down my throat. The tea is hot and strong and wipes away my permanent headache. After that it's on to a further large tent whose floor is littered with rolled-up sleeping bags.

I climb into the first one I can get my hands on and lay my head on my pack. I'm warm, fed and content. Uncertainly and fear gnaw away at some numbed part of my mind, but the only thing that matters is how I feel at this moment.

And I feel good.

I don't close my eyes, because tired as I am, I'm not ready for sleep.

The lamps are extinguished, as are the floodlights outside and we are left alone. There will be guards of course. But who is going to run when you are fed and warmed like this.

I remember the last time I slept with a crowd.

Underground station. Laura about to be abducted and sold...

Laura.

I close my mind because I can't dwell on what has happened to her because if I do I will go crazy. All I can do is lay back and enjoy the moment.

Someone touches me. I start and roll over to find a body close up against me, small, shivering, smelling of the army-issue soap we had showered with and that other sweetness, woman scent.

"Pete, I'm scared." Diya says and instinctively I put my arms about her and draw her even closer.

My lips press on her scalp where there is no longer thick dark hair but bare, recently shaved skin, faintly stubbled. It doesn't matter, she is warm and soft and she is a woman and that's enough to rouse hungers in me that I know should stay hidden. Without thinking about it, without wondering or debating, I unzip my sleeping bag and she slides inside and, exhausted and grief-beaten as I am, I can't control myself.

I feel her breath on my face and her lips and we kiss, hungrily, desperate for comfort and pleasure. We are quiet, urgent then gentle, awkward and unfamiliar but in need. Christ how in need. There's no time for guilt, not here or now.

"They're not going to send us to fight," Diya whispers, later, when we're done. "They can't, we're not soldiers, we're just ordinary people."

Isn't the whole army made up of ordinary people, people who have been conscripted and trained and turned into soldiers? Dominic, my son was an ordinary person Diya, but he would have been sent into battle anyway.

"You're right," I say instead. "We'll probably clean latrines and peel potatoes," Not such a bad prospect, if it was true.

Diya doesn't answer. I can tell from her breathing that she is asleep. I kiss her forehead and remember that I used to kiss Ruth's forehead like that.

Ruth, only a few days dead and here I am wrapped around another woman.

I try to feel guilty. I try to summon some shame, but there is none.

A bitter, bitter wind slices through the parade ground as we shuffle and stumble into some sort of order. Sergeant White struts around and between our ragged lines like a bantam cock, back straight, chest puffed out, swagger stick under his arm.

"Today," he shouts at last. "After your breakfast of croissants and preserves, and natural low-fat yoghurt, you will learn how to shoot."

I'm suddenly uneasy. My instincts are right. Why do we need to know how to shoot if we're going to peel spuds? I want to glance at Diya who is a few places to my left, but I daren't so much as move my head. White is a fearsome presence, the type of character you find yourself obeying even when you know you don't need to.

"Shooting's very easy," White continues. "Nothing to it. But there's always at least one ham-fisted cretin in every batch of recruits who spoils it for the rest of us, so, because of the cretins amongst you everyone else has to spend the day on their bellies blasting the shit out of little cardboard targets."

He's right. And there is no time to think about it because we are virtually run into the mess tent to shovel in our full English breakfasts and down as many mugs of tea as our stomachs can cope with before being taken across at a fast jog to a far corner of the camp where there are man-shaped targets and a stack of rifles.

The weapons are light, short and designed to be held and carried easily. Firing them is as simple as White told us it would be; magazine clips in, like so, safety catch off, aim and squeeze trigger.

Squeeze don't jerk you wanker!

We lay on or bellies in the cold, oozing mud and squint through our sights, awaiting White's order to fire. When it comes, I *squeeze* the trigger. The gun jumps and bucks and spews tracer in the general direction of the target. The sound is more mechanical than explosive, the discharging of the bullet itself, a sharp crack, nothing like the loud bangs you hear on films and television. The weapon is hard to keep under control, but after a while I manage to hold it still enough to hit the black and white cardboard man at the end of the shooting gallery.

What the fuck am I doing?

What choice do I have?

No one has told us anything. We have been scooped up out of the wilderness, tumbled out of a lorry and into uniform and now we are learning how to fire a gun. We're kept away from the other soldiers who hardly even bother to stare at us let alone mock us whenever they do happen to cross out path. We are kept together. We are harassed and hurried and shouted at and abused and we shoot until our eyes are blurred and our shoulders and our trigger fingers ache.

More food follows then more marching and shouting, and more shooting. We are made to run, until many of us are sick and four or five collapse and are carried away and never seen again. We are given dummy grenades and told how to pull the pin then throw and get down. We are then given real grenades and once that pin is in my other hand I stare at the lethal, segmented little spheroid and I can't let go. I'm trapped. The thing makes me tremble. I'm not the only one. But the NCOs yell and shout and eventually I hurl it into the desolation and it explodes with a disappointingly small puff of smoke and brief orange flash.

It rains as we are marched back to the range to shoot until it is almost dark. Then we're back in the mess tent. There is one more activity before we return to our sleeping bags. A film show. We settle down, satiated and ready to fall asleep in the lightless cinema tent. The film is far from an easy watch however. It's called an army information film, but is, in fact, propaganda, blatant and unashamed, and it chills me to the soul because it is footage of the aftermath of an EoD massacre.

Red Cross field hospital, behind the lines, every helpless patient, every unarmed member of the medical staff, gunned down in cold blood.

This folks, is the evil you are fighting.

I recognise the hospital and the bodies.

And almost empty my full stomach onto the tent's wooden floor.

I've barely seen or spoken to Diya today. Baz-on-Bass, as I've come to call him, has been as much of a companion as it's possible to have been and now I lay in my sleeping bag alone and wonder if last night was just reaction and need. I'm shocked at how lonely I feel without her, how much I want her to come to me. But the lights go out and the minutes pass and I begin to feel sleepy and realise that, no, she isn't coming.

Christ. I've only known the woman a couple of days.

And what about Ruth and my family, shouldn't I be grieving over them and not lusting after a stranger?

In the real world, the sane and civilised world, yes. But this is an insane, primal, bestial world. The rules don't work here.

I doze then after some uncountable time, in the near silent dark, I feel someone climbing into my sleeping bag and everything is okay again.

Two more days of marching, running and shooting.

Then, on the morning of the fourth day they wake us before dawn. I don't know what time it is.

There is lot of shouting and kicking as we struggle out of our sleeping bags and reach around for discarded backpacks and uniforms. Diya scrambles out, clutching her uniform to herself in a vain attempt at modesty. I glimpse her naked for the first time, our encounters have always been darkness and touch, and see that she is thin and frail.

I fumble the laces of the boots they've given me, flinching under the torrent of yelled abuse. There's a tension. There's something in the atmosphere, in the feel of this, that isn't right. Sergeant White moves among us, strangely quiet, leaving all the noise and bluster to his corporals. I catch his eye and see that he is pale and haunted. He nods to me, the gesture barely visible.

"Good luck," he mimes and turns away. I think he's crying.

Diya finds me again and stays close as we stumble out of the tent. I hold her hand for as long as I can then we're back in the square and making some attempt at standing to attention.

An officer appears, he too is in battle kit. He nods to his sergeant, a tall broad slab of a man who yells an order that makes us swing round in a ragged turn. We march and stumble and shuffle towards a set of trestles that line the edge of the square. They are laden with helmets, the full visored type, and rifles and magazines. We have to try on the helmets to find one that fits and the whole thing deteriorates into a Harrods's Sale scramble. My eventual prize smothers me and although the visor is transparent from the inside, is utterly claustrophobic.

Finally we're given green armbands and instructed in no uncertain terms that we are to put them on and not shoot at anyone wearing a similar accessory. We are, however, allowed, nay obliged, to shoot at anyone not wearing one or wearing an armband of a different colour.

An exercise then, a surprise treat for us on this freezing, wet morning.

Another short, sharp march and we're climbing into the backs of a handful of hulking armoured trucks that have caterpillar tracks instead of wheels. They are windowless and coffin-like. The only light is from two small portholes set into the rear doors. Someone groans, someone else cries. I can't tell if it's a man or woman.

I don't blame them whoever they are, because this is nightmare, and this is terrible.

A hand finds mine, small, trembling.

"They've given us guns and bullets," Diya says, voice hoarse with tension. "I think they're going to make us fight."

The officer strides into the clearing formed by the four armoured trucks that have brought us here. The visor of his helmet is raised so we can see his face and he looks very young. In the midst of the crash and rumble of battle, despite the smoke that rolls across the small corner of the war-sculptured wilderness in which we stand, there is an odd silence, a white, featureless roar that seems to blank out every other sound.

The officer takes up his position in our midst, flanked by two sergeants, one of them, his pet brute, the Brick Shithouse, the other, a lean, gaunt bastard with the most vicious eyes I've ever seen.

"I am Lieutenant Emery," the officer says. His voice is as young as his face. He sounds nervous, like a best man unaccustomed to public speaking. "And in a short while, under my command, you'll take to the field to serve your Country."

The groans and cries of protest that erupt are reflex, nothing the sergeants or anyone can do about them. They're like the stab of shock brought on by the first glimpse of a beloved's coffin, the terrible made real.

"Enough! Shut up the lot of you!" Shithouse barks at last. Emery seems content to let him have his say. All part of the little pantomime they've probably performed a hundred times before. "There's no use moaning now, you should have thought of that before you broke the law and deserted your homes. Think yourselves lucky you're not in prison. At least you're getting to do something useful with your miserable little lives."

Emery, the good cop now, motions the sergeant to stop. "Whatever the reason you're here, you should feel honoured and proud to be part of this."

Christ, I can't believe this crap. No one here is proud of anything. Most of us are confused by the drugs I'm convinced they put in all that food they've forced down out necks, exhausted and just want to get away.

"I know that in the end you'll do your best. And when this is over you can go home again, the slate wiped clean."

They mean it don't they. We are actually going to march off into all that smoke and fire, and fight. Men and women who have been in uniform for three miserable days, who can't even salute properly, are being sent into the meat grinder to add our bones to all the others that litter this fucking place.

Silence has returned to the ranks. I can hardly stand up for fear, Diya is one side of me and Baz the other. He's muttering and after a moment I realise that he's praying. I hardly know either of these people yet I feel as if they're lifetime friends. Their presence stops me running round in circles screaming.

The memory stick. Must never forget that. It's still buried in my pocket, still my purpose. My only purpose now because Laura has joined the long list of the lost. I want to take Diya and Baz with me. But we have to survive this atrocity first.

"All right," Emery says. "You can stand easy."

None of us know how to do this so we slump or make some attempt at the leg apart, rifle-butts-on-the-ground stance we've seen in films and on television.

"In a few hours we're mounting a big push –"

Did he really say that? A Big Push, like *Blackadder's* Big Push, like the bloodstained, status quo-maintaining Big Pushes of the First World War?

"– which is designed to punch through the EoD lines at their most vulnerable points. Our job is to be part of a diversionary assault on their centre. It is hoped that it will draw strength from the positions against which the real attack will be made. Is that clear?"

Incredibly we all murmur some sort of assent. British politeness? Drug-induced acquiescence? Fucked if I know. All I do know is that the moment I see a way out, I'm running.

"Very well." Emery reaches up to pull down his visor and I notice that his hand is trembling. Not inspiring, terrifying in fact. "Follow me and whatever happens, keep moving and fire at anyone who gets in your way, don't think twice. Kill, do you understand me?"

"You heard him," Sergeant Shithouse yells. "Slaughter anything that's running towards you. And you know what that means don't you. If you turn back and run you'll be slaughtered too."

He sounds as if he hopes that some of us will turn back.

There are a few ragged cheers. I shake my head and heft the rifle into my arms and wonder if I could get away with shooting Emery and his sergeants.

As we begin our ridiculous advance, a ragged, close-packed mob, tripping and stumbling over the broken mist-shrouded earth, I curl my finger about the trigger and lift the barrel and feel my already racing heart step up a notch.

A few short seconds that's all it will take. A few bullets.

But now I'm confused, I can't tell who is who, we are spacemen, suited and anonymous as we shamble over the surface of this alien, alien planet. The figure ahead of me could be Sergeant Shithouse, but it could also be Diya or Baz.

Someone screams and gesticulates wildly at us to spread out and a few loyal souls do so. But I'm staying close to the others, struggling to keep them in sight.

The sun has only just appeared and the light is bad. The visor steams up. I raise it and wipe it time and time again and the action becomes a nervous tic.

It feels as if the ground is sloping upwards. My legs ache, my arms ache and my head pounds. I'm hungry and thirsty. And disorientated.

There's nothing ahead of us but destruction, I see a few ruins, piles of rubble rather than buildings, more fragments of road, even a broken tree or two. Now there's a car, on its side, all paint burned away and its metalwork rusted, another, this one still upright but tyres long-gone.

I think we're entering a village or small town of some sort. The ruins of London are positively pristine compared to this. Nothing is recognisable as a building. The only familiarities are the wrecked vehicles.

And bodies, burned corpses, solders, civilians? I can't tell. I see a lamp post, still upright, its glass lamp-cover miraculously intact, its base amputated by the mist.

Heartbeat fills my head. Perhaps I should run now, just dart off into the ruins and hide until the company or platoon or unit or whatever we are has passed by.

A gun rattles.

Startled I stop walking and freeze. I'm not the only one. Several others lurch to a halt and look round. Someone shouts, another rattle joins the first and then the grey is filled with sparks.

They stream out of the rubble, out of shell holes. They move impossibly fast and straight. And when they hit the figure to my left they cut straight through, tearing great gobs of uniform and flesh out of his or her back.

Now I understand.

I throw myself down and glimpse others doing the same.

I hear the bullets, cracking through the cold, smoky air just above my head. Only inches away, one move, one breath and they'll rip out my life. Shrieks and yells erupt. More firing. I move my head, see someone on their belly, firing back, must be one of the sergeants. I feel the rifle in my own hand but I can't move enough to do anything with it, so I lay there, smeared over the ground, teeth clenched, waiting.

A tearing sound breaks through the endless clattering and banging and ends in a deafening, ground-rocking explosion. I feel mud and bits of rubble pummel my back. Another explosion, another and suddenly the universe has been grabbed by its corners and shaken and nothing is stable or makes sense. Hammer blow after hammer blow rips through the ground and I cling on as though I'm about to be thrown off.

What light there is, is swallowed by dust-filled, black smoke.

It lasts forever and it lasts for a few seconds and when the final detonation fades away I realise that the gunfire has stopped

The shells were ours.

Figures clamber to their feet, others are encouraged with kicks and rifle butts.

Up, up, fucking up.

I have my pride, I don't want any of them anywhere near me, so I struggle to upright and stand, confused, blinded by smoke, coughing on dust.

The rubble ahead of us has been pounded even further to dust. There are a few half-hearted fires, feeding on what combustible materials actually remain in this desolation.

Two figures, laden with huge backpacks push past us. Hoses are connected to the packs, which I realise are actually tanks of some sort. Flame spills from the first of them and something burns on the ground. The other moves to a shell hole and pours more liquid fire into the crater. I smell roasting meat.

So this is why all the bodies I've seen have been charred and unrecognizable. The dead are burned.

Why?

Sanitary measures? Too many bodies to bury, too much risk of disease?

I hear another flamethrower roar, and this time a cry, brief, lost in the oily, searing blast.

Christ, they're burning the wounded.

Oh God, oh fuck, they're cremating living people.

No time to think or protest. We're moving on. The light has improved. The sun, bloody and weak, has left the horizon and is climbing laboriously into the grey.

It is going to be a crisp, clear winter day. The kind I like.

We move out of the village, down torn and splintered tarmac into the swirl of fog and billow of smoke.

A mile, an aching, stiff-gaited, endless mile.

One of my comrades-in-arms moves close and reaches out to take my hand.

Diya. She's still alive, thank God. I look around for Baz but can't tell which of the anonymous, shambling bulks he is. I remember the first man to fall. He had been close to me…Christ.

Ahead a soldier raises his hand then indicates for us to move off the road and get down. We do, messily, throwing ourselves onto the earth and resting, no attempt made at taking any sort of defensive position. The Sergeants move among us shouting, pushing and contorting bodies into some semblances of soldiery.

I pick up my rifle–

The world disappears.

A row of shells drop through us and cut the unit in half. I see figures picked up and hurled bloodily through the air. I see tumbling limbs and heads and torn lumps of flesh that spill guts.

I feel waves of heat and see sheets of flame.

And then, out of the smoke, other figures are running towards us. Help? Medics? They open fire, spit lines of sparks at us. I grab at Diya and as I do so her head explodes in a shower of helmet metal, bone and blood. I scramble away, shouting, making a noise. The attackers are close and I grab my rifle and squeeze the trigger and spit my own bullets back at them but my firing is wild and panic-stricken and they're too close and I have no idea if I actually hit anyone.

I grab at soil and rubble, crawling and gibbering. Bullets patter in the mud around me. The maggots had done that. The maggots Dominic catapulted into Chalk Lake. Patter patter patter, just as deadly, enticing the unthinking, instinct-driven fish into the killing zone.

Except we didn't kill them. We let them go.

Let *me* go, for fuck's sake leave me alone and let me go!

I get up onto my feet and realise I've dropped my rifle. I tear the gore-smeared helmet from my head so I can breathe and hurl it away and all around me human shapes are falling and running and screaming and frozen and helpless and another one has removed her helmet and is shouting at me.

Bald, small, female. Screaming shrieking and running towards me. She holds a rifle but doesn't fire.

"Traitor!" Laura screams. "EoD fucker!"

I swing round, breathe hard, hear my own mindless moans and gasps.

Laura stumbles to halt. Her armband is blue. Mine is green.

That means she's an enemy. I have to kill her. I've dropped my gun, where is it? Damn it, where did I put my gun?

Wait, wait. Think.

Laura was rounded up by the SSU like me, so how can she be EoD? And how can I? It doesn't make any sense and while the ground rocks and roars and bullets hurtle around us nothing can make sense.

Except the fact that we could be killed at any moment.

Panicked now, I stagger towards her. She backs away, waving the rifle dangerously in my direction. I shout, my voice lost in the apocalypse erupting around us. She steadies the weapon, its muzzle, a tiny black eye.

I stop. A stream of tracer whips past the back of my head. An explosion rips open the ground about twenty yards to my right.

Laura shakes her head, then the rifle is lowered and she drops it and in a moment she falls into my arms and we go down into the mud.

I can feel her crying and hear her shouting but the words are a strangled noise that comes out of her crying. I hold her as tightly as I can and she holds me and bullets patter and shells tear the earth and faint sounds of death and fear emerge from the hell.

And then it quietens and stops and all I can hear are moans and cries.

It takes years for me to find the will to raise my head.

Little has changed. The ground has been more deeply wounded, the air further choked with stink and smoke. Things burn, not much moves. There are bodies but they've become lumps to me, bundles of broken skin and bone, more nothing.

I sit up, rub my face. My ears are ringing, my hands shaking, my mouth full of dust

Fires flare, brief, stinking.

Soldiers emerge from the murk, laden with tanks and hoses. The stench is beyond anything I've ever known, worse even than the field hospital.

They burn everything, the dead and wounded.

And the deserters, no doubt, and the possum-players.

I shake Laura who seems to be frozen to the ground. She starts, protests incoherently.

Whoosh, stink, whoosh stink.

They're getting closer.

I tug at her, shake her, prod her until she groans and rolls over. I stare at her unable to believe she's here, with me, astounded that I recognised her and she me. Both of us anonymously bald and gaunt.

"We have to get out of here," I say and she responds at last, struggles up onto her hands and knees. I haul her to her feet.

A shout. "You, stop!"

There is smoke and we plunge into it and trip over bodies and almost fall headlong into a shell hole. Shots ring out. I force Laura down under me then press my face into her back. Two more shots, a bullet thuds into the ground a few inches from my right ear.

A shouted curse then the flamethrowers resume.

Getting closer.

One of our fellow corpses moans. Wounded, about to be burned. It's a woman, her abdomen a bloody ruin. I want to help her, but I can't. I can barely help myself and Laura.

We have to go now. I shake Laura again and she groans but I manage to get her moving. We crawl, and slither over the ground, over bodies and vitals and blood and slime. As the curt roars of the flamethrowers grow more distant we crawl and eventually I deem it safe to get to our feet

Laura cries out and falls against me. I feel something smeared over her side. I move my hand and see blood.

Blue on Green

I get her to the nearest shellhole and we huddle against its earthen wall. I still have my first aid kit and cut away the material of her uniform, field dressing at the ready. All I can see is blood, which seems to be pouring out of the wound. Just a flesh wound though, has to be, because she'd be unconscious or dead if it wasn't, wouldn't she? I don't know, I don't fucking know. My hands shake as I try to reveal her flesh.

There's a hole. Christ, a hole that's half the size of my fist. I see the edges of her skin, other red matter, all wet and bloody. I push the dressing against it but it seems too small and is soon sodden with blood. I tape it in place anyway, a clumsy, ineffectual job. I find Laura's kit and use that as well until I've just about filled the wound with dressings. There's a morphine ampoule. I jab it into her arm and hope for the best.

Laura calms, her breathing less tremulous.

"British…" she says.

"What?" I ask and my fear and panic makes me irritable.

"We…like…we're British, the army. You…you were with the EoD."

"No, no, you don't understand. It's the other way round. They lied to you Laura. *You* were with the enemy."

She looks at me, her eyes growing heavy. "We can't both…both be on the same side."

Can't we? Perhaps this whole thing is some sort of hoax, or game. A fucking big, gruesome game.

No, too outrageous, too terrible.

But then again, no one knows who they're fighting, we wear visors and hide our faces and all the bodies are burned.

The hospital…it wasn't burned. Propaganda. EoD atrocity.

"Did they show you a film?" I ask her. "Laura, Laura listen, wake up, did they show you a film about the hospital we found?"

"Mmm…yeah…hosp…film yeah."

I'm forgetting that she's hurt, badly. I'm getting worked up, excited almost.

"That's why the SSU separated everyone. They know. And the politicians. What about the high ranking officers and the MoD, do they all know? The fucking SSU choose me for one side and you for the other, like choosing a school football team. Christ's sake the whole war is being fought between soldiers from the same army. It *was* an RAF *Panther* that attacked our office. I knew it, I fucking knew it. Laura, maybe there isn't any EoD, maybe it's all a lie. I can't believe this. The whole thing is a set-up, a fucking conspiracy."

And has no one worked this out or do the drugs and subliminal propaganda close everyone's eyes?

I want to tell them, now. It can't wait. I get to my feet, claw at the walls, shouting.

"Stop! Stop fighting. For God's sake –"

Laura's hands are on my leg, tugging weakly. She's mumbling to me, pleading.

She's right. They won't listen. They'll kill us instead. I can't stop it on my own.

My son was going to die for this? My wife and family were killed by *our* side? Christ I can hardly bear to even think of it. And all the rest, murdered by our own armed forces, who are also murdering each other.

That's why we were given drugs to confuse us. Everyone stumbling round with no idea what they're doing, who they killed. No ordinary soldier would go out and kill other British soldiers.

Never.

My rage is beyond calculation, beyond comprehension. I want to kill. I want to tear someone apart with my hands. But there's no one, just Laura and me and the burned corpses with whom we share this shell hole.

So the bombing *is* systematic and the towers *are* a way of getting everyone under control. All in the same place, to make sure the government, or whoever the hell is calling the shots now, knows where we are. What about the people from outside the cities? All dead? Hiding in holes in the ground? Shipped in to the towers, in a sort of mirror image of the Cambodian killing fields?

We have to get help, find a voice, anything.

"I can't leave you," I say to Laura. "Not again, but we have to get to Orford. There are people there."

She doesn't answer. She's finally succumbed to the morphine. Okay, we'll rest now, travel at night. I wrap her in the lightweight sleeping bag I find in her back pack and then climb into my own. The kit and the bags are identical.

Laura is still alive when it finally grows dark. I hear her mutter and feel her struggling to sit up. I'm stiff, wet and shivering and curled around her, holding her tightly.

"Pete…"

"I'm here."

"Oh Jesus…"

"Does it hurt?" A stupid question but I have to know.

"No."

She's lying but I convince myself she isn't. She gives out a quiet hiss of pain as I release her. In the brief light of a nearby explosion that sends shockwaves rippling through the earth, I see that there's more blood on her uniform. The dressings are a useless mass of gore.

But she is still alive.

I touch her, gentle, hesitant dabs at her with my huge, filthy hands. I don't know what to do, how to help her. She moans softly. I hold her hand and stroke her hair. Another detonation and I see her look up at me, a painful drag of her head. She smiles weakly. Her face is white. As gently as I can, I heft her into my arms and pick her up and hold her tight against myself and carry her.

Numb, exhausted I head north-east. I have a little food, standard rations that are not going to last long and are probably laced with some sort of narcotic. My water bottle is already half empty. Laura's is still full but we must ration our supply as carefully as we can.

The night is far from dark. Explosions beat at me, the closest only two hundred yards away. Flares sparkle in the sky. I glimpse figures, soldiers, hunched and silhouetted in the glare. None close and none paying us any heed whatsoever.

Guns rattle and I freeze. I see tracer, arcing out of a row of shell holes way off to my left. The stream of lethal sparks race off into whatever no man's land lays beyond the position.

The ground is dangerously war-ploughed. I trip and stumble over the churned earth and debris. There are shell holes everywhere, some filled with murky, stinking water, death traps because falling into one of those would be the end.

My body burns with pain. My head spins. Laura is now an impossible weight in my arms. I groan and mutter to myself as I fight my way through the endless hell. There is no escape from this fucking place, every inch, every foot, every mile is exactly the same. I can't go on much further. I'm on the verge of collapse. The dark and light flicker around me, the noise beats down the walls of my mind. I want it to stop.

A little further, a little further. A few more steps, that's all, come on, keep walking. Another step, another…

There's something large and hulking ahead. It draws me, pulls me into its black, incomprehensible shadows and geometries. The thing is rectangular, sitting at an odd, careless sort of angle. When I'm almost there a violent flare of light shows it to be an armoured vehicle of some sort, a troop carrier perhaps, about the size of a big white van, like a Transit. I gently lay Laura down on the wet, cold ground and hear her cry out in pain.

Good sign, it means she's still breathing, still with me.

The back door is open and the slow, irregular stroboscopic illumination of the war lights up the corpses draped over its metal floor, one hangs out, arms akimbo. No one has had to time to burn this little pocket of evidence. I grab at a limb and pull. The corpse is stiff, dried almost. I jump aside as it spills onto the mud. Mouth tight shut, stomach heaving I clamber inside and get to work on the others. There are three more to dispose of. The work is hard, the bodies heavy and awkward. They stink, they are messy. I manage not to be sick this time.

When the truck is empty I turn my attention to Laura. When I wrestle her up onto her feet she screams. I shuffle her back and sit her on the edge of the van then as gently as I am able fold her inside. She shivers and moans. I pull a sleeping bag up and around her, try to give her some water, most of which dribbles down her chin, then I lay down with her and hold her tight until she calms and the trembling stops.

Outside again, I forage through the dead soldiers' back packs and find water bottles and some rations. The water is probably tepid, the food bad. But it's better than nothing.

Back inside I talk to Laura for a while. I tell her about Ruth. I tell her how I met her, when I visited her school as part of a campaign to scare kids out of getting themselves into trouble with the law. I'd volunteered for the scheme as part of the deal I made to avoid prison. I'd given this talk scores of times by now, but I was always terrified, a shaking, nervous wreck suddenly pushed to the front of the stage in the huge hall of an Acton Comprehensive, confronted by a horde of near-rioting teenagers. I was accompanied onto the stage by a stunning blonde teacher with a wonderful, heart-melting smile. After introducing herself to me as Ruth Hambling, she turned her attention to the mob. Within seconds they were quiet and calm and to this day I don't know how she did it because she barely raised her voice above normal volume. Then she introduced me as…

"Mister Peter Allman, here today to tell you of his experiences with the police and why he doesn't want any of you, yes, that includes you Michael Warren, all right? Finished being a five year old yet? Good. Why he doesn't want any of you to make the bad mistakes *he* made as a young man. Thank you Mister Allman, over to you."

She touched my arm, the lightest contact, barely felt through the sleeve of my jacket and denim shirt, but electric nonetheless.

I started, as I always started, with a poem.

Jaws dropped, frowns appeared. I was supposed to be the big bad guy, the drug-sodden, violent thug who had been arrested more times than most of them had been to the local corner shop, and here I was spouting poetry.

It was Ted Hughes' *A Motorbike*. Nothing to do with drugs or thuggery, but the poem I felt had changed my life.

"I was in deep shi…deep trouble. I was angry all the time, and one night I got so drunk I didn't know where I was anymore. There was a bad fight in a pub and after beating some poor idiot unconscious, I started on one of the police constables who came to break it up. I ended up in a remand centre and….Well, I'm claustrophobic, see, so being shut in a cell is the nearest thing to Hell for me. There was no booze, there were no drugs, and without those to prop me up I thought I was going to go insane. If it wasn't for the prison counsellor, a little bloke with a comb-over." Giggles. "I would have done."

They were listening, reasonably attentive. I kidded myself that it was my charismatic personality that had them in its thrall. The real reason was probably the presence of the lovely, but uaccountably fearsome, Miss Hambling, sitting behind me on the stage.

"Mister Comb-Over loved books and one day he quoted that poem at me because he found out that I liked motorbikes. He gave me the book." I held it up, a tatty old paperback. "It's called *Moortown* and that was the start. I would bury my head in it at night when I was locked in and it helped me forget that I was trapped in a little brick coffin. I began to read more, poetry, and novels. Science fiction, ghost stories, thrillers, it doesn't matter, books are books and that means that they're good. Reading made me see that my horrible little world wasn't the only one there was. Okay, it didn't change me overnight. I was still angry, but I didn't want to be angry anymore. Reading calmed me down, made me think. And that's something I'd never done before. I just did what I *felt* all the time. If I was angry I'd take it out on someone else. If I was depressed I'd smoke something or sniff something or get rat-arsed. I was lucky, that little bloke with the comb-over saw something in me that no one else did, so I made an effort to behave and work as hard as I could and educate myself, I even learned how to use and repair computers, and in return, he made it his business to speak up for me when I finally went to court. I ended up with a suspended sentence. Like I said. I was lucky. It's better not to get into a mess in the first place. It isn't fun, or big, it's shit. It's miserable and frightening. And you know the best way to keep out that sort of mess? Education, listening to people like Mrs Hambling here…"

When I was done and the entire audience was converted to the Pete Allman Way of Living, Ruth Hambling ordered a round of applause for me. By the time she took my arm and led me off stage, I was in love.

We had strong black coffee in the staffroom and sat down and talked for a long time. I can't remember what we talked about, only that she was from a stable, happy family and I was from a messed up, violent tribe. She wanted to give something back and so did I, though our reasons were different. Hers was because she felt that she had lived a privileged life, me because I'd been given a second chance.

It was time for Ruth to return to her class.

I got up to leave. We said an awkward goodbye and shook hands. I went to the door, hesitated, mumbled another goodbye and she said thanks again. Out in the corridor, I stopped sighed then set off towards the exit. I heard a door open and shut behind me and I turned round to see Ruth walking quickly in the opposite direction. She had a bundle of books under her arm.

"Excuse me," I shouted.

No, no you idiot, get out, go, now –

She stopped and turned and because I was too far away to talk to her properly I had to walk back. The walk took a thousand years. She watched and I was sure she was laughing at me. Eventually I was close enough. My mouth worked. Nothing came out.

"Uh," someone croaked, the sound like the opening of a rusty door. "Um…Would you like to…you know, to come out for a drink, tonight. I mean if you can't…"

She smiled then said "Yes, that would be nice. Can you pick me up from my flat? Can we go out on your motorbike…"

"On my motorbike," I say and chuckle and the chuckle almost becomes a sob. "A schoolteacher who wanted to go out on a first date riding pillion with a long-haired maniac." I pause. "How can you not love someone like that? And I did love her, like crazy and I still do. I want her back Laura. I wish she'd come back for me."

I pause "But why should she? I didn't go back for her." I kiss Laura's head. "I won't leave you," I say over and over again. "We stay together Laura, I'll never leave you." She's cold. I hug her more tightly and try to keep her warm.

Later I unfold myself and clamber over the seats into the front of the truck. Thankfully they are unoccupied. The key is in the ignition. I rattle the huge gear stick into what I assume is neutral and, resigned to failure, twist the key.

The lights flick on; diesel heating coil, ignition and oil.

Too easy.

I crank the key over and something groans under the stub-nosed bonnet. The groan ends in silence. I try again, another groan, a bit more lively this time. Shaking now, my hope a form of panic I try again and again. The groans become a whine. It won't bloody fire. And the battery is going to die before long. I feel around and find a light switch. The headlights flare into life, their beam directed downwards by some form of damper. The dash lights up and I see that the tank is about half full. I switch off the lights again. A moment, then I twist the key once more. The engine groans over and over and over. I don't let up this time. The groan starts to fade. Come on, come on come on…

It coughs, judders then dies.

Christ. It almost caught.

I wait a moment until I have the strength of mind to do it again. Then twist the key. Another long wait and it coughs. The engine mutters, jerks, then seems to find its rhythm and suddenly it's running.

For a moment I simply sit there listening, breathing hard. A vehicle I have a vehicle!

Now to get it out of this hole.

I crunch the gear into what I think is reverse, work the clutch and throttle and feel it shift forwards. I ram on the brake and wrench it into neutral. Wrong way. I try again, the gears protest. Clutch, accelerator, and movement.

Reversing.

I hear the big, balloon wheels whine against the mud. I pump the accelerator, the vehicle rocks and roars so loudly I'm sure every soldier in the area must be converging on us.

Something bites, the vehicle hauls itself backwards, mud flies, wheels spin but we're moving and the world straightens and we're on level-ish ground. I switch on the lights, catch my breath again then check my compass by the dashboard glow and we're off, bouncing and lurching over the broken landscape with me steering wildly to avoid shell holes and wreckage, immediately exhausted but too exhilarated to care.

"We're on our way," I shout to Laura. "Glory, glory, glory!"

I launch into a strangled version of *Blue Mink's* "Listen to the Band". I sing loud and with a sort of desperation that borders on the crazed babbling of a madman.

I stop when I'm too tired to drive another yard and the darkness is turning dawn-grey. I sit, motionless and sweat-drenched for a long while, still unable to believe our luck. I check the fuel gauge. Under half full but still enough for many more miles yet. We're parked in the lee of a huge pile of earth, displaced I suppose by some immense explosion. It's about as near to a hiding place as I can manage.

The sound of war seems distant now and I dare to hope that we've drawn away from the battle front. Not that we're safe here. Nowhere is safe anymore, not even home and hearth.

I lean back.

"Laura?"

No answer.

She's still sleeping then. I should let her rest. I pull some food from my ration pack and force it down my throat, wash the remains away with a swig of water. One swig, no more.

Stiff and knotted up I open the door and climb out for some exercise before I sleep. The world is almost silent, the light growing brighter, the war now a drum beat of muted thuds and rattles. The ruin stretches out in front of me, mist softened, cold and so utterly bleak. I can see no end to it.

I walk round to the back of the truck and open the door. Laura is still curled tight in her sleeping bag. I sit on the back, reach in to stroke her forehead.

She is cold.

And it is a total, devastating coldness.

I whisper her name and when she doesn't answer I realise that she has been dead for a long time.

I gather her up to myself and hold her, tight but I don't cry. I have known her only for a few days, but it seems like a lifetime and the loss of her rips deep into my soul.

Yet I can't cry.

There's a spade in the back of the truck. Snow begins to fall as I plunge it into the mud. The blade hits something hard. Tarmac I suppose. A fragment of road. I move away then try again and again until the blade bites into what I hope is soil. I will bury her. I have been unable to bury anyone else but I will bury Laura. And by burying her I will bury Ruth and Dominic, Amanda and Rachel. I'll bury Dave and Diya and probably Baz-on-Bass. I'll bury my work colleagues, Hendy, Frances, Katie, Jamie and Andy. I'll even bury Gary Marshall who shot my son but was trying to help us.

I whisper their names as I dig.

The horizon flickers with war, the ground thrums. No doubt there are soldiers all around me. I'm in uniform. If they find me they'll kill me because there are no sides, only bands of brothers ordered to fight other bands of brothers. It is all a lie, a deceit, a horror of unimaginable depth and vileness. Why? Why the fuck would a Country destroy itself? And why doesn't anyone else step in? The Americans, the EU, any-fucking-one?

Or are they all doing the same to themselves?

I ask the question as I work. I ask Laura, I shout and rant at her and plead for her to give me an answer but she lies there, wrapped in her army-issue sleeping bag, staring up at the clouds. I ask Ruth who is standing on the other side of the grave, next to Diya, and Dominic and Amanda and Rachel who are arm in arm, afraid and close. No one speaks to me. There are others, behind and around them, I see Andy, smoking. I reach towards him for a turn on his cigarette but it is shadow and light, it is explosion, flare and shadow-dance.

Again and again I drive the spade down, my arms and shoulders ache, the impacts jar into my elbows and wrist. The ground is too hard. I slice and lever and cannot get down far enough.

"She has to be safe," I explain to Ruth, who nods. Who is quiet and beautiful, and watching me as I work. "She has to be deep you see, because there are rats, and probably dogs. Dominic, give me hand, yeah?"

He nods as well, but doesn't move. I ram the spade at the ground until the implement falls from my hands and I drop to my knees utterly exhausted.

I can't even dig a fucking grave.

After a while, shivering, I get up, cross to Laura and heft her up into my arms for one last time.

"It' okay," I say to her. "No one will find you, you'll be safe."

She smiles up at me. "I know, thanks Pete."

I stumble to the shallow dent I've made in the earth, tripping as I do so and spilling her into her bed. I rearrange her then I push soil and snow back into the grave. Soil covers her face and her smile and smothers her last words to me. I panic and scrub the soil away. But her face is cold and still and her eyes stare and there is nothing but flesh.

Afterwards, I sit by the mound I've made over her. The others are still here. They are dancing, a slow waltz. Andy is dancing with Ruth but I don't mind because he has more right to her than I do.

I think I can hear the music, an orchestra, slow and sweet.

I hum the tune and smile and watch them until the watery sunlight shatters them into a swirl of snow.

I head east, looking for the sea. I'm not sure where I am in relation to the coast but it feels as if it is time to turn that way. The truck bumps through the snow and over untold and unthinkable obstacles. When the snow thins out I see four huge columns of thick black smoke on the horizon to my left. I see aircraft as distant specks. I see soldiers, marching as to war. The snow here is littered with burned remains. The landscape is as desolate as it has been since I – we, Laura was with me then – entered this place.

I can't understand time anymore. Flame, smoke and snow are all I know. The truck has become a cocoon, the extent of my universe, everything else is observed but not felt.

Until the explosion.

It wrenches my reality apart and lifts the right hand side of the truck off the ground before releasing it to crash down again. Everything is wrong. I'm covered with glass, I'm bleeding, my ears roar. The engine is screaming but the wheels won't turn. Things patter against the vehicle's metal hide. Bullets.

Fuck me, *bullets*.

I batter at the door, barging and struggling, but it won't budge. I crawl across to the other side. The passenger door gives. Another volley rattles against the vehicle's armour plating, more glass waterfalls inwards and over my head and back.

I wait. The soldiers will be coming now.

Make it quick you bastards, come on, one shot to the head…

I wait.

Nothing.

I look up, cautiously, peeping over the edge of the door and out into the freezing air. I see grey, smoke, explosions, all further off. I think I can see bodies sprawled in the snow, a red splash on the white.

Grabbing my backpack I push open the door and slither out and onto the ground. Another wait. No bullets, or shouts. Just the thud and crash of a battle, close but not close enough to swallow me, it seems. The destruction of the truck was just an act of wanton violence then. It moves, so shoot it.

I get up into a crouch then stand.

No one is interested.

It rains, a messy, sleety rain that seems to ooze from the sky rather than fall. I'm cold and wet. But I will not stop. The light fades and it's night again out here in Armageddon.

I walk because I can't do anything else.

The sea is a storm-whipped desolation every bit as awful as the one I have just crossed. I stand on a cliff, topped with snow-smothered heathland. The beach below is mostly pebble. I can see no ships, no soldiers, nothing. To my right is a white-grey dome. Smoke or steams issue forth and I understand from my map that I'm looking at Sizewell power station. This then is Dunwich, or Dunwich Heath, as there is no sign of a village. There is a lonely white house on the cliffs, deserted and relatively undamaged.

The power station doesn't appear to be damaged either.

It makes perfect sense of course. This isn't a real war and we need electricity.

Looking north I can see Southwold Lighthouse

The whole area seems to be untouched by the destruction.

Orford is not too far from here, a day's walk, perhaps less. But I'm too tired to attempt it now so I go to the white house and find one of the doors open. I enter what looks as if it was once a café. There is a counter and display cases, some containing a green fluffy slime that was once food. There's a sink, chairs and tables, many of which are host to more rotting muck.

It's as if the place was abandoned with *Marie Celeste* suddenness.

I have a vision of SSU, bursting in, shouting and bullying, of all these diners and brisk-walk sea-siders rounded up and taken to the towers. For their own good, no doubt, for their own safety. How did the SSU get them all into the lorries? A threat of imminent air raid? A nuclear attack due in eight minutes? Or was it rifle butts, bayonets and cattle wagons?

I find the stairs, go up and discover a bedroom, somehow bland and characterless. The duvet is dank and mouldy but it is soft and I lay down on top of it. There is a bedside cabinet, home to an alarm clock, long stopped and a damp-swollen paperback edition of *Interview with a Vampire* by Anne Rice.

I close my eyes and Ruth whispers poison into my ear. I wake with a shout and realise that there really are voices in this house.

Edge of the World

The voices are gruff, barked orders, mingled with the sounds of equipment, the rustle of uniforms. Boots crunch over the floor. I slither out of the bed and under it. Stupid place to hide, I know, down here with the dust and grit, because I've trapped myself. I draw back as far as I can go and immediately feel claustrophobic.

Footsteps on the stairs now, loud, louder. A shout from the bottom.

"Get a move on!"

Muttered swearing then the door opens and all I see are the boots. The boots come towards me. Light flares briefly and I smell tobacco smoke. My craving is suddenly so strong I almost crawl out to beg a drag on the soldier's cigarette, just one drag, one lungful and then he can do what he wants.

I stare at the bastard's feet. What is he, blue or green? Does he know?

The bed creaks as he sits down and suddenly it's a scene from a farce, the lover under the bed, the big fat husband taking his ease, pushing the springs down onto the hapless lothario.

Except there is no wife in this farce.

You took her you cunts. You murdered her…

I shiver, with fear, with rage. I'll kill him. I'll beat and claw at him with my bare hands and my teeth. I'll have his flesh and his blood and he can feel my pain for a short, short while and then *his* loved ones can weep for the rest of their fucking lives.

But he's Dominic isn't he, he's Dave before the war took away his sight, he's Gary Marshall before his arm was torn out of its socket.

He's a nobody and an everybody. Trembling I let the madness subside. I'm breathing hard, my chest wheezing. He must be able to hear me so why doesn't he get on with it?

He coughs and there's something wrong with his breathing. It's irregular, a near gasp. Then I realise he's crying. He sounds young, a lad, eighteen perhaps? The poor little bugger is broken into pieces.

His rifle clatters onto the floor, startling me. A moment later, he's on his feet, turning and crouching down to pick it up and about to look under the bed. Without thinking, without knowing why, I grab the weapon. His face appears. Our eyes lock, his red-rimmed and wet.

"Ssssh," I say, the rifle aimed at his forehead.

He's on his hands and knees, armband visible. Green. On my side then.

"It's okay mate." I try to keep my voice gentle, reassuring, as I bring my arm out to where he can see it and point at my own armband. "I'm with you."

"Fucking deserter," he mutters, but doesn't do anything about it.

"Yeah," I answer. "I couldn't take anymore."

I see him swallow and for a moment I almost laugh at how ludicrous this situation is, me under the bed, the boy-soldier peering in at me.

"And nor can you from the look of you son," I say.

The soldier shakes his head, wet, red-rimmed eyes wide.

"You finished yet?" Yelled from downstairs. I can almost see the NCOs anger-mottled face, the corded neck.

"Almost Sarge!" He makes no move however.

"You'd better go," I say. "But before you do, listen to me. This war, this hell they are putting you through, it's a fake, it's not real. You're fighting your own mates, do you understand me? There *is* no EoD. You probably think I'm talking shit but it's true, okay? Absolutely fucking true and if you keep your eyes open and your brain clear you'll see that I'm right and that it has to stop."

The soldier doesn't answer but seems frozen, breathing hard, on the verge of collapse. Carefully, carefully, I turn the rifle round and hold it out to him.

"Mirza! Fucking get down here. Now!"

Private Mirza grabs the rifle by its stock, pauses for a moment, then scrambles up onto his feet and hurries to the door. He rattles downstairs and there's more shouting, door slamming and stomping around. I wait, tense, trying to resign myself to the inevitable.

"There's a deserter upstairs Sarge, out of his skull and hiding under the bed."

A century later the voices move outside and, eventually, all I can hear is my own heartbeat and the sea.

I almost spend the rest of the night under the bed. I'm afraid to come out. It's the silence of the house. I've spent too long shivering through the darkness in shell holes and ruins, the rumble of war my lullaby. There are too many ghosts as well, too many whisperers and accusers.

But I can't stay here. The bed is a coffin lid. The old claustrophobia returns and it's almost a friend now, a link to the cowering thing locked inside me that is *me*... So I drag myself out and curl, dog-like on the duvet and wait for my family and my friends to step out of the shadows.

The snow has turned to slush, the air drenched with fine, unrelenting rain. I walk slowly along the shore, heading south now. The shingle crunches under my feet, which are blistered and numb. The sea thrashes at the beach, reaching and retreating, reaching and retreating. I can almost feel its frustration, its need to break away from the forces that bind it and smother the dry land that offends it so. My hands are deep in my pockets, my right one curled tight about the memory stick.

I pass the power station, an oppressive and inscrutable complexity of concrete and steel. I'm visible to anyone who might be looking. There's nothing I can do about it. But no one calls out, there are no shots. Something hums from deep inside the power station's heart; got to keep those kettles boiling, got to keep those televisions on and the masses numb.

Then once more I'm trudging along empty beach, bordered by heathland then marsh. This is a beautifully bleak and lonely place. If only I had known about it before. Ruth would have fallen in love with its isolation and rawness. I would have held her here, on this beach and drawn warmth and strength from her and kissed her and become high on the heat of her sweet, sweet breath.

I reach another village, intact but deserted, brooded over by a bizarre house built on a wooden pillar. The village reaches down to the beach, none of its houses new, and all following a similar black-and-white colour-scheme. There is something artificial about it despite its established, elderly clothing.

Thorpeness, according to my map.

There are no shell holes, no burned ruins. The place has that same *Mary Celeste* feel I experienced in the white house on the cliff, as if, at some predetermined moment every living soul was snatched away. Isn't there some prophecy in the bible about people being swept up to heaven in the "twinkling of an eye"?

There are cars, but I leave them alone. No one drives around here anymore. A vehicle would arouse suspicion.

A couple of miles further on I find Aldeburgh. Another quaint little seaside town, a place of ancient buildings and fishing boats, now turned into mouldering emptiness by the war. Oppressed by the sheer loneliness of this place, by the blank corpse stares of windows and death-rictus of forced open doors, I pass through as quickly as I can but find my way blocked by a river which forces me to turn inland.

Orford is yet another dead body. There is a castle, or the remains of one, because it consists of a single, flint tower. There are more picturesque houses and more slush-greyed desolation. The village ends at a river which separates Orford Ness from the mainland. Beyond the Ness is the North Sea, against which the Friends, if they are still over there, have their backs.

The Ness looks uninviting and deserted, more giant shingle bank than landmass. It's dotted with concrete blockhouses, grey stained and long-disused. There are other strange structures that resemble concrete pagodas. There was some sort of establishment over there once, government, military? I'm not sure. And neither do I care, just as long as they're not still in residence.

It's late. The light, which has not been good all day, is deteriorating fast. If I'm going to cross to the island then I have to do it now or spend yet another night alone and try in the morning. No, I can't do that. Never again. I'm going.

There are boats pulled up onto the muddy shoreline and I move among them, trying to choose something suitable, knowing nothing at all about rowing or sailing. Most of them look as if they are beginning to rot from neglect. Some have engines, one or two, masts and sails, alien, intimidating machines that mean little to me. The first wave of panic sweeps in. I have to cross the water, I have to make a choice.

Then I see a rowing boat, tossed onto the shore and abandoned, its paint and varnish flaking. I struggle over the mud to take a better look. There are oars, Christ, a complete kit. There is also a pool of filthy, stagnant water in its belly.

I can't help that. This has to be the one, small, uncomplicated with no engine or sail. I grab hold of its nose/bow/prow, and pull. Nothing, the craft is jammed solidly into the mud. Shit, hell. I try again, this time driven by desperation. I pull and rock at it and slowly, slowly it begins to slide over the murky, adhesive slope towards the water.

Seagulls mock me and other, smaller birds chirp out their derision. Perhaps they're right. They're the winners after all, no more humans, no more filth and noise and clatter, only the river and the sky.

I stumble into the water and almost fall. It quickly penetrates my boots and trousers and it is agony, cold, broken glass on flesh, knives. But the boat is afloat, and it *is* floating, not sinking. I haul myself aboard, an ungainly scramble that sets up a precarious rocking and bobbing. I settle onto the dank, sodden bench and struggle the oars into the rowlocks.

A breath, a moment then I pull on the oars and feel the boat crawl over the river and know that I am going to reach that bloody Ness or die trying. I haven't eaten, I'm weak, but something bubbles from deep down, some strength. A final burst of energy.

I've rowed on boating lakes on sunny Sunday afternoons with Ruth, and the children when they were small. I've punted down the Cam on a lazy Bank Holiday Monday. But this is real. The work is quickly back-breaking, the oars cumbersome. My right arm's greater strength causes the boat to veer right or to starboard or whatever it is. I can't see my destination, only the shore that I've just left.

The water is choppy, grey and cold. There is a current that tries to drag me away from the village and the Ness. I correct my course but it takes a tremendous effort. The distance is much greater than it looked when I first stumbled down onto the muddy shoreline.

My arms and shoulder soon ache, my hands are sore. I'm weak from hunger, exhausted from my trek. But I pull, over and over again. Bobbing and bouncing over the river. Occasionally looking over my shoulder to make sure I am actually heading for the island and to see how much progress I'm making.

None.

That's what it seems like anyway. Yet the Orford shore is pulling away from me, the gap is widening.

I see a figure.

There, scrambling down towards the river then merging with the shadows, then gone.

Imagination. One of my ghosts.

My feet are wet. I look down and the last shreds of light show me that the boat is leaking. I pull harder, I strain and swear and haul. The boat is getting heavier, lower in the water. It would be funny if it wasn't winter and night and dark and oh so cold. I haul and drag and my body is aching and I'm scared.

The far shore finally disappears into night black and there are no lights.

I look behind me, the island is a dark mass, closer, yes, but not close enough. I want to stop, I'm cold, wet and miserable. But I keep on. Driven. The ghosts are back, walking alongside the boat. How can they do that, how can they walk on the water? I mutter to them, ask for help. Please help me, please…They whisper, their voices watery. It starts to rain.

And then I can't row anymore. The boat seems to drop away under me. My legs and feet are numb, there is water everywhere. Don't stop, not now, come on you bastard. Come on.

I heave at the oars, my back straining, they bite, the boat moves. I haul again and again. I grunt with each stroke, swear and curse and feel my muscles tearing and the blood pound through my skull. I stop for a moment and retrieve the memory stick and drop it into my chest pocket. Safe. My purpose, and the reason I start rowing again, the reason I drag at the oars and grind my teeth and pull.

Small movements, the boat, rocks and dips to my right, what's that, starboard? Yeah, starboard. A starboard list cap'n. If it goes over I'm fucked.

Another pull, the oar drags through the syrupy, near solid mass of the river. Another, another. The list gets worse. Water laps at my shins. And I shiver with a cold I've never experienced before.

The boat drops way from me. The sensation bizarre. It drops and there's nothing but water.

I rear up onto my feet and scramble about, panicked, shouting for help even though there is no one anywhere to help me. I feel myself falling and by instinct step out of the sinking boat, the *sunken* boat. My boot slams into solidity, muddy, murky but solidity. I waver, almost fall again but stay upright. I turn, and see I'm only a few yards off the shore. I force myself towards it, the cold stealing my breath, staggering and almost falling, which I mustn't do because the stick is on my pocket and it has to stay dry.

The water shallows, there seems more land than river. I finally let myself fall forwards and land heavily on my hands and knees on wet shingle. My boots are still in the river but I'm here. I'm here, I'm here!

"Don't move, don't fucking move an inch okay?"

I look up to see figures, dark against the dark. They have guns, everyone has fucking guns.

Light, a torch, flashes quickly over me, into my face where it blinds me

"Soldier," someone snaps.

"You alone?" A woman this time but till brusque.

I nod, manage a yes.

"What do you want?"

"Got some…got something."

I make to reach into my pocket.

"Keep still. I'll get it."

The woman moves close. Her clothes are bulky, taking away any shape or form.

"In my chest pocket," I say. "From Gary."

"Who?" the man asks.

"Marshall. Gary Marshall."

I feel their shock. Then a hand gropes into the pocket and the woman draws out the memory stick. They have it, at last they have it. I let my arms give way and collapse down onto the beach.

"What the hell is it?" the woman says.

"Memo –"

"I know that but what's on it? Why have you brought it?"

"Gary… Mason." I can't think or speak. "Death List…SSU."

"Jesus."

More of them appear. There are hands and help. I'm lifted, carried, hauled over the shingle and I let them take me. I make no effort, offer no help. My feet drag through the stones.

Hours, or perhaps only a few minutes later, I'm lying on a table, half blinded by harsh lighting. I see wires looped messily over a concrete ceiling. The air is cold but not as cold as it was outside. I'm wrapped in the same type of army-style foil blanket Laura and I salvaged from the death hospital. The people around all wear uniforms and for a moment I'm afraid. But then I see how worn and tattered and faded their uniforms are, how much-repaired and improvised. Some are augmented by items of civilian clothing, sweaters, jackets and coats. Mixed, muddled and warm.

"Here, drink this," It's the woman from the beach. She's tall and slender with long salt-and-pepper hair. There's a scar running diagonally across her angular, high-cheekboned face. There is some compassion in her eyes, but her mouth is set hard, jaw clenched, angry.

I sit up and take the mug she's offered. It has a zodiac sign on the side of it, Aries the Ram. The drink is tea, hot and strong and laced with so much sugar it's almost syrup.

"How did you find your way here?" The woman asked.

"Walked."

"From where?"

"London."

"How do you know Gary?"

"Dave, Dave Miller."

No response.

"He's a veteran, my best mate. Gary was with him." I tell them, as much as I can, sketchily and haltingly. I'm tired, but aware that I'm a stranger on their shore and owe them this.

"So you're telling me that you managed to get out of London and find your way here, on foot."

I nod and drink and wait.

"Do you know who we are?"

"Friends. That's what Gary called you."

The woman nods, seems to consider this, then says; "We've checked your stick. There is a list of names and we do recognise some of them. Gary sent us a message a week or so ago, he told us there was a death list, that Veterans were being murdered. We haven't heard from, him since."

I don't tell them why, because my presence at his death will need a lot of explanation.

"Look, I'm Rainer, Captain Rainer, not that that matters much anymore. Everyone here is either a deserter, a veteran who managed to escape, or people like you who got out of the cities and made it across the war zone in one piece. There are not many of those."

No, I wouldn't imagine that there are.

"This isn't the only refuge, but none of us are allowed to know where the other ones are, security."

"*Who* doesn't allow you to know?" I ask as I sip tea and draw warmth from the Aries the Ram mug.

Rainer smiles and it is an attractive smile. "*We* have friends. Friends of Friends. Where do you think the diesel for our generators comes from and our food and clothes? Look, we're the people who understand what is going on, and who don't want to fight anymore because of it. Our organisation was founded by a high ranking officer who deserted and took a Company with him. They came here and set up this refuge. Once it began to grow, splinter groups were sent out to establish more of them. The Colonel has *links*, allies in high places, people who feel the same way as us and are prepared to cover for us, and arrange supplies and support. They also spread the word about the refuges. Nothing specific, we're a rumour you see, a legend. Not many people have the courage or will to find out if it's more than that, but those who do are always the strong and capable and, as such, welcome. Survival of the fittest, Darwin rules okay."

"What is this war?" I ask. "Why is it happening?"

Rainer shrugs. "Good for business, good for a government who want to regain control of their Country. What better way to repair a broken society than give them a purpose and an enemy. The Nazis had the Jews to persecute, we've got the EoD."

I finish the tea.

"You can stay here if you want. We're the rats in the sewers. It's a hard life. We grow our own food, go out on raiding parties, get killed regularly. But that's our life. We run it on military lines, early to bed, early to rise. It gives us some sort of structure and purpose."

I nod. Yeah, I'll stay with them.

"The law here is hard too. Anyone steps out of line and they end in the North Sea."

"Can't we tell the truth?" I say. "Use your *friends* to spread the word."

She stares at me. "The majority are not fighting against the war. The majority are not taking to the streets or shouting. Is that because they want it, because war gives the people a purpose as well?"

"The subliminal messages –"

"Oh that works to a point Pete, but not everyone is susceptible. I don't think anyone actually wants to know the truth."

Rainer leaves me and I lay down again. The table isn't exactly the height of luxury, but it's a bed and I'm warm and I don't have to move or think anymore. My journey is over. I've only just met these people but already I feel as though my fate is tangled with theirs.

I think I sleep because suddenly I hear a voice, female, Ruth…I open my eyes and I'm confused, there *is* a woman leaning over me, talking to me. Captain Rainer

"…need to show you something afterwards."

I sit up, bleary-eyed and disorientated.

"After what?" I ask her. My mouth is dry, my head aches dully.

"Food, my God you really were asleep. It's supper time."

Hungry, I follow her through a series of corridors, all with concrete walls, low ceilings and illuminated by temporary lighting strung up on lethal-looking wiring. I get the feeling we're under ground and have to fight that old claustrophobia as I struggle to match Rainer's energetic, brisk stride. After a dozen identical turnings and junctions and a set of rusting, clanging metal stairs, we arrive in an open area that serves as a mess hall. There are probably about two hundred people in here, men and women, but no children, all dressed in various combinations of uniform and civvies.

I'm welcomed, my hand shaken.

We sit at long tables, perched on institutional plastic chairs and eat some sort of broth, heavy with vegetables and meat. After that there's a huge wedge of apple pie and a gallon of custard, washed down with copious mugs of tea and coffee. My shrunken stomach protests under the assault but I'm too hungry to care and I keep shovelling it in until I start to feel sick.

When it's done people wander through into another cave-like communal area adjacent to the mess.

Something doesn't feel right. I'm uneasy, sensing layers of motive and agenda. Everyone here seems friendly enough, scarred and battered and grim maybe, but they make me feel welcome, and God help me, I can't resist that after what I've been through.

But...

We settle down in an assortment of battered old armchairs and sofas, probably looted from the abandoned houses across the river in Orford village. Cards appear, a few dog-eared paperbacks are opened and cigarettes ignited. Someone produces some cans of beer. One of them is handed to me and I hold it for several minutes before pulling at the ring tab and putting it to my lips.

So good. Everything so bloody good.

I'm invited into a game, poker, played for cigarettes which are shared out at the beginning of the session. There's banter, friendly squabbles and a lot of laughter, skin deep though, the scars on the faces around me mask the real wounds, and I sense that they are far too deep to be healed by a simple dose of late-night camaraderie.

No one asks me any awkward questions. I'm offered a job helping tend the vegetable garden, which is hidden on the sea-ward side of the Ness. That sounds fine to me, fresh air, mindless labour. Someone gives me a potted history of the place. It was a weapons testing station, established during the First World War, sensibly placed by the sea, as close to Germany as it's possible to be then finally decommissioned and closed down in the early 1970s. A radio station operated on the island until this war started. There were also experiments in over-the-horizon radar carried out from here. The National Trust eventually bought it and preserved the place as it was on the day it was closed down. The National Trust have been closed down now, for the Duration.

There is a lighthouse at one end of the island, defunct, abandoned but useful as an observation post.

I nod, express fascination and let the conversation wash over me.

The room feels stifling even though it's concrete and cold. A few gas heaters add a muted roar to the general hubbub but they are not the cause of my discomfort. It's the walls, the people. I'm locked in. Escape means re-crossing the water, and then…

What?

This is too much like the locked doors and shared cells of the remand centre. This is the proximity of bodies. Okay, there are women here, who soften the hard male edge of the place, but it is still eyes that watch and flesh that sweats and mouths that talk, and fists and boots. I can't believe that there are no flare-ups, no explosions of frustration and cabin-fever-driven violence.

But I have to endure it, adapt to it, because I'm here for a while.

I'm also beginning to understand another of the many layers of tension in this room.

These people are waiting.

There's a feeling of transience. The card games, the paperbacks, all have something of the fighter-pilots-passing-the-time-between-scrambles feel to them. Yes, the people here are mostly soldiers, used to a life governed by orders, activity-then-boredom, but that atmosphere of imminent explosion is too strong for this to be mere habit.

It's my turn to deal.

I don't have many cigarettes left, which is okay. I'm not trying to win because I think that cleaning-up on my first night would be a bad idea.

At some point people begin to drift off to bed. I notice couples. The absence of children must mean that there is a ready supply of contraception, or do they dash the newborn against the walls of these bunkers then cast their tiny corpses into the grey North Sea?

Probably the former, *hopefully* the former, supplied, I suppose, by those *allies*. Another couple of hands then I make my own excuses and ask if any of my gambling buddies know where I'm supposed to sleep. Once of them, an energetic, slight-built character tells me to follow him.

He's amiable, talkative, the one who had given me the history of Orfordness in fact.

"I didn't mind the army really," he says as we walk. "I mean, it was that or prison. The Judge gave me a choice, so off I went." He fixes me with his glinting, stone-hard eyes and grins. "Well? Don't you want to know what I did?"

"It's your business, not mine."

"I like that, too many people want to know too much. Especially in a place like this where we live on top of each other all the time." He raises his hands which are curled into fists. I see faded tattoos. "Too handy with these bastards, and I had a temper. At least in the army you can beat the shit out of people legally. Trouble is, I found out we were beating the shit out of our own side. I couldn't take that…"

My bed is in a large, mixed-sex, dormitory area. A couple of lights are still on, the occupants mostly asleep, although a few still talk and read. There are about thirty beds in here, basic, hard mattresses, sleeping bags instead of covers, Army-issue I suppose. Again, they must have been supplied. Stealing this amount of equipment would have meant a massive operation.

I lay down and I'm suddenly wide awake. The ceiling is high enough, the walls a sensible distance away, but there are no windows. This room is underground, I'm sure of it. There is soil, or sand or concrete above that ceiling, tons of it pressing down.

Come on, you've slept in a pitch black Underground Station, you've ridden in a metal water tank, buried alive in rubble, you can cope with this you weak bastard.

The last of the lights goes out and the room fills with oily, gritty darkness.

The sudden explosion of light and shouting is a relief. I haven't slept at all. I'm tense and trapped and sweating. God knows how much time has passed but it has been a hell of claustrophobic terror, of frustration and a need to get out, away, for space and sky and solitude.

"Delivery! Delivery, wake up, fucking delivery!"

The shouter sounds like a sergeant of some sort, bullish, relentless. I sit up and see that he is a big, broad man with red hair who is yelling and shaking any lingering slumberers.

I'm up, quickly, struggling my feet into the battered-but-sound boots I've been given and following the others as they stumble and swear their way out of the dormitory.

We end up outside, on the seaward beach. A savage, snow-scented wind batters us as we stand in huddled, complaining groups. The waves crash and roar, contemptuous, enraged. I glimpse figures with powerful torches, shining them out across the heaving blackness. A moment then a light flashes in return. More signalling then I hear an engine, another, boats, coming in. Shapes form behind the brief light-sentences. There's a ship out there, lightless and invisible. The three, no four, large motor boats, launches, whatever you call them, are its offspring. Flat-bottomed, surging out of the waves to beach roughly at the seething waterline.

I follow the others as they rush in, the red-haired sergeant yells us into a chain, people move in the darkness with alarming efficiency and I allow myself to be shoved into position, about six places from the boats.

Crates and sacks are hurried down the line, some bloody heavy. There's no time to feel what any of them might be, but now I know how the luxuries and necessities of refuge life arrive. Snatches of shouted conversation reveal strong accents, alien language. East European, Middle Eastern, French or Gaelic? I haven't a clue but the implication is alarming. Someone is taking advantage of our self-destruction. Someone is easing their fingers into the slowly opening door.

I'm astonished at just how much can be carried by those boats. The cold eats at my flesh and bones and the exertion drenches me in sweat. When it is finished and the sounds of the retreating engines finally merge with the rage of the sea, I know that my insomnia is cured.

It isn't over yet. The goods have been piled inside the doorway of a large warehouse, shelved with Dexion and already packed with the same kinds of boxes and sacks that we've just unloaded. Before we turn-in we are bullied and harangued into stacking the cargo onto its assigned shelves. Rainer is there, along with an older, impressive-looking character with a leonine mane of grey, a wind-roughened, hawk-featured face and the hardest, clearest pair of blue eyes I've ever seen. He wears a khaki greatcoat and from his bearing and the sheer energies of authority he generates, I take him to be the Colonel Rainer had mentioned when I first arrived. He doesn't speak, just watches. After a moment Rainer says something to him and I feel the full weight of his ice-hard stare burn into me. He nods, then after a few more moments, turns on his heel and strides off.

Rainer walks over to me as the last of the sacks is hefted onto its shelf.

"Wait," she says then dismisses the rest of the party with a single, sharp order.

"You're in deep Allman," she says once they've gone. "Do you understand?"

"Yeah, I do."

"Do you know who we are?"

"Friends, that's what Gary Marshall called you."

She appears to consider this for a moment. "Well, depends which side you're on."

She motions me to a corner of the warehouse and hands me a screwdriver. "Open that crate."

I'm tired and cold and I want to go back to bed, but I do as she says, fumbling the job but eventually removing the Phillips screws that holds the metal lid in place. As I pull it away I see that is sealed and made waterproof by a thick rubber gasket. I also see that it is filled with the same, snub-nosed rifles I had been taught to fire during my very brief time with HM Armed Forces.

"There's only one way to stop this war," Rainer says.

"By fornicating for virginity?" I answer.

She frowns.

"Something someone said: 'Fighting for peace is like fornicating for virginity.'" I think it was Jake Thackeray. He was a folk singer and never played heavy metal but I liked him. "So what are you planning? A revolution?"

"You could call it that."

"And what are your *friends*, the ones who are giving you this stuff, going to want in return?"

"We'll worry about that when the time comes, first we've got to stop the fighting and killing."

I nod towards the crates. "By killing more people?"

"If that's what it takes, yes." There's no bloodthirsty relish in her voice, which is reassuring, I suppose.

"You can't take on the whole Country –"

"Why not? The army is bogged down with this fake war, most of our soldiers are conscripts who don't want to fight and like I said before, there are a lot of us, scattered throughout the Country, waiting for the signal." She stares at me, hard, fixedly. "If the bastards want Enemies of Democracy, their *so-called* democracy Allman, they've got them now."

An icy wind tears off the North Sea and burrows through my newly acquired, though well-worn coat and deep into my flesh and bones as I work. The previous owner of the coat is probably dead, but there's little time for niceties in the refuge.

I'm harvesting brussel sprouts from one of the EoD's many, carefully concealed vegetable plots, this one in the lee of a huge, plain concrete wall, out of sight of the mainland and hardly noticeable from the sea, not that I've seen any ships since I arrived two days ago.

Apart from those night-time delivery vessels that is.

The work is mind-numbing as well as body-numbing, but I don't care. This is all I need at the moment. There is too much to ponder and, for me, the best way of dealing with it is to not think at all.

We are the EoD. Fantasy become life. The irony occasionally makes me chuckle out loud, other times it terrifies me. The people here are, for the most part, decent. Oh they're hard and tough, brutalised by their experience of war, but their intentions are honourable, their motivations honest. They want to end the conflict, they want to stop the murder.

But I'm afraid for them, afraid of the powers that supply our home comforts and our weapons, Afraid of the price they will exact for their friendship. The EoD revolution will not be the end, but the beginning of yet more bloodshed.

I will have a decision to make. When the day comes and the action starts I'll be expected to take my part. But can I? Is there another way out of this? Shouldn't we move out into the battlefields and try to spread the truth, disrupt the war, run around with megaphones singing *Imagine*?

Yeah, the day is coming, but it isn't today, so for now, I can heal my wounds and ease my mind with gardening and doing my share of general maintenance work. The EoD have boats hidden away on the island. I told them I used to be a mechanic, so repairing and servicing their outboard motors has become another of my chores.

I enjoy it.

I can't lie or pretend that my life here is taken up solely with mental torment. The company is fine, I'm accepted, befriended. We laugh and joke, eat good food and drink beer, well, as okay as tinned beer can be.

The light is fading, the evening and the night of the fifth day. I straighten and rub my back. Then grab the handles of the wheelbarrow and push my harvest round the building towards the kitchen area. I used to hate brussel sprouts, but now they're a luxury, green nectar.

The soldier who told me the history of Orford Island is called Ed. I don't know if it's his real name but it will do. He's friendly enough and has taken me under his wing. He has a girlfriend who is black and named Tanny. That isn't her real name either. Tanny was a medic in the infantry and still plies her trade here at the refuge. She's tall, feisty and well able to handle Ed and his shenanigans.

I've got to know one group quite well, a handful of men and women who sit together in the mess hall then play poker in the evenings. Ed and Tanny of course. William Ong, quiet, intelligent, a bit argumentative at times, but solid. Deana, a tall, elegant communications expert who can silence you with one deftly placed verbal bullet, and Haze, lover of, and expert on, reggae in all its forms. Big grin, affable but prone to sudden long silences during which his face collapses into a mask of pain. No one tries to bring him out of it, they just leave him alone and I soon learn to do the same. Everyone here has something, a locked-up secret, a grief or trauma that has to stay hidden and dealt with as best as it can be.

The last member of our gang is a civilian like me (okay I spent a few days in the army, but I don't think that makes me a soldier). He calls himself Harry and he is a Doctor of Engineering. Like me, he lost his partner in a bombing raid, simply walked away and found his way Out. He had money, so he didn't need to play the pimp to get what he wanted.

Harry is affable, spare with his words, though every sentence counts when he does talk. He has a sharp sense of humour and a seemingly boundless knowledge of every subject on earth, even motorbikes and heavy metal.

He saw the original *Black Sabbath*, fronted by Ozzy Osborne way back in 1975 during their *Sabotage* tour, something I missed and can only wonder at. He's lent me a couple of poetry books and I've found some comfort there. One of them is a collection of First World War poetry by John "Woodbine Willy" Kennedy. The other is John Betjeman and makes me want to weep for what has been torn from us.

No one's picked a fight with me yet, I think it's because I'm too big, although a couple of bastards keep giving me the angry eye. Don't know what I've done but I'm not rising to the bait. There are boxing matches on Saturday nights. I'll take them on then if they insist. I think I'd enjoy it. I think I need it.

We eat, talk, play poker, talk and laugh then smoke and sip beer and talk again until we're lulled into a vague, soul-soothing daze.

I walk before I turn-in. I need a few moments outside, on the surface of the earth, where I can breathe real air and feel its energies on my face. I walk across the beach and down to the water's edge. The wind has dropped a little, the sea, that heaving black mass that seems to rise up and threaten to swallow the island at any moment, is still angry but not raging. I look up at the stars, and wonder at the beauty of it. You never see stars like this in light-drenched London, even during the blackout.

I follow the shore then move round the end of the main complex and across to the river, where I light up another cigarette and stare at the dark blur that is Orford village.

We are the EoD.

That old dread returns and I'm suddenly crushed by loneliness. I want everyone back, all those lost souls whose deaths are already retreating into my past -

Something, on the river.

I freeze and peer into the dark.

Nothing, just the lap of water and roar and hiss of the sea on the other side of the island. I make to go back, then stop, there *is* something, a faint sound.

I strain to listen, but the wind is too strong, and the dark too impenetrable for me to see anything. Perhaps I should warn the others. Even if it's a false alarm it doesn't matter, they've managed to stay hidden this long by being cautious.

A slap.

Something hitting water.

An oar?

Another deserter battling his way in?

I scan the darkness. My eyes accustomed, managing to separate the sky from the mainland, the water from dry ground. Just ripples and shadows.

No, there is something or someone out there. I'm sure of it now.

Not wanting to take any risks, I break into a jog, heading for the complex –

Light floods the beach, engines cough into life. I'm frozen in the glare. I force myself to turn round. The brightness blinds me but I can hear, clearly now, a boat, racing in.

I shout but my voice is lost in the noise. There is a *thump*, a deep, coughing sound. A moment later the night is shredded by an explosion that erupts against the wall of the nearest block house.

I drive myself on, shouting and yelling but already figures are emerging from the refuge. I wave at them to get own. Another mortar shell slams into the beach between them and me and all is light and noise and I'm wrenched from my feet then hurled back down against the shingle and left, ears ringing, gasping for breath.

Shouts and gunfire, the enemy are storming the beach now, filling the night air with white hot metal. A helicopter clatters overhead then come more searchlights, more dazzle and noise and confusion.

I get up and run towards my friends, who are on their bellies, firing back from behind ragged coils of rusting barbed wire. Tracer whips towards and past me and I realise that running like this is stupid if not suicidal, so I go down again and crawl.

I clutch at the beach, cheek pushed hard against the cold stones. I feel the crack of bullets as they pass over me. I force myself to move, a slow, slow crawl, not daring to lift any part of my body above ground level, hoping, praying the EoD gunners will recognise me.

Another explosion brings a brief flare of daylight then thrums through the earth. It feels as if the ground wants to throw me off, shrug me away. I move, pushing my carcass through the shingle, daring to look up and see that I'm now only four or five yards from the defenders. Something is on fire, the glow silhouettes the barbed wire. I see heads, rifle-flash.

Another shell rams into the beach about twenty feet to my right. A rain of stones rattles over my back, smoke swirls. There is chaos, light, dark, shouts and screams. I scramble to my feet and run.

Any moment now, any moment now, *any moment now…*

Gunfire rattles and snaps. I'm pounding through smoke into a shifting hell of flame and destruction. The barbed wire is torn, there are bodies. I stumble, drop to my hands and knees then someone helps me to my feet and shoves a rifle into my hands. The defenders are pulling back, hunched, shadows, occasionally spinning about to fire at the invaders. I join them, shooting wild.

Figures erupt out of the dark, running at us fast. A scream to my left, a gasp of pain to my right. The shingle is whipped-up in tiny eruptions that sting my legs, concrete chips shower me from behind. The ground rocks and lurches as more explosions erupt behind me. A helicopter sweeps over and our defence line is shattered by its machine guns.

I drop, hug the ground.

Then I'm up and running, almost at the complex. A door is open, people scrambling inside.

The door disappears in a fury of smoke and flame. I see bodies hurled outwards and away. The blast smashes into me, followed by a wave of searing heat that leaves me clawing for air.

No hope now, all I can do is run. I look back. Shifting orange-white light illuminates the beach and the waves of attackers as they pour through the gaps in the barbed wire. I see them fall as surviving defenders open fire, from doorways, rooftops, from the shadows and darknesses that remain.

I also see a film crew.

For a moment I stand and stare.

There's a cameraman, someone with a microphone and portable sound equipment, running awkwardly into hell. A fucking film crew.

A pair of fireballs hurtle out of the dark and smash against the walls of the complex. Rockets I suppose.

I retreat, not knowing where to go, just needing to get away from the noise and destruction, heading towards the sea. Perhaps I'll keep running until the cold, cold water takes me.

A gunfight flares up behind me, fierce but silenced quickly by a series of skull-fracturing detonations. The EoD are being overwhelmed. It's over.

I stumble out of the complex and onto the seaward beach.

Then hear someone call my name.

"Pete! Stop, Pete!"

I do so, stunned into stillness. I turn and see a figure, black and featureless against the firelight.

"Pete," Mason shouts again. "It's okay, put down the gun, your job's done. You're a hero."

I'm walking towards him, rifle aimed at his chest. He appears to be unarmed. I don't care, I want to kill him. And I want to be close enough so that when I pull (squeeze, don't jerk) the trigger I hear him scream. I want him to see his own blood and guts spill out onto the ground.

Mason raises his hands. "This attack, this eradication of the EoD is *your* work Pete. *You* led us here."

I don't know what he's talking about. I just want him on his knees, pleading for his life, begging and sobbing and craving my forgiveness.

Which I will not grant.

"Kneel," I say and am surprised by how calm my voice sounds.

"Pete –"

"Kneel."

He does so, slowly, carefully, hands on his head now.

"You led us here Pete, yes, you. That operation of yours, remember it? There was no infection. It was a routine procedure that was accomplished without a hitch. It was also the perfect opportunity for us, for the forces of democracy. The NHS took something out, the government put something in, a simple radio transmitter. That's right, we've known exactly where you've been for almost the entire time since you were in hospital."

"You're a fucking liar," I say.

"Oh come on. How do you think you managed to get here in one piece? How do you think you escaped from the police, remember the angry driver after the London Wall raid, and the car crash in Oxford Street? We lost you a few times, you shouldn't have been press-ganged, now *that* was a near miss. But we found you again, and transferred the idiot SSU lieutenant who picked you up and gave you to the army."

"Why me? I'm nobody, why not some SAS hero?"

"The EoD would have spotted a plant right away. We needed someone who actually believed that they were fighting back. You're not the only one Pete, but you're one of the few who've managed to get through and find any of the EoD refuges. We needed someone tough and resilient and bloody minded. Given your unsavoury past and subsequent redemption and your outspoken opposition to the war, you were perfect."

I shake my head, unable to remember the Pete Allman who was so vocal in his pacifism, the one who was part of the war but who agitated against it.

Mason must sense my confusion because he says; "We used some rather effective mind-scrambling drugs on you, the same types we put in our troops' food, only much stronger. We didn't just need daze and confusion, we needed complete memory loss. Mixed with a little hypnotism they worked very well on nearly all our agents. We also needed a trigger to start the process, a phone call. Do you remember a wrong number, early one morning, just as the sun was dawning?"

Oh yes, I remember that. The phone call, the curtains, the smoke columns, my family…

"Then we fed you the Death List. That wasn't exactly a lie, and it has come in useful, but it wasn't as important as you believed. I think they call it a red herring in those old whodunits. Or is it the muguffin? Your colleague Andy was very helpful, he had a thing for ladies of the night. His wife didn't know, and never would, as long as he got you to the *Hammer and Nails* on a lunchtime when you could bump up against your old mate Dave Miller."

I raise the rifle, sighting it on his forehead. He looks up at me, unflinching.

"It was risky Pete, and costly. You are a stubborn bastard my friend. We had to do a lot of damage to get you on the move and we had to take a lot of risks. That first air raid almost killed you. The aircraft struck before you were safely off the fourth floor didn't it. You were still cautious, even after that, still not moving as fast as we wanted you to. And then suddenly we had your family, all together, the final straw, the touch paper –"

"Cunt!" I scream at him and jab the muzzle of the rifle against his forehead. Its metal breaks skin and blood begins to run down his face. His eyes lock with mine. I see sweat in the shifting light, I see fear, but he won't beg, not Mason, he is sure that I will not pull the trigger. "Filthy, murdering fucking scum!"

Somehow the words have lost meaning, suddenly I'm tired and empty and going through the motions.

"What's done is done Pete. We have a new life to offer you. The Country needs a hero or two at the moment, just as the government needs something decisive to keep the public behind the war and to win them the election in the spring. What better than the destruction of a major EoD headquarters, all captured on film, and with a hero thrown in.

"Everything about you was right for us Pete. Your friendship with one of the Veterans we mistakenly allowed home. Your absolute devotion to Ruth –"

"Don't say her name you bastard. Don't you ever put her name in your filthy fucking mouth."

"– and your family, because they have been your salvation. They were weren't they Pete. You won't kill me because Ruth would never countenance such a barbarous act. You can't pull that trigger, it goes against everything she stood for, everything."

I see him tense, feel the tremors of his fear through the gun. I curl my finger about the trigger and squeeze, carefully, gently.

"We had to do it Pete, just as we had to start the war. The Country was going to hell, the streets were paved with shit, the economy collapsing. We needed purpose and control and we needed industry back on its feet. We needed to gather up the chaos and shovel it into a place where we could sort it out and start afresh. There's only one way to do that. War Pete. Man's natural state –"

The trigger gives slightly under my finger. I'm aware of soldiers running towards us. I don't look up. I stare at Mason, waiting for the shot, the flash and crack of bullet as it rips through bone and blasts his brain into the freezing, boisterous air.

Ruth

Between me and the sea, Ruth cold and huddled in that grey coat-cardigan she wore on the night she died. The wind plucks at her hair, she is calm, stern.

No Pete.

Yes Ruth, for you, for Dominic and Amanda and Rachel –

You're not one of them. You're not an animal, you never were. Don't, please…

Another increase of pressure. Mason is trembling violently now but he won't take his eyes off mine.

Pete…Please…let it stop…

Stop, it has to stop. Christ it must stop.

Slowly, slowly I lower the rifle then let it fall onto the ground. I don't raise my hands, even though there are soldiers yelling at me to do so. I will not raise my hands and I will not kneel.

"Don't shoot." Mason snaps out, "Leave him alone, it's all right."

The film crew have arrived. I'm bathed in light. A microphone is shoved into my face. Mason is back on his feet, an arm draped about my shoulders.

"This is Pete Allman," he says. "And because of his courage and determination we have dealt a decisive blow against the EoD tonight. Peace is within our grasp."

"It's a lie," I say, quietly at first, then more loudly. The microphone is still in my face, picking up my words. "It's all a fucking lie. The war is a fake. The air raids are carried out by the RAF. Only they don't realise what they are doing, no one realises what they are doing."

"Pete, Pete, it's all right, its over now, it's all right." Mason turns his bloodied face to the camera. "I'm sorry, the interview will have to wait, the strain, you understand…"

The soundman withdraws the microphone, the camera, however is still running.

"It's a fucking lie, a hoax, a game! Listen to me. *Listen.*"

"No one will listen while you're alive Pete," Mason says calmly as the crew finally begins to move away. "You're a crazed fool, raging about conspiracies and cover-ups, broken by your mission. You're a free man Pete." He nods toward the camera crew again. "Enjoy it."

The announcer, I recognise him as the tough-guy actor who hosted *Officer Quest*, leads the crew back into position to growl a questions at Mason. I am ignored, alone.

Alive.

Yeah, alive and an embarrassment, a ranter and raver…

Even the solders begin to move away, ordered out by a familiar bark. The night, its heartbeat the relentless beat of the sea is returning to swallow me whole.

One of the soldiers lags behind, staring at me.

"You heard me," I say to him. Then fight down my terror and continue. "And you believe me, don't you, Private Mirza, because we've talked before."

He has not yet lowered his rifle, the one I stole then gave back to him when we collided into each other's lives in that white house on the Dunwich cliffs.

... alive...an embarrassment, a ranter and raver. But dead, now that would be another story. The more serious-minded sometimes listen to what the dead have to say. Think Oswald and Ruby, think Dr. David Kelly...

"Mirza," the sergeant snaps. "Come on you dopey bastard."

He makes to go, unable to take his eyes off me, afraid, torn. I follow him. Calling out to him, pushing, provoking.

"You know the truth, that's why you were crying that day."

He stumbles to a halt once more. The rest of the platoon slow, look round, bemused. Even the sergeant has stopped and is staring.

Please God, don't let him intervene, one last favour eh?

"Leave me alone," Mirza says and sounds close to tears. He makes to walk away, shouts at his comrades. "He's crazy, I've never met him before. I swear it, I don't know who he is. We've never met."

"Yes you have," I say as I jog after him. "We talked and I told you the truth and you believed me."

He spins round, and in the shifting firelight and film crew glare I see that he is crying. "No."

"What's going on?" the sergeant says. "Mirza, what is this man talking about?"

"Yes Private Mirza, tell him." I raise my voice to address the others. "He believed me sarge —"

There is a flash, a brief burst of flame from the muzzle of Private Mirza's rifle.

Time slows, darkness is coming, in a moment, in less than a heartbeat, but it's long enough, for me to wonder if, in the end, Mirza fired to keep my mouth shut or because he understands what I understand. It's also long enough for me to see Mason's interview startled into silence.

Caught live on TV, the execution of Pete Allman
Think Oswald and Ruby, think Dr. David Kelly...
And it's long enough for me to reach out and grasp Ruth's warm, strong hand.

www.ingramcontent.com/pod-product-compliance
Lightning Source LLC
Chambersburg PA
CBHW061535210726
48287CB00006B/1960